—There was no **sky**
in that world.

——The **conceptual rewrite** had affected all of the ladies present.

From **big-breasted Lolis** to **proper racks**—this was a place abounding with **boobies and dreams**...

"It's a **spirit arm** using **big boob essence** to **conceptually** give someone big boobs, it is...!!"

Ah, fiction tells us *Evil never prevails...*

However, sadly enough, in reality, *evil always prevails*!!

Sora sang evil's praises so gallantly, his face twisted in a demon lord's smile——

THE TEN COVENANTS

The absolute law of this world, created by the god Tet upon winning the throne of the One True God. Covenants that have forbidden all war among the intelligent Ixseeds—namely.

1. In this world, all bodily injury, war, and plunder is forbidden.
2. All conflicts shall be settled by victory and defeat in games.
3. Games shall be played for wagers that each agrees are of equal value.
4. Insofar as it does not conflict with "3," any game or wager is permitted.
5. The party challenged shall have the right to determine the game.
6. Wagers sworn by the Covenants are absolutely binding.
7. For conflicts between groups, an agent plenipotentiary shall be established.
8. If cheating is discovered in a game, it shall be counted as a loss.
9. The above shall be absolute and immutable rules, in the name of the God.

10. Let's all have fun together.

CONTENTS
10

No Game No Life

YUU KAMIYA

10

YEN
ON

NEW YORK

NO GAME NO LIFE, Volume 10
YUU KAMIYA

Translation by Daniel Komen
Cover art by Yuu Kamiya

NO GAME NO LIFE Volume.10
©Yuu Kamiya 2018
First published in Japan in 2018 by KADOKAWA CORPORATION, Tokyo.
English translation rights arranged with KADOKAWA CORPORATION, Tokyo, through Tuttle-Mori Agency, Inc., Tokyo.

English translation © 2020 by Yen Press, LLC

Yen On
150 West 30th Street, 19th Floor
New York, NY 10001

Visit us at yenpress.com
facebook.com/yenpress
twitter.com/yenpress
yenpress.tumblr.com
instagram.com/yenpress

First Yen On Edition: February 2020

Yen On is an imprint of Yen Press, LLC. The Yen On name and logo are trademarks of Yen Press, LLC.

The publisher is not responsible for websites (or their content) that are not owned by the publisher.

Library of Congress Cataloging-in-Publication Data
Names: Kamiya, Yu, 1984– author, illustrator. | Komen, Daniel, translator.
Title: No game no life / Yuu Kamiya, translation by Daniel Komen.
Other titles: No gemu no raifu. English
Description: First Yen On edition. | New York, NY : Yen ON, 2015–
Identifiers: LCCN 2015041321 |
   ISBN 9780316383110 (v. 1 : pbk.) |
   ISBN 9780316385176 (v. 2 : pbk.) |
   ISBN 9780316385190 (v. 3 : pbk.) |
   ISBN 9780316385213 (v. 4 : pbk.) |
   ISBN 9780316385237 (v. 5 : pbk.) |
   ISBN 9780316385268 (v. 6 : pbk.) |
   ISBN 9780316316439 (v. 7 : pbk.) |
   ISBN 9780316502665 (v. 8 : pbk.) |
   ISBN 9780316471343 (v. 9 : pbk.) |
   ISBN 9781975386788 (v. 10 : pbk.)
Subjects: | BISAC: FICTION / Fantasy / General. | GSAFD: Fantasy fiction.
Classification: LCC PL832.A58645 N6 2015 | DDC 895.63/6—dc23
LC record available at http://lccn.loc.gov/2015041321

ISBNs: 978-1-9753-8678-8 (paperback)
       978-1-9753-8679-5 (ebook)

10 9 8 7 6 5 4 3 2

LSC-C

Printed in the United States of America

⏻ Re:Start

This is the story
of an empty puppet and a flightless white bird
who joined hands and looked up at the sky.

The sky told them they could go anywhere.
But the sky would not let them go anywhere.

I am the sky. The empty sky. Your sky.
I promise.
I will be your sky. I will let you fly.
I will take you anywhere you want to go.

So said the puppet, admiring the white bird.
In the end, the puppet could not keep that
promise.
They ran from it and everything else.

In the western region on the continent of Lucia—the former Kingdom of Elkia—Immanity had lost everything except for a single city in the last country they still controlled. But by now that was a distant memory. In a stunning recovery of their territory, they'd brought the Eastern Union, Oceand, and Avant Heim into a three-country, six-race commonwealth, a great power that had to be acknowledged. By now, however, that was yesterday's news. Now word had spread that the monarch who had led this staggering advance had suddenly disappeared.

It's all too familiar in history what happens when a country loses its wise king, its great leader. The administration stalls. Factions fight for power. Chaos reigns. *And the country splits.* Sooner or later, the great power declines…until, inevitably, it is said to have fallen…

…But that's assuming the existence of a wise king or a great leader. When it's a monarch who is neither wise nor great, then that's a different story. For instance, a slacker king who dumps all the work on someone else. Or a shut-in leader who undermines the dignity of the state. A monarch who bets the Race Piece as if it was nothing and picks fights with higher races under policies a half step away from a reign of terror. If such a tyrant disappeared, that would be a completely different story. And that's the tale of the Kingdom of Elkia—oh, sorry. The Republican Dukedom of Elkia.

It was as peaceful as could be. More stable than before if anything. …With some exceptions. For example:

"…Are you listening? You have three choices."

For instance, on the main road at a rest stop far northwest of the capital.

"You give me back my boobs, you cough up where you're getting the drugs, or you *die*!! Do you understand?!"

Black-haired and flat-chested, she screamed with tears in her eyes in front of the open-air stall. Such a happy and lively town it was, filled with the hustle and bustle of merchants enjoying the *boom in trade*…

"Chlammy? Why, I told you, that drug was nothing more than barongrass extraaact."

Next to young Chlammy Zell of the modest bosom stood Fiel Nirvalen of the ample bounty. The Elven Fiel gently admonished her friend.

"Barongrass is a spiritually active herb that merely inflates the breasts with air for a short period of tiiime."

"That's why I'm investigating this spurious substance!! Fi, can you understand how I feel?!"

Chlammy was furious. She wept profusely in her yearning to pummel the bastards responsible for this outrage against all that was right and proper. She, after all, had never been blessed when it came to matters of the chest. She had lived her life looking down at a wall that could never be surmounted, doing her best to cushion the blow with pads. But in her heart, not far from the surface, she knew more profoundly than anyone the greatness of voluminous breasts.

Three weeks earlier, the king and queen had abruptly gone missing. She and Fiel had searched for them high and low, across every plain and every mountain. Even Elven magic proved of no use to trace their whereabouts. Then, the previous night, they'd arrived here, and Chlammy had found *this*. It took no time for her to empty her purse.

——Hastily she clutched the bottle labeled Bosom Enhancer. With her pinky out, without a second of hesitation, she gulped down the vial with a grand gesture.

——......

It did not take long to hunt down the stall's supplier. It was a little shop on the corner of the thoroughfare, and indeed it seemed to be doing brisk business. The line and the crowd were so massive that they could hardly even get close. Chlammy snickered as she made out what it said on the sign: Apothecary of Dreams. She slipped into the side street and reflected on the irony.

"Heh... Yes, quite. That night certainly was a *dream...*"

...It wasn't as if Chlammy had trusted the concoction to be genuine in the first place. She had placed her hopes and dreams in the Bosom Enhancer with doubt—nay, with a near-certain conviction she would be disappointed. However—

"Yes, cleavage as if in a dream... I couldn't even see my navel when I looked down."

—her breasts had *actually grown*! Ah, to have boobs most plentiful! She couldn't even hear what Fiel was saying! It was time to rush to the inn, have a toast, and feast until her entire torso was swollen!! *Wait? Where do they even sell lingerie big enough for these?* ♥ *Ha-ha!*

"It was a nice worry to have, if you will, bouncing about in my chest as I went to sleep. A most pleasant night..." Chlammy whispered, her eyes gazing far off into the distance. She made her way to the back of the shop—and without a second thought climbed over the fence of the garden where it appeared they were growing their medicines. As they faced the door on which was written For Stakeholders Only, Fiel raised her voice to rein in Chlammy.

"Ch-Chlammy? Wh-why, I don't think we should trespass..."

"What are you talking about, Fi? It says 'For Stakeholders Only.' In other words, for me."

Chlammy thought, *"Apothecary of Dreams"? Fitting indeed. Yes, dreams. That which vanish the moment one wakes*—nothing more than dreams.

She put her hand to her chest, which had been so cruelly brought back to reality after a dream-filled night, let the grandest of tears fall from her eyes now devoid of brightness—and asked:

"Are you saying that, with this void returned to me, with this emptiness in my barren bosom, I have nothing at stake?!"

A charlatan selling fake boobs on one hand, and Chlammy's boobs on the other. Good and evil. What more did Fiel want to be at stake?! Sobbing uncontrollably, Chlammy started trying to kick down the door as Fiel hurriedly put her arms around her.

"Chlammy, y-you must calm down! Why, surely you knew it was a fraud?!"

"A monetary fraud, yes! But if you're going to defraud me—**don't puff up my boobs in the firrrst plaaaaace!!**"

Ah, psychological fraud…first filling the chest with joy, and then emptying it of all hope. To *lift her up* with a dream that could never be, and then to *drop her* from such unprecedented heights—it was a sin deserving of heaven's wrath!! Chlammy freed herself from Fiel's grasp and unleashed her righteous fury.

…Only to freeze in the wind-up when she heard someone's voice behind her.

"…Well now. I did plant quite a variety of seeds for the medicines…"

Chlammy and Fiel turned, and their eyes opened wide.

"…but I don't recall planting seeds for washboards or weeds. How curious. ♥"

They looked back on that venom-tongued being, the most curious of all, with strained smiles.

A diabolical angel with a halo over her head of prismatic hair—the *thing* had appeared without sound, and now she casually opened the aforementioned door.

"*Master!* ♪ Your humble servant Jibril has returned from deliveries! ♪"

"Yeah, good work—hey, it's Chlammy and Fiel. *C'monnn in.*"

"...*Welll-cooome*... What are you...doing...here...?"

Ah, yes—those two voices answering merrily from beyond the door were, in fact, those of the long-lost king and queen. The very ones for whom Chlammy and Fiel had been searching for three weeks. The black-haired, dark-eyed older brother, an apron over his "I ♥ PPL" shirt, some sketchy implement in his hand. The white-haired, red-eyed little sister, standing on a stool, stirring a similarly sketchy cauldron. Sora and Shiro, those two siblings who epitomized sketchiness. At last, Chlammy gave them a friendly smile and said:

"That's my line... What are you doing *mucking about* here?!"

Indeed, they were *the very malingerers who had abandoned their administration without notice.* They looked at each other. Sora apologetically took in a deep breath.

"Sorry...but actually, this isn't muck. This is medicine. We've got all kinds. How 'bout it?"

He handed her a list of goods, among which was a Bosom Enhancer. How kind of him to offer a written confession of the outrage against all that is right and proper that he had committed upon her. Employing the momentum of her urge to strike him, she took the list and hurled it into the cauldron...

■■■

What were Sora and Shiro doing, you ask? Sora had a ready answer: They were *killing time!*

"I mean, we got chased off the throne... We'd be in trouble if they knew we were still in the country."

He flinched not at the murderous gazes of Chlammy and Fiel. Though Sora told a sad tale as he sat in his chair, Shiro on his lap, his attitude was upbeat. More than upbeat, it was grand—it was with pride that they smiled as they continued!

"We got fired from our monarch job! We're unemployed and penniless! Devoid even of the slightest *desire to work*!!"

"…Loser…shut-in gamers… That's…us…!"

"But we don't have a house to shut ourselves into! And you ask us what we're doing? Is this not foolery?!"

"…The real…question is…what *can* we do…?"

"Oh, and when I said we were in trouble, I wasn't kidding. We're just about finished *as human beings*."

Chlammy couldn't help but clear her throat in the face of their zeal. They sneered.

—*Why are you all surprised?*

They had already been the scum of society, Sora and Shiro… "Just about finished as human beings" was far from the lowest they'd gotten! At the bottom of the valley, they'd dug a hole into the ground—and fallen through to Disboard, basically.

"But, you know, when we got to this world—*we were just back at the start*, right?"

"In, other words…'*New Game*'… Playing again…"

"——!"

Yes, they had lost their throne, their home, and their power, even their value to society. But all that, to them, was *just* that. Seeing their faces, Chlammy couldn't help but remember who they were, and it took her breath away. The personal effects they had—smartphones, tablet, portable game console—were vestiges of having lost everything. Those were all they'd had when they landed in Disboard, and now those were what they were playing with.

Those were all they'd had. *And now their smiles and the fingers that played with them* were the ones that had played the world. Those of the world's ultimate strategist—" " (Blank), greatest gamer among humans, two in one. With their smiles and fingers—what was the point of worrying even if they lost everything else? They made it clear that the world was the game and they were the ones playing. And now—

∗   ∗   ∗

"So, when you play the second time, it's about everything but the main quest, right?! Like…"

"…Crafting…smithing, farming…and shopkeeping, duh…!"

"You haven't even *finished* the main quest! Beat the game once first!"

They were done with conquering the Ixseeds and challenging the One True God for the time being. Chlammy made clear she was none too happy about their declaration that they were going to mess around with the world's economy, but they completely ignored her. The only answer she received came from the medicinal products arrayed in this establishment Sora and Shiro were apparently running. Fiel looked about the compounding chamber, narrowing her eyes at the pharmacological ingredients she saw.

"Barongrass… Prana… Kama leaves… Why, *none* of these herbs are found on this continent, are theyyy? ♪"

"——!!"

Those elves and their foresty ways. Sora and Shiro chuckled as Chlammy gasped. Fiel had the eye to identify at a glance the effects and habitat of each herb—and to discern that Sora and Shiro's claims were not worth trusting. If they were so broke and homeless—*then how did they start this shop*? Chlammy searched their faces for the truth. She was met with a smile.

"Ah, you see, I simply shifted about the globe to collect what was needed and used magic to grow them in the back garden. ♥"

"What do you mean, 'New Game'? More like *'Cheat Activated'*!!"

Despite Chlammy's protestations over the obviously broken character, Sora calmly raised a hand to silence her.

"Must you accuse me so unjustly? You should know that you get to *bring new stuff along on the second playthrough*."

Yes—who cared how broken and OP she was?! If the devs said you could use her, then why not use her?! That's right—!!

"So, on the second playthrough, we get to start with Jibril!! Thus we graduate from being broke, unemployed, and homeless! We sold materials and raised funds, and then we developed our own products and went into business! *You see?!*"

"...Jibril, well...have you served..."

"It was a mere trifle. Ah... I deserve not this honor..."

"...All right... I see what you're doing now," Chlammy murmured to Sora's bombast, Shiro's thumbs-up, and Jibril's wing-folding genuflection. "*Basically, the usual*—cheating and swindling, right?!" She'd been holding back her urge to yell, doing her best to hear him out, but she'd reached her limit.

Sora said:

"...Sorry. Which case of cheating and swindling are you talking about? There've been so many, I'm not sure."

"You're clever to blow me off while acting apologetic, but could you stop?! I'm talking about your Bosom Enhancer. Your most wicked ruse yet, to *hawk phony breasts*. Give me back my dreams!!"

Chlammy screamed with tears in her eyes. But Sora looked back more quizzically than ever.

—*Huh?* He took out a vial of the Breast Enhancer.

"*Just take another dose.* If you take it every day—congratulations! You've got big boobs."

"Yes, I'll have *big fake boobs* that will shrivel as soon as I stop taking it, won't I?! Does your underhandedness know no bounds?!"

Chlammy censured him with a plaintive wail. Regardless, she took the vial.

"...Big *fake* boobs...? Ohhh, I see. You're saying it's not fair because the boobs are *fake*...are you?"

As if he'd finally figured out why she was angry, Sora nodded several times and said...

"All right, Chlammy... What sort of breast enhancement is not fake?"

Chlammy took in a breath, intuiting from the heavy sound of Sora's question that something was up.

"Chlammy... You have my memories, so you should know. In our old world… Yes. We have *many methods* of bosom enhancement—of *bust-building…* However—"

Yes, having received Sora's memories in the game of existence, Othello, Chlammy should have known. The many and various and dreamlike boob technologies that existed in their old world—for all that—were all—nothing more—than the likes of the Bosom Enhancer——!

"All forms of breast augmentation are essentially *just pads*!!!"

"———————————Ah… Ahh!"

You could stuff your breasts with fat or with silicone. In any case, it was just stuffing. Just *pads!* The only difference was whether you put it under your breasts or under your bra!! And she was saying that to inflate them with air was fraud?! Then *all breast enhancement was fraud.* Why, you ask?!

"Even if you manage to get big boobs, just as you yourself have realized, they will be fake!!"

"No—stoppp!! I don't want to hear this. I—I don't want to admit it!"

"You say you *want to have big boobs—* but that just proves you *don't.* Ultimately, thinking that just proves your chest is flat as a board!! It doesn't matter how many pads you stuff in there. That fact will never change!!"

"———No… Nooo… Oh, stop—stop—stopppp!"

It was a hard truth…but a truth she had to accept. Shiro, Fiel, and Jibril all looked down silently. Though Chlammy covered her ears and shook, the devious Sora continued mercilessly.

"You have a meager chest! You are impoverished! No matter how hard you try, you will never be well-endowed. *So, if you're not going to take pride in fakes that look realer than the real thing—"*

Yes… If she were just to smugly, proudly deceive herself and say: *I can have real big boobs*, or put on bouncy fake boobs and tell herself: *These are real boobs—*

"Then what you have—*is even worse than fake.*"

* * *

Chlammy slumped to the ground without a word. Fiel broke the silence:

"Chlammy…? Please listen caaarefully…"

Fiel gently embraced Chlammy. The Elf, the race most skilled in magic, said:

"Why, we *do* have magic that can make your breasts bigger… Buuut…"

They had all kinds of means, she was saying, from sex-change spells to camouflage spells. But as Chlammy had seen herself, and as Sora had told her, no matter what:

"In the eeend…they're alll fake… Dreams are just dreams… you see."

"…Ugh… Egh… Waaaaaaaaaaaaaaaaaaaaaaaaaaaaaaaah!!!"

—*To turn fake into real*…was impossible even with magic. It was only a dream. Chlammy bawled as it dawned on her that the true nature of reality is despair. Even Sora's and Shiro's eyes glinted ever so slightly with tears.

"Yeah—they're just dreams. Just dreams that vanish when you wake—*but then*…"

Sora and Shiro wiped their tears and proudly corrected their sitting posture, announcing with a glint yet fiercer:

"…That's, why…there's, demand…"

"And the nature of business—is to always supply a demand."

Yes—in every age, in every world, it was a commodity always in short supply. An intangible commodity subject constantly to the most severe of shortages—namely!

"*It's left to us to sell it*—sell *dreams*. *Drugs* that make you dream for a short time!!"

That was why the sign said "Apothecary of Dreams." He went on.

"You know why dreams are called dreams? *Because they don't exist in reality!!*"

Indeed. Dreams were dreams—mere fantasy, mere fiction. It wasn't for nothing they'd written on the label, "Do not take more than the specified dose"! Those dreams packed so tight in that little bottle of medicine—

"Ah, even such a paradox as a *big-breasted Chlammy*!! A less realistic proposition than world peace!! A wild fancy contrary to Brahman! A dream ridiculous even as a dream! Even such a dream, one is free to dream."

"............Excuse me."

"Dreams are the spice that adds zest to an otherwise unpalatable reality. All right, so it's no wonder drug. It's fake. But there's no end to the demand for recreational drugs like this—it's a dream ocean!!"

"Excuse me, Shiro. Do you have a drug that will help me realize my dream of punching Sora?! Name your price!"

Sora nodded deeply at his own statement that had brought the collapsed Chlammy back onto her feet.

Yes. This was proof: Even despair buckled under the rage of dreams! That's why he was here, supplying those little wishes people had, like being popular or having big boobs. And that alone would suffice.

"And this keeps our business steady on the rails. Look at the sea of people outside our door!!"

"...So steady...the crowd...scares us misanthropes, from going outside... A critical hit!"

"But, you know, we're shut-ins anyway. *It's not like we were going to go outside!* We just have Jibril warp the goods to wholesale customers! And we sit here like courtiers fanning ourselves! Haaa-ha-ha-ha! Look at all those suckers!!"

"It is a natural consequence of my masters' wisdom and business talent. ♥"

Jibril knelt before the cackling siblings. Chlammy and Fiel nodded jadedly.

No wonder we couldn't find them anywhere...

Chlammy narrowed her eyes yet further, vowing not to look the other way this time.

"—Enough *business*. Get back to *governing*!!"
Chlammy's booming howl shook the small shop. And then—
"If you're so talented, then *why did you get chased off the throne*?!"
—she thrust before Sora and Shiro the reason they were chased
out—rather, the manner in which they *managed* to get expelled.
For Immanity's greatest gamer, the unbeaten ruler—" "—to *lose
the position of agent plenipotentiary*—it had seemed impossible, and
yet—
"It's because of how you used the Covenants to force the Commercial Confederation to bend to your will!! It's your relentless oppression
that gave them an excuse to band together in a coup d'état!!"
...Yes. Basically, that's all it had been—a coup. Sora and Shiro
chuckled.

■■■

Three weeks earlier...
A placard reading CLOSED FOR BUSINESS hung from Elkia Castle.
And there were a number of people in front of it. A ragtag band from
the commercial associations, guilds, and various upstart nobles,
who collectively called themselves the Commercial Confederation.
Making a show of being on strike, they demanded of Sora and Shiro
a simple game. Holding the country's infrastructure hostage, they
proposed a simple game—simply rigged for them to win, that is...
And that was the story. That was enough for the greatest gamers to
turn down the match and leave the throne.
The trick to never losing was *never playing a game you couldn't
win*. And thus the smoothly executed coup d'état turned Elkia from
a monarchy to a constitutional dukedom. It was a parliamentary
system in which capitalists and lords used their money and connections to influence state affairs.

"Oh well, it was bound to happen sooner or later anyway. Don't
worry about it."
"You *should* be worrying about it!! Hey, are you listening?!"

Snapping out of flashback mode, Sora determined that they'd met their achievement quota for the day. Chlammy chased Sora as he started up the stairs to the second floor, where his living quarters were. But Jibril and Shiro, ascending at either side of Sora, dismissed her.

"For instance...the Eastern Union needs continental resources. Normally, Elkia would be able to sell them at exorbitant prices—"

"...But under the policies, of a multiracial commonwealth... Elkia's got to, keep its prices, fair... Only a matter of time..."

"I'm...well aware of that...!"

Yes...Sora and Shiro's ultimate goal lay in their plan to challenge Tet, the One True God. Their plan to create a multiracial commonwealth that would unite all the races without domination sounded good. No one would lose out, they had said—indeed. But what about those *forced* to sell goods otherwise commanding high prices at appropriately low ones? The merchants would suffer a loss in revenue—so clearly, they'd lose out. Chlammy had known that the discontent couldn't be suppressed forever. But even so...

As the three reached their bedchamber on the second floor and sat on their respective beds, she asked them:

"Isn't it the job of the government to suppress it anyway?! Why did you have to *troll* them?!"

It wasn't oppression she was talking about but negotiation that Chlammy expounded. Sora, Shiro, and Jibril all grinned with increased ferocity.

"Come on, Chlammy... You're asking a gamer why he has to *troll* people?"

"...We're...not, politicians... You should, know, why we troll them..."

Politics was for the politicians. They'd leave aside a certain redhead. Sora's and Shiro's grins warped with malice—and the two of them explained how a gamer thought.

"The coup d'état event's gonna happen anyway. So—"

"...We get the *flag-setting...out of the way...* ♪"

* * *

——.

Chlammy and Fiel both knew better than to underestimate " ". You could see on their faces what they thought as they listened to Sora and Shiro: *I knew it. They'd sparked the coup d'état* on purpose.

Having tracked down Sora and Shiro to confirm this, the two were ready to move on to the next question: *Why?*

"Chlammy. After the Commercial Confederation chased us out, what happened *here?*"

"......? Are you talking about how trade exploded after your regulations were loosened?" Chlammy answered suspiciously and carefully. Sora nodded gravely.

"In particular—at a certain waypoint along the trade route: here. This is the *center of distribution*."

The Commercial Confederation's capital lay mainly in the trade business Sora and Shiro had restrained. The goal of the coup was profit. And therefore, it could be inferred, free and unregulated trade. Anyone should be able to see what would happen—so, all they had to do was *exploit it*. In other words—!

"...You know all those stories about shopkeepers in alternate worlds? Don't their protagonists piss you off?"

"...........Huh? The what in the what?"

"They win the contest of flavor using their knowledge from their old worlds to make mayo or miso and try to sell their product on the merit of taste alone? Ha!! These suckers don't know how to think big! And they're too slow! They think business is about having the better product. They can't see the big picture!!"

"Huh? Wha—wait—what are you talking about?! It's not?!"

Sora grinned, unconcerned with Chlammy's bewilderment by his sudden change of subject and heated speech. To meet demand, you supplied the best products. Indeed, that was normal. Exceedingly appropriate.

And for that very reason, Sora laughed in its face!

* * *

"It doesn't matter how good you think your product is. *If no one buys it, it has no value!*"

Yes... Fundamentally, it was the reverse. Not supply, but demand was everything!

—Even if you set up a bunch of jewels on a deserted island, who were you gonna sell them to?!

—In a desert, water would go for more than jewels, wouldn't it?!

You had to read who was gonna want what where. That came before questions of quality. So!!

"I'll just come out and say it!! As long as you understand the fundamentals of business, you don't need quality products, or even fake-boob drugs!! You can just take an empty bottle and slap on a label that says, 'Ion-Enriched Air,' and sell it so fast your crappy little hole-in-the-wall becomes the next big thing in three days and your series ends after one volume!!"

As Sora pontificated, he sat back on his bed, and his eyes glinted dangerously. He revealed the foundation and the secret of business. The truth. That being——

"...If you want to sell your supply, first you make demand."

Yes—all you had to do was goad the Commercial Confederation to mount a coup d'état. And then you didn't have to predict demand. You just had to *create* it. That's right—!!

"You gotta understand the flow of people and things—locations and trends!! Especially where it's gonna boom when the Commercial Confederation loosens regulations!! You gotta know what's going on with new currency being issued to smooth the flow of trade!! You gotta know before anyone else, and then frankly it doesn't matter what you're selling, you're already rigged to win!!! ***Dooo youuu understaaaaand?!***"

—staaand!

......staaand...

.............*staand...*

Sora's voice echoed.

"Why, it couldn't possibly be that you really think us such fools as to take you at your word when you say that you sparked a coup d'état to run a medicine shop, could it?"

"You must know *what's really going on* with Elkia right now... I won't let you say that you don't."

Fiel and Chlammy looked back with subzero eyes. But Sora and Shiro laughed to themselves. They didn't think them fools.

After all, it actually was the case.

And what was really going on with Elkia?

They didn't have a clue... And so—

"Yeah, I don't know what to tell you... We're just commoners now, just medicine sellers."

—to be honest—he'd known what *would* happen, he thought with a sneer.

"Our game is selling drugs. What else can we do now?" asked Sora sarcastically, lying in his bed.

A voice answered:

"Proposal: List of options selectable by Master. Bath. Meal... This unit."

Gaaah! Sora managed not to scream out loud. He leaped from his bed, where— Wait, let's rewind.

She'd riffed on the conventional blushing-new-wife line, "Do you want a bath? Dinner? Or...*me?*" Sitting up from within the sheets was a girl with violet hair—or rather, *a machine that looked like one.* Glossy naked skin peeked from between the sheets along with mechanical parts here and there.

"Recommendation: Sequence. Process specification: Devour this unit in the bath. Unit recommends highly."

The thing closed the distance with Sora. Another carryover from the last playthrough.

"—E-Emir-Eins?! How long have you been there?!"

"Reply: Always."

She answered immediately as she crawled toward him. Sora shook his head and screamed:

"Come on, not *always*! What about your job?! Weren't you supposed to man the shop?!"

"Report: Inventory exhausted. Therefore, at 15:09, this unit initiated nude standby. Nude... Nude?"

Despite her placid response, she seemed to have just realized the situation she was in.

"Error: Embarrassment far exceeding predicted value detected... This unit ready... *Sofort?*"

...In other words, it was much more embarrassing than she thought when she tried it, and she wanted him to get on with it at once. Her glass eyes shimmered. But unexpectedly, the one who answered was—

"Oh, I see... It's true, you'd never be the ones to deal with customers..."

—Chlammy, who'd just finally figured out what it was that had seemed amiss.

Who'd been dealing with the crowd? And...

Chlammy and Fiel narrowed their eyes. *So this is the Ex Machina...* Fiel eyed Emir-Eins warily, Chlammy pityingly. On the verge of tears, Chlammy spoke:

"Heh... *What* now? You've *got* a friend, haven't you? Good for—— *Eeegh!*"

"...Not *a friend*...an enemy—!! What happened...to your other, jobs...?!"

"Interesting. Being disconnected from the cluster affected not only your basic performance, but also your memory, did it? ♥"

Shiro's outburst and Jibril's murderous smile transformed Chlammy's speech into a shriek.

—And, "Ah... This again?" Sora whispered as he looked up at the sky with the melancholy that had become his daily routine. Regardless of him and without response to the hostility of the two, Emir-Eins crawled out of the bed. The next moment, she transformed back into her maid costume. She bowed deeply to Shiro and Jibril.

"Report: Shop closing procedure completed at 14:09. Currency transfer to exchange counter completed at 15:03, using optical camouflage."

She'd even cleaned the shop, made orders—and performed tasks that Shiro normally would, such as market analysis. She'd finished them all, she was saying. Continuing her report inexpressively, she tilted her head.

"Riddle: During same period, which incompetent one *sat uselessly* beside Master? Hint: Birdbrain."

Emir-Eins faintly sneered, though to be fair, Jibril had also been floating some of the time.

"Dear me...? What could possibly be more useless than an Ex Machina with her Lösen abilities disabled...? How astonishingly inscrutable. ♥"

"Acknowledgment: Productivity even lower than this unit alone in safe mode. Exceeds analysis capacity of this unit in state disconnected from cluster (32 percent of normal computational/analytical performance). Incompetence of Flügel astonishing. Wow."

The two ridiculously powerful beings matched wits as Shiro remained so silent as to be even more unsettling.

Sora felt sure he heard the earth rumbling. Emir-Eins made to throw fuel on the fire—or to announce the end.

"Conclusion: Plan to restrict and interfere with operation of this unit by *task overload* failed. High confidence."

She flashed two V-for-victory signs coolly, and appended a single word coldly.

"Taunt: *Sieeeg*."

Having declared her victory, Emir-Eins walked away, leaving Jibril and Shiro twitching. With a curtsy, she sat down next to Sora. It seemed that even the ingenuity of Shiro and Jibril had been insufficient to avoid this. Another day of this sad routine had begun... Yes.

"......Focus... Staaare..."

* * *

Emir-Eins stared at Sora. That was all. That had been the routine for three weeks—making Sora very sad. Yes... Before, she had been taking a more seductive tack, and that was all right. Well, no, it wasn't. But the much bigger problem was this. Emir-Eins just sat next to Sora—and, without expression—

"......Ecstasy...... Mm. ♥"

—she just stared at him happily with a slight blush. He was doing his best not to give her free time, because this was always how she spent it. And that was a problem because—

———

"............Uh, excuse me? May I ask...just what is this atmosphere?!"

"Don't ask me! That's what I wanna know!! Why do I have to lie on a *bed of nails*?!"

—it always created *this atmosphere*, such that it made Chlammy scream and Sora roar back.

"...Hey—you're Emir-Eins, right? ...Don't tell me...y-you're—in *love* with Sora?"

Chlammy's expression was probably like that of the first person who ate a sea cucumber. It was impossible, Chlammy thought, yet her question was answered in less than a second.

"Acknowledgment: This unit loves him. This unit loves Master. This unit will say it once and say it again. This unit loves him. *Liebe*."

Yes—she would not deny her love. She was just doing what she said she would some days ago.

...A girl whispering her naked love, beautiful as a doll because she was one. It would be only natural for a male's heart to flutter and for desires to surge under these circumstances. But Sora could solemnly swear: His heart would never flutter, nor would his desires surge. They were not doing so. Because they couldn't. Not in a million years. Because—

"**Are you out of your mind?! How could you possibly**—? Waaah, Fiii, help!"

"It's all riiight, Chlammyyy—**I'll give my life to protect you!!**"

—yes—with one look from Shiro, Jibril, and Emir-Eins, Chlammy burst into tears. It was *this atmosphere*, which even put Fiel into a life-or-death state of mind!! The heart could never go aflutter amidst this malevolent, hostile silence. It would be more likely to sto——

"Oh, man! Sorry, Emir-Eins! I forgot to ask you to go take care of the crops. Sorry, but—" Sora cried out, searching desperately for an excuse to escape the situation. But Emir-Eins smiled back gently.

"Interrupt: Anticipated. Completed at 15:01. This unit will remain on standby by Master's side. Ahhh."

She thrust despair in his path. However...

"...Apology: Yet incomplete. One remaining crop: Could not determine whether to pick—"

"All right, let's go get it! Hey, I'll go myself! Shiro, come on! Okay, what crop is it?!"

Sora literally scooped up Shiro under his arm and started running. But Emir-Eins's reply—

"Reply: *Only head* protruding from Earth. Small Ixseed. Cultivar——Dwarf."

——made him frown: *Huh?*

■■■

Ixseed Rank Eight, Dwarf... A higher race, with magic aptitude just below Rank Seven, Elf's. The race lived in Hardenfell, second-greatest country in the world, in both size and power. And in the production of magical tools—machines using spirits—none of the other Ixseeds, not even Elf, could rival them. A well-known race of which they'd heard many times, and which they'd even seen on the monitors of the Eastern Union. But...

"...Let me just check. Dwarves aren't something you pick out of fields, are they?"

"...Is this world, faithful...to the classics, that say...they're created, of earth...?"

In a corner of the field, there it was, sticking out next to the lettuce they'd planted on a whim. A head, with brown skin and silver hair slightly peeking out from under a hood. Sora and Shiro looked quizzically at it. They'd never heard of such a thing. Jibril was less cautious.

"My, I don't recall planting such unusual seeds as Dwarf seeds—what's this?"

She pulled out the presumed Dwarf—and a slip of paper fell. Sora and Shiro casually picked it up and looked it over——

——.

"...Hmm. A Dwarf came all the way from Hardenfell to visit you...'just medicine sellers.' Some timing, isn't it? I wonder what this could be about?"

Chlammy ironically prodded them for the truth. Sora just barely managed to answer with a smile.

"We're medicine sellers, so it's got to be about medicine, right? We've been waiting. It's just..."

Looking back at the piece of paper, Sora stopped smiling, as Shiro looked down.

No address, no sender—no. There was a terribly stupid-looking signature, and there was some extremely sloppy Immanity script that looked as if it had been written by a child. Just one short, concise line, scratched insistently and brutally.

It's me. Gimme the drugs, on *credit*, ya *outsiders*.

"...Seems like this customer might be tougher than we expected..."

"............"

Countless memories flooded the minds of Sora and Shiro, outsiders to this world. Things they'd turned their backs on as they ran from and trampled over everything.

Their past was catching up to them to collect on the tab they couldn't pay. Yes...flashing about in their heads as their hearts creaked in pain......

⏻ Chapter 1: Another Age
Relativism

When first the puppet met the baby bird,
upon the bird's back were great wings.
Those white wings could surely go anywhere.
The empty puppet wished:

I want to see what this bird sees.

The dazzling bird had everything the puppet did not,
yet it had no home. Surprised to find
that it could become the bird's home,
the puppet smiled and swore from the heart:

I will be your home.
We'll always be together…
They crossed their little fingers and swore…

Sora and Shiro, having thought long and hard, got back to the problem at hand. The problem was the presumed Dwarf lying on the bed in front of them. The Dwarf—of yet indeterminate gender—was draped in what looked like a firefighter's coat. Actually, that wasn't even the biggest question. If Emir-Eins hadn't told them, Sora and Shiro wouldn't even have been sure this was a living thing. This "Object X" looked more like a backpack. They'd had Jibril pick the object from the ground, carry it, rinse it off, and dump it on the bed… And now—

"It still won't get up. What do we do?"

"…Brother… Are you…sure, it's alive?"

—they weren't even sure whether this stone-still thing was alive or dead. As they grew increasingly nervous, Jibril solemnly knelt on one knee and informed them:

"What is picked from your field *belongs to you*, my masters. I do believe that you may dispose of it however you like. ♥"

…For the sake of absurd argument, let's assume that ridiculous hogwash to be true. *Even so!!*

"You're saying this aspect ratio–skewed, bearded thing belongs

to us?! *Noooo, thank you!* **I just wanna wake it up and tell it, 'Please go home.' But how do we do that?!"**

Sora howled as he remembered the disappointment of the day he had first observed the appearance of Dwarves.

…Indeed—he'd had hopes. In this world, the Werebeasts had been animal girls. The Sirens had been mermaids as opposed to fish monsters. The Elves had been pale, blond, and long-eared, just as one would hope—this world had brought his dreams to life! Under the circumstances, of course he'd imagined the Dwarves as super-strong manga girls or porn-game legal Lolis!! Who would've thought they'd be buff and bearded regardless of sex as in the classics?!

…But dreams were only dreams. Sora wept at the bitter reality.

"If I may, Master, please, please give the matter more thought."

Jibril folded her wings and put her hands together in prayer.

"—There is no greater thing in this world than a Dwarf."

……

……*Hold up. Is it about to start raining meteorites?* Shiro and Sora compulsively looked out the window, fearing for the day's weather prospects.

"After all, *they use catalysts such as this* to bring out magic."

Jibril waved a hammer of mechanical structure—a giant hammer, about the size of Sora, that had been buried in the ground with Object X. They didn't know the details of this "catalyst" thing Jibril was talking about, but…

"What…? You're saying they *can't use magic without some magic wand–type item*?"

"…? You call that, great…? More like…weak sauce…amirite…?"

Instantly reminded of Sunday-morning cartoons, Sora and Shiro were both skeptical. Magical girls were always given items to fulfill their great destiny of selling toys. What great destiny did this Dwarf shoulder? their eyes asked.

"There are spiritual materials in the bodies of Dwarves. Their bodies are protected by mithril hair, and their eyes are made of orichalcum." Jibril swallowed. "When they manipulate spirits in their bodies, the mithril naturally amplifies the spirits…which in the worst case may cause an overload—a *loss of control.* Therefore, to use magic, they use their orichalcum to synchronize the spirits externally, with catalysts."

Sora and Shiro narrowed their eyes further at her reply.

Ah yes, I see, that's magic…also known as bullshit. It could never be understood in its details by normal humans like Sora and Shiro. But basically, was she saying that Dwarves couldn't use magic without their wands? No, she was saying that they were just so powerful they couldn't control it without their wands.

…Sora understood, at least, that this was the stuff of every little boy's dreams. He was impressed.

"Furthermore, they combine multiple catalysts with intricate seal-rite patterns, structuring the rites to be mobile, adjustable, and *modular.* By synchronizing with the catalysts that form the core of these mechanisms, Dwarves are able to cast multiple spells at once, allowing them to emulate the Elves' unique specialty of multi-casting. What makes this possible, in short—"

Jibril paused her magical technobabble to raise the hammer before Sora and Shiro before concluding.

"—are these spirit arms."

——*Spirit arms…*

So, the countless components of this mechanical hammer were all catalysts. And the fine patterns on each of them were seal rites or something? And a Dwarf would combine those to…like, *cast some übermagic or something…* Having translated it into terms they could understand, Sora and Shiro felt strangely relieved to recognize that, yep, this was some bullshit. But wait:

"So, Jibril? That means this Dwarf can't use magic without this hammer, right?"

"That is correct. Indeed my master is wise. It should be no surprise that you would deduce this fact independently."

Jibril swallowed again. Sweat ran down Sora's and Shiro's cheeks.

—*So if it's so important—*

——*why is* Jibril holding it?

"I excavated and claimed this hammer. Yes…*I was able to claim it.*"

…*She'd been* able. *Yes,* able. *And what does that mean?*

"In light of the fact that the Covenants render theft *impossible,* that means this hammer is *lost property* and now belongs to me, who *found* it—which in turn means that it belongs to *you,* by the Covenants!!"

"Uh… But isn't it still obviously against the Covenants to make off with lost property?"

"…If the Dwarf says… 'Give it, back'…we'll be forced to… return it…"

Sora and Shiro felt compelled to say what had to be said to the impassioned Jibril, but they got what she was saying. Jibril had a logical basis to assert that the Dwarf belonged to them.

"Yes. If the Dwarf says, 'Give it back,' then **you** will be forced to return it. However, *I,* like the hammer, am merely your property, and *I myself have no right to return it!!*" Jibril beamed. "And therefore, even if the Dwarf asks **me** to return it, I will have *no obligation to do so!* ♪ Though it may be impertinent, I would ask that you vacate this place for a brief time, so that I can *compel* the Dwarf to indulge me in a little game by the Covenants—and with that the Dwarf will be yours. It is as good as done. ♥"

Indeed, she would *make* the Dwarf play. She could enforce it. But how?

"Since, without the hammer—without magic—the Dwarf could neither leave this spatially severed room nor win at my game. ♥"

Which would leave the Dwarf with two choices: refuse a losing game and never leave, or accept and become property. Having laid out her diabolically brilliant plan, Jibril looked up at them, hoping for praise it seemed.

—Heh. That Jibril… She's learned a thing or two.

Getting teary eyed, Sora and Shiro smiled and were opening their mouths to give her the compliments for which she so yearned, when they noticed the way Jibril gulped as she crept upon the Dwarf.

Gulp. It was the gulp of one who was drooling. They closed their mouths without speaking.

"In which case, my masters? Before you depart—you see, in the Great War, useful materials such as mithril, which amplifies spirits, and orichalcum, which synchronizes souls, were *quite easy to procure*, but since the Ten Covenants, they have become quite hard to come by. And here we have a *walking mother lode...*"

Thinking back on Jibril's words, they realized there was no need to worry about those meteorites.

—There is no greater thing *in this world than a Dwarf...*

"How shall I reconfigure this Dwarf?! Please, instruct me! Geh-heh! Eh-hehh!"

"At least recognize it as sentient, okay?! How 'bout we return that hammer right now?!" Sora cried out as Jibril gripped her blade of light and begged him to tell her how to harvest these materials. He was surprisingly echoed by two people of different races who had been observing in strict silence from the corner of the room.

"Why, I never... If only that devil had the sort of multicellular brain necessary to achieve tasks other than killing."

"Acknowledgment: Object cannot be reconfigured. Critical gap in Flügel intelligence. Confirmed. Stuuupiiid."

As soon as he heard Fiel and Emir-Eins, Sora looked to the heavens: *Oh no, not again.* Through the raging flames of malice, his sadness had come to pay a second visit for the day.

But then...he dropped his gaze from the ceiling, made eye contact with Shiro, and thought.

—Flügel, Ex Machina, Elf—and Dwarf...

...Was he imagining this? Here, in this bedroom above this little shop in a corner of Elkia—all were present to resume the Great War of the ancient past...or was it...just him————?!

"Uh, ummm!!! Emir-Eiiins! ♪ What do you mean when you say, 'cannot be reconfigured'—?"

"*Oh, Master.* ♥ It is simply the inaccurate reading of a long-obsolete machine. Please pay it no mind. ♥"

Sora was doing his best to stay positive toward Emir-Eins, to be sure that the Great War never needed to be numbered. But Jibril shifted right into his line of vision. Sora and Shiro each wondered: *The explosion that shook the building earlier—that was just my imagination, right?*

"...Conflict: Mithril, orichalcum. Only Dwarves can process. Obvious."

"No, Master. It is quite feasible to process them as long as we have the fire of the Old Deus Ocain. ♥"

"Ridicule: Seizure of Holy Forge. Equivalent to control of Ocain. Requesting plan data. Resource not available. No surprise."

"Why, we've no need to trouble ourselves. ♥ We need only dispose of it *deeep* underground so as not to pollute the soil. ♪"

"Rejection: Can collect raw material. Recommendation: Disassembly. Sale. Profit."

The two of them discounted each other's claims, their animosity swirling through the air, as they all argued for the same kind of thing.

"Come on, doesn't anyone care to remember the Ten Covenants? Why is murder even on the table?!"

Sora howled out the lone objection to what otherwise was a consensus to kill the Dwarf.

Just then, a trio of blasts shook the shop.

"Hey—that time it wasn't my imagination, right?! *That was seriously an explosion*, right?!"

The heat made it clear it was no illusion as Sora scrambled to protect Shiro. Had they failed to prevent the second Great War? Sora was more than half-serious in his panic.

"......Looks like...it *happened*...?"

"Estimate: Dwarf simulated sleep for escape attempt. However, spirit arm failed. Rite failure caused explosion. Boom."

Shiro and Emir-Eins pointed to the burned "backpack" trembling in the corner of the room. Apparently, it had long been awake, watching for a chance to escape. Then its escape spell blew up, and now it was shaking there, clutching its broken hammer and its head.

......That made sense. Suppose you were the Dwarf. You wake up and hear that all of a sudden Jibril is plotting how to despoil you of your rights. While the Flügel, an Ex Machina, and an Elf are arguing about how to kill you. What a nightmare. Sora and Shiro had respect for this hero who managed to get back the hammer and at least tried to escape. Meanwhile, however...

"—? My... How could this happen? How perfectly unfathomable."

"Jibril, if you're saying that after talking seriously about killing the little d00d, that's pretty damn freaky!"

"Oh, no, Master. It's not that... If you'll please observe—"

Jibril gestured as she murmured with sincere confusion. Sora and Shiro gaped.

While the Dwarf shook in terror, around the Dwarf countless blurs zipped about, too fast for Sora and Shiro to follow or identify. But they could manage to get the gist of things: It was like a video playing in reverse of the *once*-shattered hammer coming back together as its countless components flew through the air as if being juggled.

"As you can see...Dwarves are exceedingly dexterous."

"...Mm...not that, we can tell...since we can't...*see* it..."

"Mm-hmm... I can see that at the very least their dex is *broken as shit*..."

Sora and Shiro looked on in disgust at the repairs proceeding literally faster than the eye could see. Apparently, they were also faithful to the classics in nimbleness. However:

"A Dwarf *failed*? At a seal rite? It boggles the—"

"Sorry to interrupt. But could you please explain *that* mind-boggling phenomenon first?"

"Why, even without spirit arms, you moles can use magic, too, you knowww? All you have to worry about is the possibility that you might explode due to internal spirit overload!! But you'll certainly die otherwise, you knowww? Why, this is your one chance to gamble on escape!! Why, I'd looove to see how dashing and heroic you can be! Go, Mole! ♥ Go, Mole! ♥"

Their buxom counterpart appeared interested neither in letting the Dwarf escape nor in letting a chance to kill the Dwarf escape. She hopped around the Dwarf with a radiant smile—as she indirectly told them, "Hurry up and die! ♥" They struggled to explain the Elf who was trying to goad the Dwarf to use magic while interfering with the repairs.

"Since when is Fiel that kind of character?! Hey, Chlammy, this is you, right? **Stop her!!**"

"——Huh? Uh. I've never seen her like this, either! Hey! Hello, Fi?!"

Fiel's bizarre antipathy toward the Dwarf had left Chlammy almost transfixed in the corner of the room. Having been woken up by Sora, she shrieked and rushed to intervene.

So what Sora was asking Jibril was, if humiliating Jibril once had been enough for Fiel to forgive her for annihilating the Elven capital in the Great War, how would you explain the cementitious obduracy of Fiel's hatred of the Dwarf? Jibril hung her head.

"Well, Elves and Dwarves. Their mutual opposition is iconic, like that of oil and water or cats and dogs."

Indeed. The strife between Elves and Dwarves was and had ever been legendary. However!!

"Which of you assholes *don't* hate each other?! You think you can justify her being this OOC with a canon statement that applies to anyone?!"

Thus Sora raged at those who moments ago were racing to resume the hostilities of the Great War, when—

"Warning: Spirit overload detected. Master advised to seek shelter beneath this unit's skirt. High urgency. *Herein.*"

"Ah. Master. It seems the Dwarf has elected to attempt escape, despite the high probability of a fiery death."

"Make it stop! Chlammy, get Fiel away! Jibril—"

—The two weapons' casual report of the Dwarf's impending demise caused Sora to yelp. The rapid-fire orders and entreaties of Sora and Shiro, as well as Chlammy, filled the room…

■■■

…and that was that. Those whose presence was like a bomb with a lit fuse were politely escorted off the premises, and Jibril was made to sit. The only ones left in the now-peaceful room were Sora, Shiro, and—

"Uhhh, all right, I'm not going to let anyone kill you, okay? Sooo… are—are you okay…?"

—the still-huddled-in-terror Dwarf, who gingerly looked up at Sora. The Dwarf's eyes cautiously inspected the room for safety—and then made contact with Sora's involuntarily. What did those pale blue eyes see in Sora's dark ones from under the hood of their coat?

It was a soft whisper:

"……You're Sora, you are…"

"Yeah. Nice to…meet——?"

Sora replied reflexively, but then frowned suspiciously.

"Wha…? *Did I ever tell you my name? —Hey, whoaaaaa!*"

"Waaah! I was so scared, I was!! What do I dooo?!"

The "backpack" leaped upon him, knocking him to the ground as it wailed.

"I—I was ten thousand meters below the surface…when my subterrane broke, just when I was coming up! I—I dug on and on without rest or sleep…until I saw the sun and thought, oh yes, I'm saved—yet then I found myself in hell, I did!!"

"Oh, Master. A subterrane is a ship used by Dwarves to travel through the ground."

"Oh. Thanks for the footnote—but is that all you have to say after freaking out the little d00d like this?!"

Sora remonstrated appropriately with the cause of the little d00d's frightened tears, as he began to go over the facts in his head.

* * *

—All right. So the Dwarf didn't actually grow out of the field.

Regardless, the Dwarf continued to cry on his chest, clinging with great unease.

"I—I can't see why you would save a grubby mole such as me, I can't!! Wh-what do you want from me?! Wh-what can I do for you not to kill me?!"

"Ah, Master. Since the spirit arm is broken, the Dwarf is as good as yours. ♥"

"Oh. Thanks for the footnote—but, Jibril, isn't it your fault the little d00d's pleading for their life?!"

Sora shouted at the absurdity of being begged for clemency by someone trapped by Jibril.

Okay. So the Dwarf couldn't run, because they needed the hammer to do magic and that was broken. Therefore they had accepted as an inevitability that they would be Sora's property.

However, they had determined they needed to somehow prove that the rights to their ownership were worth fighting over with a Flügel, an Ex Machina, and an Elf. And they were begging for their life with the conviction that this was the only way.

"I'm ready, I am!! I'm nothing but an unwanted mole, with no home to call my own! I'm ready to live in exile, whether as a slave or a pet! If it will save my life, I'll even be your chair—Whaaa?!"

But their prayers turned to a squeal and disappeared at the same time as the Dwarf's weight from Sora's chest. Sora's sister had pushed the Dwarf aside and now was sitting in their place, squinting.

"…This…is *my* seat…! Who is this *girl*…?!"

Shiro's voice was like a hiss, making Sora realize too late:

—Ah…indeed, the voice of the backpack that had pushed him over wailing—

—was like that of a girl.

And on top of that, she was already in unconditional surrender mode, like, *I'll do anything.* That did explain it. Under normal circumstances, Sora would have bit at close to the speed of light. Though in this case, there was the disqualifying condition of the race of stumpy girls being bearded in this world. But that didn't seem to stop his sister from getting a little jealous because she was, technically, a girl. It warmed his heart, and he smirked.

"Yeah, okay. That's a good point... Let's start with self-introductions, shall we?"

Sora sat up and put Shiro on his lap where she belonged.

"*Once more*—I'm Sora. This is my sister, Shiro... Sorry. I'm my little sister's reserved seat."

He patted her head as she continued to growl, and he affirmed her behavior by starting introductions. The Dwarf either realized her impropriety or simply felt Death's blade hanging over her.

"Sir—!! I-I—I apologize, I do!! I—I failed to even show you my face—!!"

The Dwarf hastily righted herself and saluted. She opened the backpack—rather, the coat that covered her head to toe...and—
——.

"I—I! I'm a *grubby mole of a travesty of a Dwarf*, I am! My name—"

Sora watched as she revealed her face—and her body. Distantly, abstractedly, in ecstasy and distraction, he listened as she said her name......

■■■

Shiro sat on her brother's lap. Her brother appeared in drunk rapture, as if his soul had left his body. Seeing the Dwarf appear out of the backpack-like coat—

—she couldn't blame him. It made her gasp, too.

The Dwarf was neither bearded nor stumpy. Her brown skin glistened as only the paltriest excuse for clothing covered...her exceedingly young-looking body. A pair of horns emerged from her hair. Her hair, in contrast to her body, sparkled of silver—no, mithril. Her enchanting pale blue eyes flickered with faint flame, doing justice to the name of orichalcum. And her sheepishly, nervously wavering voice and fragile expression—

"I—I! I'm a *grubby mole of a travesty of a Dwarf*, I am!"

—and the plaintive way she struggled to make herself heard—it all was just the thing to arouse the desire to protect. Shiro thought it not unreasonable that her brother would be entranced. In fact, it was necessary—perhaps even inevitable. *And for that very reason—!!* Shiro left reason behind her and moved. Yes——

"My name—is Tilvilg by clan, Nýi—— ......Um... What?"

Tilvilg.

Shiro now knew the name of her sworn enemy. She etched it into her memory and took prompt and appropriate action, reaching out her hand to *clear that flag by force*. Reaching for those components of unfathomable use on the garment that covered that flat body all too little, those *string-like suspenders...*

...Yoink, yoink, yoink...

"...My sister... Would it be all right for your brother to ask you what you're doing?"

Sora was brought back to reality as Shiro silently tugged. But *Shiro herself* could not answer his question. She tugged on and gave an evasive answer.

"......Buttons, exist to be pushed... Cords, exist...to be pulled."

"Yeah. I get that. I almost want to ask you to let me do it, but—Shiro? Hellooo?"

"Uhhh, excuse me! I'm not sure why, but I feel as if I'm being gravely humiliated, I do!"

Shiro ignored their objections and kept tugging as her thoughts raced furiously.

How had she come to this thought? Despite her typical excellence in inductive reasoning, the question hung over her unsolved. Her intuition insisted without clear evidence that the girl before her eyes was the *biggest threat ever*.

"... By the way, Jibril? I have a grave and serious question for you. Please answer with due consideration."

Her brother, at this very moment, was investigating this question with a solemn voice.

"If memory serves, Dwarves are supposed to be stumpy and bearded...correct?"

"Yes, Master... Wha—?! Oh... Oh! I am so sorry, Master!!"

...It was the question of how Dwarves were supposed to look here—that was the source of her unplaceable restlessness, which led her to this thought:

————*Oh, shit...*

"From your words, I should have deduced that you *were only familiar with male Dwarves!*"

Yoink, yoink, yoink... Shiro pulled hard. Yes—that was it... *That was the problem...!!*

"Dwarves exhibit pronounced sexual dimorphism... For example, females tend to have less hair, relatively speaking—and they have horns that extend from their foreheads."

Yoink, yoink, yoink... Shiro ground her teeth. Yes—and thus every time she pulled the string, a round stomach was revealed that proved this: Female Dwarves *were not fluffballs.*

"Also, while both males and females are *short in stature*, the adult form of females is what we might see as—*youthful.*"

Ah—so, if we were to just lay it out there on that ironing board—!!

————They were *dark-skinned Loli monster girls......*

And from what Jibril said, they were even legal.

"I see. In that case—Miss Tilvilg? Allow me to rephrase my request."

If he had on glasses, they would have glinted. Shiro found her hands shaking.

A girl—already in unconditional surrender mode, like, *I'll do anything.* Under normal conditions, her brother—virgin, eighteen—would most certainly take the bait at close to the speed of light!

NYOOON
(YOINK)

"There's just one thing I ask. As I said, please go home. And…"
As evidenced by his creepy words as he spread his arms and flashed his teeth—!

"From today, your home is here… Welcome back…*Til.* ☆"
——As far as he was concerned, this was almost as awesome as animal girls.

…But…*how'd that seem, like such a big deal…even now…*? She hadn't felt so shaken even when they conquered his favorite type with the Kingdom of Animal Ears. She couldn't explain this panic—the screaming of her instincts that *Seriously, oh, shit.* What was it? What basis did she have to know that the belly before her represented a *foe unprecedented*?!
"D-did you…pick me up without seeking anything in return?"
Shiro once again observed Tilvilg—Til—from her words to her expressions. She scrutinized the data to identify the danger lurking within.
"I-I'm but a grubby mole, I am! N-no skill at building spirit arms, no place to go home to, just an unwanted mole, I am!! I'll assure you I'll be of no use whatsoever, I will!"
From the feeble gaze and voice that inspired such sympathy, Shiro began to form a hypothesis.

——*Hypothesis*: Because she's useless? A pincushion of flags from the start indicating that this was the easiest girl in the game to get?
"O-or could it be…that tugging at my clothes is somehow of use to you?"
Seeing the Dwarf's face flush uncertainly, Shiro internally called B.S.

——*Hypothesis*: Because she's an exhibitionist masochist? Embarrassed, was she? Then she didn't have to go out practically in underwear, now did she? "Failed to even show her face," did she? Then couldn't she just take off her hood to show *only her face*?

...Why'd she have to open up down below? Seriously! What was she after, flaunting her Loli body to Lolicon Brother?!

...*Yoink, yoink, yoink, yoink—!!!*

"Uhhh, hold on a sec... Hey, Shiro?! A little girl getting red-faced as she glares like a monster while endlessly sexually harassing a little Dwarf girl, it's kind of—it looks kind of bad, y'know?!"

".............!!"

Her brother having pointed out her aberrant thoughts and uncomposed expression, Shiro abruptly let go. But the exchange that followed as Til ducked behind her brother's back made her narrow her eyes to knife points.

"You don't have to be useful. You just have to be mine."

"A-all right, then I'll be your...slave? Or pet, is it?"

"It's neither!! We are absolutely not turning this into porn, okay?!"

"Sir. I-in that case, I am yours, I am—and exactly what is it you would have me do?"

——.

"...........Yeah, what do you do after you get them?"

Such is the fate of the man who wishes for game. The virginal big brother had never considered *what he would do if he actually had it*.

"Eavesdropping: Opposite-sex body conformant to sexual preferences. Assessing motivation to possess: Relief of sexual frustration."

A voice answered with exactly what Shiro was thinking.

"Corollary: Risk of compromising Master's fidelity to this unit. Reminder: Disassemble and sell parts of Dwarf. Go away."

"Hey, Emir-Eins... I thought I told you to leave. Did you use your optical camouflage again?!"

"Oh dear. You offer yourself as a slave to *my* master? Are you truly so disenchanted with life? ♥"

"I'll never be a slave, I won't; I wouldn't even think of it, I wouldn't!! S-Sir?!"

"Uhhh, wait, wait!! ...F-friends... That's right!! Friendship is legendary, like—you know?"

"Just as you say, Sir! As of this moment, I am your friend, I—"

"Request: Disclose justification for *possessing friend*. Also, evidence for feasibility of opposite-sex friendship... Can this unit achieve friend status?"

Translation: *Yeah, let's hear this alleged motivation you have other than sexy time.* As Sora found himself caught between a rock and a hard place, Shiro's panic and questioning deepened.

——*Hypothesis*: Because Brother's just getting too popular recently?! No. Because it wasn't even a recent development at this point! Shiro shook her head in agony. She was extremely reluctant to admit it—*but that was old news!* The very day they'd arrived in this world—that very night, he'd already had that redheaded doormat fall right into his hands!! And Jibril just didn't realize how she felt, given Flügel's lack of emotional sensitivity and her perception of the relationship as master–servant! Like Emir——like—Emir-Eins——?

The hypothesis Shiro now arrived at cooled her head instantly. Knowing that she'd identified that *unprecedented threat*, her thin smile bore deep into her face like a crevasse.

...It had just been Jibril and Emir-Eins competing for one role, that of servant. Izuna and Holou comfortably shared the pet role. Steph had the role of doormat all to herself. So then—

—what was *Til's* role—?

As fate would have it, the weepy Til herself confirmed Shiro's hypothesis.

"Um! S-Sir! A moment ago, you referred to yourself as your little sister's reserved seat, you did!!"

......*Oh yeah? ...Right...*

"Th-then allow *me to be your little sister, too*—oh. I am eighty-four years of age, but will this be acceptable?!"

"What the hell kind of family circumstances lead to a little sister sixty-six years older?! No, I mean, my only sister is Shiro, okay?!"

"Then allow me to be your big sister or mother or—I-I don't know, I feel as if I am being glared to death, I do!!"

Shiro's eyes, fixed on the commotion, seemed to see the entire story that lay ahead.

A useless simpleton with no role, the type who triggered a person's desire to protect. The type you bedded as soon as she appeared. Okay, that's nice—what next?

She wanted to steal the little sister role. And the white-haired role, and the Loli role. All of her brother's favorite things... Something in Shiro audibly snapped. She sneered ferociously as her hand thrust forward...

■■■

Sora and everyone else turned at the sudden *bam*. Shiro's fist was buried in the wall next to Til, who was trapped as Shiro closed in.

"......This is your final warning... I won't, say it again...so listen...up."

She seemed to whisper, but with a malice that brooked no argument. It was an ultimatum—no room for compromise or negotiation. If Til didn't comply—

"*...I am, the little sister here! Me!!* ...I won't cede that role to anyone else... Okay?"

—Shiro would annihilate her.

"——Y—y-y-y-yes, Ma'am!! Right as rain, it is!!"

Til shrieked at Shiro's ghastly smile, then saluted, her expression that of one facing certain death. And then there was silence.

——.

Then: ......*Uh—*

"A-all right, calm down, Shiro! Well, yeah, your brother should've been the one to calm down, but!!"

"............*Fffff... Hssssss...!!*"

Having crashed and then restarted in his mind's return to normal operation, Sora shouted foolishly. He lifted Shiro out of her position dictating to Til the proper settings for her headcanon, while silently he screamed at himself.

When I think about it, this isn't even the time to be deciding her role!! Til wasn't his slave, or his pet, or his sister, or by any means his mom! And in any case...*they hadn't even played her yet—so they hadn't even gotten her yet*!! Jibril had just gone ahead and trapped her! And Til had just assumed herself she would lose!! While Sora had just gotten carried away by the beautiful tanned monster girl that came from the backpack, so strange and scandalous!! But Til, when all was said and done, was just—

——a *guest*—no. To be more precise: just the *messenger* of that *tough customer* making an inquiry with their shop. As his mind cooled down, Sora sorted out the information as he'd originally intended. It was true, she was a guest he'd been expecting—but still... Sora tried to probe carefully:

"""" .... """"

"Well, Ms. Til! What is the purpose of your visit to Elkia? Business or pleasure?!"

"Sir! Neither, I'm afraid!! I—I suppose I'm more of a castaway or a refugee, I am!"

But the pressure from around him made it difficult—the pressure from Shiro, who continued to growl in his arms; Jibril, who still hadn't received an answer as to what Sora wanted out of Til; and Emir-Eins, likewise. Til's eyes were filled with tears.

"Th-the chieftain seized me in the capital and forced me to deliver this let—ter? Wh-where is it?!"

With one eye on Til as she looked for her letter, Sora inquired softly of Jibril:

"...Jibril. Let me just check something here... 'Chieftain'?"

"Yes. The Dwarves traditionally play a game using spirit arms to decide their representative. This is meant to appoint the Dwarf with the greatest craft as their chieftain—their agent plenipotentiary."

"Here it is—so... I'm not even sure you can call this a letter, I'm not. It's more of a messy little note, it is."

Til pinched the "letter" she'd found in her pocket and frowned. Sora and Shiro had to agree with her, smirking to themselves. They'd already read the little scrap and put it back in Til's pocket.

It's me. Gimme the drugs, *on credit*, ya outsiders.

That was all that was written on the dirty little scrap, no address nor signature. It was for Sora and Shiro—but Til didn't even seem to know that.

"He said, 'Give this to the *weirdos*'...and with that just dumped me in the subterrane, punched in some coordinates, and off I went... I-I'm an exile, I am. Cast adrift...'"

—*Well, then. So the purpose of her visit was mere survival.*

"There's no place and no work in Hardenfell for a grubby little mole like me, so off he sent me to find a needle in a haystack—I'm a waste of space, I am! Being kept busy with the most thankless task until the time comes for layoffs!!"

That explained it. *No place to go back to.* An *unwanted mole.* At Til's self-abasement, so enthusiastic it seemed kind of fun, Sora and Shiro exchanged looks and nodded. Then this should be good news for Til: *the needle had already been found.* Sora and Shiro stood up to deliver the good tidings then and there, but...

"**Heh, it's fine with me, it is! I'd just as soon leave that bloody country behind, oh yes, I would!!**"

———?

"...Uh, ummm...? What now? Til—don't you want to find your needle and go home...?"

"*Not at all, I don't!!* It's a heavensent opportunity, it is!!"

Sora and Shiro were dumbfounded as Til shrieked giddily before her expression clouded over.

"—I certainly have no place in my country—but then...who's to say I have a place anywhere...?"

...Perhaps she did have a place in another country.

"When one door closes, another opens. It's true, it is!! So long, Big Papa Ocain! Out with the old gods, and in with the new! A needle in a haystack will be crushed sooner or later, it will! In which case it's *indistinguishable from the hay*, it is! I have no interest in sifting through hay. **Pft!**"

With that last part, she pretended to spit, without actually doing so. As Til smiled, at last having been able to let out all the vitriol inside her, things finally made sense to Sora and Shiro.

...So that's why she was so willing to be acquired. She'd been prepared for an exile that might have even put her life in serious danger—and just when she'd been searching for a new home, Sora and Shiro had picked her up out of the ground, literally. She'd lost any prior motivation to return to Hardenfell, and now she even had an *excuse* not to return until she delivered the letter. Her eyes glistened with gratitude as she looked at those heaven had sent her.

"I—I see... Thing is, though, *we're* going to Hardenfell *right now...*"

It would probably come as rough news to Til, Sora reflected, as he pointed out what was *right in front of her nose*. They say that you tend to find things when you stop looking for them. It was true.

"...Look at us. Doesn't it make you think of something?

......

"————I—I was just talking to the *biggest weirdos conceivable*, I was!"

...Two shut-in Immanities with a Flügel and an Ex Machina. While outside the room were an unduly familiar Immanity and Elf pair. Haystack be damned, one could hardly find a more distinctive needle in the world. This was the cause of Til's bellowing.

"I think it's actually not the case that it doesn't have an address. It's that the addressee is us—Blank."

Til looked back and forth between the scrap and her hosts.

"Ah. Um, by Sora and Shiro—d-do you mean…the king and queen of Elkia?!"

For some reason, her eyes sparkled as her voice screeched and bounced. Sora squinted dramatically at her reaction, which was much like that of a fan finally meeting her favorite star.

"Hate to break it to you, but right now, we're just pharmacists. And now, we're going to go deliver an order of some drugs."

"…Deliver drugs…COD…to the chieftain, of Hardenfell… Go."

Having told her their *existing plans*, Sora and Shiro started packing. After all, the two of them were pharmacists, and a pharmacist had only one business—pharmaceuticals. All that was left for them was *where* and *to whom* the pharmaceuticals were going.

…So the "who" was the chieftain…the agent plenipotentiary of Dwarf. The "where," they now knew, was Hardenfell. Thus they got ready to go.

"—Wha…? Do you mean I was merely sent as a gofer?"

It seemed Til hadn't been told she was merely their customer's gofer. She'd been all fired up over the idea that the chieftain was exiling her when he punched in those coordinates, and now:

"I—I was afraid I would be enslaved… Once again, the chieftain was just *teasing* me, he was!!"

Til stomped her feet, large teardrops rolling down her cheeks from the sheer ridicule.

But there was *one thing that still bothered* Sora.

"…By the way, how did your 'chieftain' or whatever *know where we were*?"

"Haven't the foggiest, I've not. Probably just a *hunch*, as usual!!"

Til puffed up her cheeks in frustration, and went right on:

"I-I'm not going back to Hardenfell, I'm not!! M-my place is here, it is! M-my home is here…it is…isn't it…?"

It seemed she hadn't been just throwing a fit over being exiled. She genuinely didn't want to go back to Hardenfell, apparently. Clinging to Sora and Shiro, she trembled like a puppy: *Are you going to abandon me?*

Sora smiled gently.

Abandon a tan-skinned, legal Loli monster girl? Nonsense!

Even after the coup d'état, Elkia remained the leader of a multiracial commonwealth. Even members of other races could immigrate if they went through the proper channels—and what was more, Sora informed her...

"Of course. It's just that *Hardenfell is gonna become ours*."

"———Come again?"

"...This order of...drugs—it's a bit, pricey..."

"Yeah, the price is—*your whole friggin' country*."

———.

Shiro and Sora sneered at the speechless Til and carried on.

"So onward we go to claim our sweet new home, that Shangri-La, the Kingdom of Brown Monster Girls!!"

"...You mean to claim them...and then...do what...?"

Shiro brought it back up with a look. Sora, virgin, eighteen, held back his glistening tears.

"*I'll think about that after I get 'em!!* The saying goes 'Opportunity has hair in front; behind she is bald'—but who has time to chase some goddess who's ninety percent bald?! Just lay a trap and get her once she's caught. And that's just where we are!! Get them and then do what? I can just as well think about that later!!"

He shouted bombastically to distract from the impurity of his motives.

"—Then perhaps we'll accompany you. That won't be a problem, will it?"

Announcing they'd heard everything, as if it were only natural, the two eavesdroppers—Chlammy and Fiel—opened the door. Having exhausted every resource *and still not figured out this was where Sora and Shiro were*, they continued on, their eyes sharply agleam.

"So you have medicine as valuable as Hardenfell. I would very much like to know what kind of medicine that is."

"Heyyy, hey. Didn't I tell you? It's the basics of business—"

Chlammy smiled fixedly at Sora with great sarcasm. But Sora showed his empty hands and replied with equal snark:

"—if you're gonna sell medicine, *first you gotta make the poison.*"

That's right: To sell your supply, first you need to create demand. Once the customers were desperate, nearly killed by your poison...

"Then you can sell empty bottles for *more than a country.* ♪"

......

"Very well—it is 9,748.7 kilometers to our destination, the capital of Hardenfell."

As Chlammy and Fiel looked on in doubt and Sora and Shiro in smug silence, Jibril just did her thing. She spoke with a bow, and the spinning of her halo sped up.

"Please take hold of my clothes and make yourselves comfortable for the brief journey. ♥"

Everyone took hold of the belt hanging from Jibril's hips as she prepared for a very-long-distance shift.

"'Kay, we're off. Look after the shop while we're gone, Emir-Eins."

"Equanimity: This unit will mind the house. Duty of wife. This unit is dedicated to the completion of its mission... Not lonely."

Except for Emir-Eins, who interpreted Sora's words in the most convenient possible way, as usual. Despite her claims, she waved a handkerchief in poignant demonstration of her loneliness. Chlammy squinted.

It made sense. They were having the spies, Chlammy and Fiel, come along with them, while leaving behind the fearsome warrior Emir-Eins. But was that really all that was going on?

Suddenly, Til butted in with her mumbling.

"Uh, um... My subterrane is out of service, it is. How will we reach the capital?"

"Mm? Doesn't everyone know about the Flügel's shift ability?"

"No. I have heard that their ability to shift to any coordinates known or in sight was a nightmare in the Great War, I have!"

Reminded of that RTS they'd played based on the Great War, Sora and Shiro smirked. No kidding—that was a nightmare. It invalidated the basic concept of a front. They laughed dryly at this angel of bullshit whose preparations were now coming to a climax. Meanwhile…

"…The capital is underground, it is. *She can't have seen it*—a—and—"

With Til's next words, not just Sora and Shiro—

"—i-is it just me, or is she *compiling a Rite of Heavenly Smiting*?!"

—but everyone there, even including Jibril for some reason, looked back as if confused. She had a point—even a long-distance shift shouldn't require this long a charge. Sora worriedly inquired:

"…Jibril…? Have you been to Hardenfell?"

He spoke for all of them. Jibril straightened her collar and nodded.

"Yes, Master. After all, Dwarf is the race most advanced in industry. The federal nation that unites them is the most developed mechanical civilization in the world. ♪"

In other words, Hardenfell—

"It is true that its capital is underground, but it is a very interesting country whose branches extend up to the surface and take a multitude of forms, from vertical cities to marine cities. I have visited on numerous occasions. ♥"

—was a treasure chest to the insatiably curious Jibril. Of course she would visit. Everyone breathed a sigh of relief to find that Til's misgivings had been unfounded. However—

"—Yes, and on numerous occasions I have visited *the airspace above the capital*. ♥"

—at Jibril's follow-up, they all froze…and then ran without another word, her voice fading behind them as she wiped the drool from her sloppy grin.

"After all those years looking down, a-at last I have received authorization to *enter*!! It will just take me a bit of time to compile the rite chain to shift us into the air, bore a tunnel with a Heavenly Smite of approximately one percent intensity, and protect my masters as—"

Jibril's declaration of her plan for an air raid made it clear that Til's misgivings had actually been perfectly well-founded. Apart from Fiel, who alone cheered, everyone else rushed out of the room.

They dashed off at full speed, all with the common understanding that they should fix the subterrane...

■■■

Far from the maddening crowd, in the Elkia Royal Castle—in the throne room—there was someone besides Emir-Eins who'd been left to take care of things: a certain redheaded girl.

Stephanie, Duchess of Dola—now Grand Duchess of the constitutional dukedom, leader of Elkia in name only.

"...Say, Aloe? I've got a problem... Will you listen?"

Despite it all, she sat not on the throne, but on the floor, a potted plant in her arms.

"It seems to me...I've not been entrusted with holding the fort, but *merely abandoned*... I must be overthinking it, don't you think? ♪"

Her sobs filled the empty throne room like a song...

The day Sora and Shiro had been driven from the throne by the coup—no, the day they'd turned down the game, stepped down, and handed the throne right over—

—*Allll right, Steph. Hope you'll work as hard as you always do.* ♪

—Steph had known without a shadow of a doubt, as they disappeared: This coup by those whom Sora and Shiro had oppressed...

...*had been orchestrated by none other than Sora and Shiro themselves.* And if they'd told her to work "as always," well, that must have been part of the plan, too. "As always," it would be a plan that could very well destroy Elkia. She'd readied herself to carry the heavy responsibility of the fate of Immanity, no stranger by now to her shoulders. It had already been three weeks—

*   *   *

"Aloe... Am I being left out again...?"

—and still there had been no word from Sora and Shiro. What peaceful days. The trauma of being left out of the game with Old Deus flashed through Steph's mind, and she buried her face in her knees. Ah... How peaceful. This was a coup d'état...a seizure of power. The House of Lords was bubbling over with the chaotic machinations of the Commercial Confederation—*but that was all there was*. Merchants, after all, put profit first. It wasn't in their interest to give the people the impression of instability. Thus the Commercial Confederation had set it up not as a "revolution" representing the people, but just as an internal altercation among the nobles—a "coup." And they issued convertible banknotes. Facilitated distribution. Liberalized trade... To the everyday man on the street, at least, it appeared as though nothing had changed—things were as peaceful as could be. While Grand Duchess Steph, divested of all actual authority, sat alone complaining to her aloe.

"...They always put everyone else before me... It's not fair..."

She bet they were off in some exotic land doing things she'd never dreamed of. Jibril and Emir-Eins had probably gone along, too. What about everyone from the other states of the Commonwealth? *It was strange how they were just quietly observing...*

"...I wish I...was with———— **What?!**"

She realized she'd been about to admit she was crying over not being with Sora.

"With whom...? With Sora?! What is my mouth doing?!"

Her sudden self-questioning led her to reflexively imagine all manner of ways she might be with Sora. She did her best to expel these lurid fantasies! *In the solitude, I've lost my mind. Come back, my sanity!* Steph sought a good wall to bang her head against.

"What's thiiis? If you find the throne so uncomfortable, I'll take your place aaanytiiime. ♪"

A girl's voice—a boy's, actually—accosted Steph. Steph screamed to chase the Dhampir off the throne he'd sat on before she knew it.

"That's Sora and Shiro's seat!! It's not mine, and certainly not *yours, Mr. Plum*!!"

Ah. To think that the first familiar face she should spot in three weeks would be, of all people, his...

"...Mr. Plum, won't you return to Oceand with everyone else...?"

She was insinuating, *You too, get out.*

"Excuuuse me? Renowned for my dutifulness, I would neeever leave Elkia at thiiis juncture."

The supposedly dutiful fraud stuck out his chest as he declared his devotion to his duty.

"I'm not like the others. I'm allll about self-interest! I intend to plot and scheme with the utmost sincerity!!"

His sworn duty being—to stab his every enemy in their sleep!! His otherwise questionable declaration was so bold, Steph couldn't doubt his sincerity. She sighed—and froze. He'd said it so naturally, it had taken her a moment to catch on.

"'Plot'?! D-do you mean—you've been playing a part in this chaos?!"

Oh no...how did I not realize?! The administration was in turmoil. Things seemed all too peaceful for there having just been a coup— but someone with the right connections in the Commercial Confederation could very well seize control of the state—it was the perfect chance to devour Immanity—!! Steph sweated as she finally realized just what she'd been meant to work hard at.

"—*Us?* Not just *uuus*... Even just as far as I've observed—"

Plum smiled a pitying smile.

"—Elf, Dwarf, Fairy, Demonia—even those reclusive Lunamana are playing paaarts. ♥"

——*?? ...?! ?!*

Steph alternated between sprouting question marks and losing consciousness standing up, utterly confused.

"Where shall I staaart...? *Blank are no mere Immanities*—"

With his troubled grin, Plum continued as if lecturing a child.

"—as other countries surmised. They've been probing their

allies, like us, to figure out their true identity—and particularly, the unbeatable trump card they're thought to have, capable even of defeating an Old Deus. Did you reaaalize this?"

"Y-yes, I did… They said that would make our *allies*, like you, excellent bait."

Sora and Shiro had rapidly expanded their power and even defeated an Old Deus, Holou. " " had done what no one else could. So they were suspected of having an unbeatable trump card. Now they were skipping a turn to let their enemies probe their allies for that risky *something*. Steph recalled Sora explaining this to her. Plum's sneer grew even more twisted as he looked at her.

"And why did you suppose that they'd probe only your *allies*—and not *you yourselllves*?"

Well, about that—

"*Everyooone* wonders whether Blank are mere Immanities… *including Immanities.* ♥"

————.

"If you want to look wayyy back, think of when Their Majesties first won the tournament to become the monarch of Elkia… They defeated an Elven spy. What would make you think that they themselllves were not foreign spies?"

—————No words.

As she felt the blood drain from her face, Steph listened to Plum's taunting sermon.

"Doubt has been brewing for a looong time… So, if it were meee, I would approach some Immanities with long-harbored resentment against King Sora and Queen Shiro—in this case, the Commercial Confederation."

Putting aside whatever agendas they declared when they colluded, if one assumed basically what they were after was power—

"I'd say: 'Pleaaase, I'll give you support to outstrip your rivals, so find out who Blank really is.' ♥"

That's right—if one won over a member of the Commercial Confederation, one could swallow up Immanity. What this meant was that Steph had entirely failed to appreciate what a crisis this was. After all—

"—You don't think *I'm* the only one who would think that, do youuu?"

In a haze of dizziness, Steph just managed to wring out a shriek.

"Th-then, the way Elkia is now—the Commercial Confederation moving to seize the reins of the administration—"

"It's spy paradiiise!! Foreign interference, information leakage, secret pacts!! A world fair of treacheryyy!!"

And Plum's next words forced Steph to look to the sky in terror.

"Or may I spell it out plainlyyy? You're three seconds away from succumbing to the poison. ♥"

…*Hard to argue there.* If everyone in the Commercial Confederation that now controlled Elkia was a spy.

In that case, Elkia…has already been swallowed up, hasn't it…?

"—No… No! That—that cannot be the case!"

Remember—those "Immanities with long-harbored resentment" to which Plum had referred—the Commercial Confederation—Sora and Shiro themselves had *built that resentment and given them an opening*—which meant!

"I'm sure of it!! All of this is part of Sora and Shiro's plan!"

"Yesss. ♪ It's a *trap*… Only we the allies know this. ♪"

Yes—those who knew who those two—Sora and Shiro—" "—really were. Those who knew that, while from another world, they were only human, and they had no unbeatable trump card.

Which meant they could anticipate this situation and *would certainly exploit it*. That would explain why the allies had been watching with such unusual silence. And it would also explain that *national missive*, hardly comfortable to describe as such, that Sora and Shiro had made her write.

—*"Hey, dumbasses, need some help? How 'bout you thank us by giving us your whole damn country?"*

Everything she hadn't understood then was starting to make sense. Which meant...

"They mussst have a plan to save and exploit the poisoned Elkia—an antidooote."

Steph sighed in relief. He agreed after all that it was part of their plan.

"...Ahem. Parrrdooon...? Why are you sighing in relief at that?"

"E-excuse me—?"

Plum's follow-up left her breathless and dazed.

"This is the very staaage on which the spies will be crushing each other looking for an unbeatable trump card that doesn't exist..."

"B-but you said it's a trap set by Sora and Shiro—"

"What is the surest way to bring down a whole pride of lions at once with poison?"

Steph started thinking about it. The Dhampir boy didn't wait. The edges of his mouth curled. With a sadistic grin, as if about to bite into and bleed his prey at any moment, he spoke.

"—It's to *gulp down the poison yourself and let them eat you.*"

——.

"It must be a poison so powerful that the other nations who fall into the trap will beg to be allowed to give up their countrieees. Simply put—it's a game of chicken. Without the antidote, everyone will die, including Elkiaaa. ♥"

Trembling, Steph covered her mouth to stop from screaming. This was more than losing the battle to win the war. It was a trap that could bring Elkia and the whole pride of lions down at once—however.

"...J-just what sort of magic potion could right this situation?"

Steph hadn't the faintest idea how that step was supposed to work. More pressingly, she had no idea what the point of it was.

"... If I knew that, do you think I'd be blabbing away to you thiiis kindly...?"

Plum smiled, making no secret of his considerable irritation.

"My plot is based on the wager that everyone will fall to their trap."

Steph grasped the meaning behind his expression and tone, then blanched once more.

"And for it to work, Elkia must be kept aliiive... Do you catch my driiift?"

That meant: Even Plum, a master strategist approaching the level of " ", had searched for the purpose of this charade, a way to resolve it, and a means to exploit it...

...and *had come up empty.*

"If you have the time to talk to an aloe plant————then *get to work.* ♥"

Even if she was a figurehead without authority, she should use whatever connections or other means she had. The situation was dire enough for Plum to worry and ask for help in keeping Elkia alive. It was an emergency that left no room for debate. Steph ran.

But she stopped and asked one last question:

"May I ask...why you chose to bet on Sora and Shiro's victory?"

Sora was a swindler, a liar, and a poor excuse for a human being. But, by now, Steph did trust him...not to cross that final line. However—this Dhampir boy, Plum, was another matter. If he thought it necessary, he would gladly sacrifice all the races—even himself. She couldn't trust what he said. She had no reason to. But then his smiling answer convinced Steph that he meant what he said, and she grinned.

"Oh, have I never told you? I like to bet on the looong odds. ♥"

—Ah, so things were going according to Sora and Shiro's plan... just as always. Just as always, it was a plan that *more likely than not would destroy Elkia!!* With a renewed sense of responsibility for the fate of Immanity, this time Steph sprinted without reserve. Yes, just as always—they'd left the politics to the politicians, just as they said they would.

"Aloe!! They didn't leave me out after all!! Did you hear that?! Did you?!"

———······

Plum watched Steph dance away.

"I wonder why she doesn't trust meee... I've never lieeed..."

That's right—everything he'd said was true, he thought with a pout. *He just hadn't told the whole truth.*

"It certainly would be marvelous to usurp their means of victory... to *take their mediciiine.* ♪"

I'm not too fooond of watching from the sidelines. The Dhampir smiled as at last, out of the view of anyone, he slipped away into the darkness.

However, those great wings
failed to reach the sky.

For there was no sky in that world.

An empty world that lied, saying
they could go anywhere.
An empty voice that would not let them
go anywhere.
An empty cage that told them how
to live—

Every time those wings opened,
aversion and curiosity,
inclusion and exclusion,
a force barred the sky.
Seeing the baby bird's tears,
the puppet said:

Let's take our time and think
how we can escape this cage.
The puppet entered the bird's cage.
Let's think together how to spread
your wings and fly.

Always together…
Just as we promised. They smiled…

There was no sky in that world…physically.

The capital of Hardenfell—a massive space said to lie ten thousand meters below the surface. Sora and Shiro got down from the subterrane and viewed that expansive underground city. Both were lost in thought figuring out how they could describe what stretched in front of them. Technically, not just in *front*. Also above, below, behind, to the left, and to the right. If they were to describe this 360-degree panorama just as they saw it.

"Let me guess. Your chieftain is the president of a corporation that rhymes with Thinra."

"…What does Demi…actually…do…anyway?"

If you did an image search for "factory nightscape," you'd probably get the right idea. A steel jungle floating fantastically with countless dazzling light sources sparkling in the darkness. It basically looked like a slight modification of Midgar from the seventh installment of that one series where both of the words begin with *F*. As if they'd used a Gravity spell to ignore all those laws of physics and stuff and copy-pasted it in every direction and there you go. What you saw was what you got—no sky, no *up or down*. The upshot:

"They even have the Mako Reactors. Just say it. The chieftain's Ruf*s, isn't he?"

Seeing a pillar of light thrusting through the center of the city, Sora threw this question over his shoulder half in earnest.

"—Oh! No, Master. That is the aforementioned fire of the Old Deus Ocain—the Holy Forge."

Jibril had been looking about, eyes agleam with excitement, but she hurried to lower her head as she spoke.

"The Dwarves are one of the rare races whose creator is alive and well, and still resides with them. The industrial utility of the Holy Forge allows it to serve as the driving force of this advanced mechanical civilization—this city."

Advanced mechanical civilization—huh. They'd seen plenty on the way to convince them of that. Such as the subterrane, which Til still wouldn't exit...

Apparently, it was a ship that used "flow differentials" to travel through the earth. They hadn't a clue what that meant, but anyway, they had traveled about nine thousand seven hundred kilometers to get here. Discounting the time Til had needed for repairs—a little under six hours. One thousand six hundred kilometers per hour...

...*through solid ground.* In their old world, that wasn't even in the range of a submarine—you'd need a supersonic jet. Did the standard disclaimer for improbable physics—"ignoring friction"—apply to reality in this world? Even Shiro clutched her head.

"...It's pretty awesome, I'll give you that. But with Jibril saying it was the most scientifically advanced civilization anywhere—"

Sora took another look about Midgar—pardon, the capital of Hardenfell. A bit steampunk, but totally sci-fi.

Yet even so... What was it? Somehow...*it didn't live up to his expectations.* Something was off—*or not exactly off, but...*

"Oh, no, Master. I merely indicated that it was the most *mechanically* advanced civilization *in this world*."

Jibril interrupted Sora's discordant thoughts with a correction and elaborated.

"If I may add—your world is far more advanced in science."

…Huh. Compared to these bullshit Dwarves who messed with gravity to build 360-degree cities? These sick freaks who'd built this city in layers with *no supports*?

"Dwarven civilization is *mechanically* superlative—but by no means *scientifically* so. In fact, Dwarf is the race furthest removed from science… I suspect this will become clear to you quite soon. ♪"

——?

Mechanically advanced, *scientifically* advanced… What was the difference? Sora and Shiro exchanged skeptical looks, but Jibril just smiled knowingly.

"With that, though with great reluctance—I shall take my leave to welcome our guests."

Her sullen voice lingered as she vanished into thin air.

And so, for now, those who remained were Sora, Shiro…and one other. That was Til, making furious use of countless tools to fix her spirit arm—her hammer. Her work had continued noisily since they were in route. "Hey," started Sora—

"Y-y-yes?! I-i-is the chieftain here? Help me!!"

—to which she immediately shrieked from behind him and Shiro. She'd taken shelter in an instant, tears in her eyes, her hammer held defensively aloft. It had been too fast for Sora or Shiro to see or comprehend.

"We dunno why you're so freaked out. But can we say what we do know?"

"…We're…positive…we can't do…*shit*, to help you."

If she had that kind of physical prowess and was still afraid…then hell if they could help her.

"*I disagree*, I do!! I-I've somehow managed to *overhaul* my spirit arm—in time!!"

As if to confirm Til's objection, her hammer made a clanging noise and emitted an intricate pattern of light beams.

Sora and Shiro narrowed their eyes and went, *Ah, I see.* Not because of the transforming, initializing spirit arm. Rather, it was the pale blue fire shimmering in Til's eyes—those eyes purportedly of orichalcum—that brought grins to Sora's and Shiro's faces. It was the determination in those eyes, that indomitable resolve burning with bright flame—

"I'm not alone anymore, I'm not!! If the *enemy* comes—"

—that iron will, bowing for no one, that roared from the mouth of that brown Loli monster girl. In other words—!!

"—**you'll hold me, you will!! And then! I'll be so ☆ very ☆ safe—!**"

"**Excellent. Come roaring into my arms! Yeah, where's that enemy? Come and—**"

With indomitable resolve, Til would run like hell from the dominant! And Sora would welcome her into his arms—that ultimate safety zone where the Covenants would repel any attempt to pry her loose—

...Yoink, yoink, yoink...

Silence arrived as Shiro yanked at Til's suspenders. Til blushed, and Sora watched adoringly. But just as soon, the silence dissolved with the appearance of one of the enemies Til feared.

"Whyyy...so this is your burrow... What a perfectly grotesque horror showww!"

The sudden visitor continued merrily as if in song:

"It rubs me quite the wrong way. ♥ Why... ♪ this would be a fine time to execute you in a dark ☆ ritual! ♥"

"Help me! This is the time, it is! Help me! I'll be *burned alive*, I—ow! Q-Q-Queen Shiro, pardon me, if you will! I-I'm safe here, I am; I've successfully escaped, I have!!"

Smiling, Fiel announced Til's imminent slaughter. Til fell on her face, probably due to having her suspenders pulled, before crawling into Shiro's skirt. Sora looked behind, unimpressed with Til's shaky-voiced declaration of victory.

"…? Oh, I apologize for the wait, Masters. But I have returned."

"Yeah… Good work, Jibril… So, sorry to spring this on you right away, but…"

The devil angel, back with the Elven menace, stood there confused.

Til and Fiel had averred that they would die were they to breathe the same air for six hours in the subterrane. So the agreement had been made that Jibril would go back to pick up Chlammy and Fiel after they got to Hardenfell. Sora praised Jibril and clutched his head again.

"…This isn't even on the level of 'they don't get along'…"

"Heh-heh-heh, yes, heh, I say! I can't see anything, I can't! Even if you glare at me, I—I won't be scared, I won't! You might as well craft a spell to hurt me and watch the Covenants turn it to mist, you might! **Pft!**"

"Fi!! Come on, Fi, don't make that face; it's scary! Please…"

Her head buried beneath Shiro's skirt, her bottom showing, her body trembling, Til taunted Fiel all the same. Fiel's face was such a storm of silent bloodthirst, it ultimately made Chlammy cry. Shiro grudgingly bore the situation as the alternative to having Til in Sora's arms. All present looked to Jibril for an explanation.

"Perhaps owing to the influence of their creator, Dwarves believe that everything exists to be forged."

She gestured toward the light at the center of the city—the Holy Forge.

"And with the fire of Ocain, god of the forge, they are capable of melting anything."

…*Hmm, quite a radical line of thought.* Sora nodded. *Everything existed to be forged*—so the world existed to be rebuilt. To the Dwarves with their all-melting furnace, the environment *was made to be destroyed.* Meanwhile…

"Why, rocks cave, trees fall, rivers dry up in their wake. The very mountains collapse."

—*And the wind? And the sky?* Sora, Shiro, and even Chlammy wisecracked to themselves as they listened to Fiel.

"The seasons dieee, and the homes of the Elves—*naturally!*—die as well..."

And as they started to hear the rumbling of intent to kill, Sora and Shiro finally understood.

"Why, to exterminate such vicious beasts...is the natural obligation of every intelligent being. ♥"

The polar opposite of the Elves, whose love and hearts died as well, apparently... Even so, Sora asserted that he was not convinced—for indeed—!

"You both destroyed the environment on a planetary scale in the Great War! Who are you to talk?!"

It was *thousands of years too late* to be saying that—!! Sora and Shiro couldn't swallow this however they tried. But at Jibril's next words—

"It is a matter of the length of their feud, I suppose. Masters? Please observe the forehead of that long-ears. Do you *see* something? ♥"

—they froze like stone. In Fiel's forehead...there were gems—*minerals*. Sweat ran down their cheeks.

—*Everything exists to be forged...*

They didn't know exactly what those gems were. But it was easy to imagine that it would be problematic for them to be mined.

"As the Elves have butchered the Dwarves for destroying their forests, so have the Dwarves massacred the Elves for their gems..."

No one knew by now which happened first, but in any case...

"They have slaughtered each other since the beginning of time, *altogether apart from squabbles over the One True God.* ♥"

"It's your fault for being born with stones in your head, it is. If you've a complaint, then come back as a liquid instead. **Pft!** That's right, I won't apologize, I won't!! I'll never apologize to a little weed, I won't!!"

"...Nooo, nooo... Fi's ignorrring me... Waaaaaah!!"

"—Ah! Wh-why, no! I wasn't ignoring you, Chlammyyy, I was just a bit—"

"Nooo! I don't like iiit! Eegh... You're scary, Fi. I hate you!!"

Til's trolling had made Fiel's malice explode again, which then brought Chlammy's fear to the breaking point, it seemed. Fiel apologized in a panic to the wailing Chlammy, who'd regressed to the state of an infant...

At all this, Sora just sighed. He gave up and decided to dismiss it. *This is beyond reconciliation or resolution...*

"'Kay. So, will you take us to our customer who wants his medicine?"

He looked back at the multilayered, antigravity, omnidirectional factory-type city as he spoke.

Actually, to be precise, by now Sora's eyes were only on the Dwarves who bustled about the city. To be more precise: only the females. Yes...the brown Loli monster girls—!! As he asked Til where to find the customer who would sell them to him, not knowing even which way was up...

"By the way, you might want to get out of there...before Shiro goes ballistic on your ass."

...Sora advised Til, who'd been squawking away with her head beneath Shiro's skirt. Til responded promptly.

"——Wha? Wha?! I-it was a brief lapse, but I do apologize, I do!!"

"......There's...a limit...to how, *rude*...you can...be......isn't there?"

Til's shoulders bounced up as she scrambled to her feet with a salute. Which meant...

...*Her skirt*—Shiro's—*went up, too.* Dazzled by the sight of her panties, belly button, and smile, Sora and Til froze.

"...The little sister...role's, not...enough, huh? ...Now you want... to be the protag...?"

The smiling Shiro was looking just as ballistic as Sora had feared. He could read between the lines.

"...You think, you can get away with...being an accidental perv...
if you're not even, the main character...?"

I see, so you want to be crushed, do you? Very well, I'll grant your wish.

**"Alll right, Til!! Let's hurry and get to Hardenfell and get back!!
Okay?!"**

"Sir!! I-I'll escort you to the Chieftain's Hall immediately! B-but I
won't see the chieftain, I won't. I-I'll wait nearby, if I may...!!"

Sora shouted at Til in the hope of hurrying her and avoiding an
unmanageable situation this time. Til saluted, while sticking to her
guns on that one point. She closed her coat up to her head—once
more in backpack form—and said as if reassuring herself:

"...It—it's all right. I'll go back home; this is just a trip...it is..."

Mumbling, she walked ahead with heavy steps. Following, Sora felt—
—a sense of déjà vu at this one who so hated her own country.

"...Hey... Why do you hate Hardenfell so much?"

"Heh... There's no place for a *grubby mole* among Dwarves,
there's not."

She sounded just as she had when they first met, when she called
herself a *"grubby mole of a travesty of a Dwarf."* She seemed to sense
the doubt of Sora and Shiro behind her.

"...We're going through anyway, we are. I'll introduce you to the
Central Industrial District, I shall."

A picture is worth a thousand words. You'll see. The ironic smile
with which she turned made clear enough what she meant. And then:

"...Sir and Ma'am, do you like this city?"

......

"To me...the capital is the worst part of Hardenfell, it is."

Til looked up at the lights like dazzling stars throughout the spher-
ical underground city. The light shone in her orichalcum eyes—but
she dropped her gaze as if she were staring *beyond* the horizon.

"——There is *no sky here*......"

Til managed a fragile smile as she looked at the dark sky reflected
in the dark-haired Sora's eyes. Sora chuckled—*Yeah, you're right...*

■■■

The Central Industrial District buzzed with noise and machines and Dwarves...and manufacturing plants. Sora and Shiro witnessed an answer to a question they'd long had for fantasy works: *Why is magic the opposite of science?*

What is science?

It is a system of records of observation of natural phenomena, inference of laws, and verification by testing. If one could observe magic, spirits, souls, or even gods as natural phenomena, then one could research them systematically. And if the results were reproducible, then wasn't that totally science? Wasn't it just one more scientific discipline, like physics or mathematics?! Spiritology!! And now we were talking about machines—devices that behave in specified ways according to theoretical laws. Who *cared* if they ran on steam, electricity, spirits, or what?! Wasn't it science regardless of the power source?! Yeah...that's what they'd thought...but...

"Now!! It's time for a demonstration of some simple spirit-arm manufacturing, easy for any Dwarf to handle, it is!!"

...Sora's eyes were already glazing over at this complete collection of advertising phrases that had never been associated with anything that was actually simple. Til shouted over the work noise and gestured below them. They were on an overpass, looking down at a massive manufacturing site... Yes...

"First! You just need some ordinary Dwarves and an appropriate amount of materials, you do!!"

...Slapped in the face from the first line, Sora and Shiro looked like they were already done with this. They watched a buff fluffball pick up a huge mass of metal as if it were nothing. *Ordinary, my ass.* And then:

"Next, you just bash it with a hammer! Do it in the way you feel is best—and there you go!!"

There was a blast as if someone had gotten frustrated, shoved a whole bunch of charges into a rock mass, and ignited them all at once.

——.

"…Yeah? So…what's that?"

"It's a spirit arm, it is. See? Simple, isn't it?"

"……I don't, like this… My, head hurts…"

Before they knew it, the buff fluffball had in his hand a mysterious machine—reportedly a spirit arm. It was as if they'd cut straight to the end. This was reality. Shiro crouched and held her head. Sora pressed on his temple and took a deep breath before asking Jibril:

"Okay… Now show us the raw footage in slow motion. With voice-over, if possible."

"Master, I'm afraid it's just as it looks. Dwarves are exceedingly dexterous."

"…Mm… *Can't even see! …I don't get it*, but…okay?!"

"I'm asking you to explain this *crazy* bullshit, okay?! Don't tell me—"

Having gone over it, there was just one thing Sora had learned, and he asked to confirm:

"You're saying they grab a lump of metal ten times as big as they are, hack at it, bash away at it—and then—"

Eyes wide open, his head shaking side to side, he screamed—!

"**—boom, you have a *mechanical ball*? There's only so far 'dexterous' will take you!!**"

"…Not just a ball…it's, almost a perfect sphere! …The precision… is on the level, of a prototype for measurement…!"

The object in the fluffball's hand, according to Til, was a spirit arm.

This spirit arm had been transformed from a metal mass to debris to a machine that operated as intricately as a gyrocompass. It had been finely engraved and gave off the luster of a mirrored surface.

"I mean, how is it possible to turn a single piece of metal into a machine with *multiple interlocking parts*?!"

Cast it. Cut it… At least assemble it! What? They just mash the material arbitrarily? They pound it and bend it and fold it, and then there's a seal-rite machine—a complete spirit arm?

At least drill it——!!!

They're "seal rites" as in engraved seals, right? So *engrave them*! At least do what the name says!!

"...Hey, you're not telling me they made the subterrane and this whole mechanical city this way, are you?"

Sora was flummoxed. Jibril replied with a correction.

"Oh, no, Master. Spirit arms are implemented by connecting catalysts that have had seal rites applied, combining them, and synchronizing spirits and souls with the cores. Ultimately, they are driven by the magic of an individual Dwarf, the spirits of the caster."

"Yes, yes! Typical machines... Oh, look over there. They're building an airship, they are."

They turned their eyes to the section of the plant Til pointed to. A fluffball who'd crossed his arms in front of a huge bulk of material, shouted "Rahhh!" and smashed it like a karate master would to a stack of tiles! And then—somehow!—before their eyes, the material turned into an organic-looking drive furnace. Then, with the sense of satisfaction at a job well done, the Dwarf lifted it up like a barbell.

"Now! Another Dwarf who's made another part as seems best takes that part—"

The fluffball tossed the drive furnace to another fluffball, who caught it with his hands—

"And thus they put together parts as they see fit until they have an airship, they do. And there you have it, you do!!"

—Steadily. At blinding speed. Tossing and heaving... Various units flew through the air and piled up on one another, connecting as they hit each other, unfolding, coupling. It seemed as if a massive structure was forming all by itself. This was unwatchable.

"Other than the seal-rite stuff, isn't this exactly the saaame?!"

...Okay. So basically, it was magical bullshit. Time to let it go. Even as Sora relaxed, his face sculpted into an archaic smile, the airship kept coming together—but there was no need to trouble oneself over how this insult to aerodynamics could fly. If you wanted to start that, what about Jibril? Screw it. It's magic. But it was a machine—so screw you, Sora roared with the baneful visage of an Asura!

"Look—*where are the blueprints*?! Where are the measuring instruments?! Where are the tools other than hammers?!"

A machine—a device that behaved in specific ways according to theoretical laws... Sora demanded to know what had become of the design documents, the engineering logic...in short, the theory. Til's voice rang out to reveal to him the quintessence of this advanced civilization.

"Sir!! If you ask what the secret of Dwarven mechanical engineering and magical theory is, there is only one answer, there is!!"

"Don't think, FEEL!" it iiiiiiiis!!"
"How can you have engineering or theory if you reject *thinking*?! Are you screwing with me?!"

—Don't worry about all that theoretical crap. Use your common sense!!

Sora gasped under the weight of this unheard-of absurdity. But Jibril kneeled and told him for the third time:

"Master, I apologize for not explaining sufficiently... Dwarves are exceedingly dexterous."

No matter how he begged for an explanation, that was the only answer she could give. And there was a reason for that.

"*I can see it, but I cannot understand it myself.* I speculate that they themselves would be unable to explain it."

Sora felt the blood drain from his face, as Shiro felt it drain from hers as she crouched trying to do calculations. So Jibril was saying that Dwarves fundamentally...

"Dwarves: the race created by Ocain, god of the forge."

It was like asking the Flügel, created by the god of war, how they could fight so well. If one were to ask the Dwarves, created by the god of the forge, how they could forge so well—

"All they need is their natural gifts—no, their *god-given sensibility*—to manufacture anything."

—one's question would be answered with a question: *How can't you?*

"They imagine what they fancy and move as they please—drawing their ideal ever nearer through pure sensibility."

Sora and Shiro gulped as the answer got shoved down their throats.

"And as a result, they *never fail*... They are a race without need for hypotheses or testing."

——So it was just that they were preternaturally talented... No. *Straight-up geniuses*—monsters of sensibility. All they had to do was move their hands the way their imagination told them to, and creation would occur spontaneously. If they'd built this civilization all out of flashes of inspiration and casual tweaks, then they didn't need theory. Trial with no error. Testing with no failure...

"...A mechanical civilization that's progressed by passing down knowledge and experience by sensibility alone...huh..."

Having finally got the big picture, Sora and Shiro looked at each other and nodded deeply.

—In that case, there's no problem!!

"So basically! Dwarves just have an OP buff?"

"......Mm! ...If that's, all it is... Okay... I can live with that..."

Sora and Shiro powerfully stood up and shook off their confusion. *All right, so they have a mechanical civilization that would sneer at science fiction. But this isn't* science fantasy, *either. It isn't science at all. It's pure fantasy!!* So the two of them thought, having at last understood the true meaning of what Jibril had been telling them.

A mechanical civilization but not a scientific civilization...huh? Ah...now they had their answer as to the difference between science and magic.

—Machines without theory... Yes, indeed, that was not science. It was, indeed, magical bullshit!!

"Maaan... Why didn't you just *tell* us Dwarves were a magical bullshit race?"

"...You could have...saved us...a lot, of...sweating..."

Beaming from ear to ear, Sora and Shiro resumed walking, ready to leave this magical workshop that called itself a manufacturing plant, while the Dwarves carried on their work below.

A race of geniuses that advanced technology without theory. So decisively incomprehensible that it was a relief. *It'd be more productive to try to understand Flügel or Old Dei,* Sora thought with a smirk. They were just fundamentally beyond human understanding—or rather...

...They were the most dangerous thing to assume you understood. Sora made up his mind about that. As they began to exit the Central Industrial District, Sora and Shiro heard someone mutter behind them.

"...Why, they're simply animals not capable of complex thought."

It was Fiel, who'd kept silent for a long while, with a differing opinion about the Dwarves... No, actually, a plain statement without the slightest aggressive intent. She sounded as calm and sure as a Buddha giving a sermon.

While Chlammy cried—*You're scary, Fi; I don't like it*—Fi's face, its emotions sealed away by magic, remained as placid as a Buddha's.

"...Fi? Your 'form is emptiness' face is kind of scary in its own way..."

"Chlammy... You must calm your mind... Why, fear is one of the roots of suffering..."

Fiel looked like a Buddha statue, and it only made Chlammy back farther away.

"By the way, Master? I hear there is a race that has repeatedly lost to *this very thoughtless race.* ♥"

Jibril looked pleased as punch.

"I have also heard that they analyzed the tactics produced by the thoughtless sensibility of this thoughtless race, and systematized them into a set of conventions that just barely allowed them to fight back, both in war and in games— Oh! That reminds me. ♪"

The terrible actor glanced at Fiel.

"I believe the link tattoos on the arm and forehead of that long-ears do, in fact, stem from a desperate theoretical adaptation of those used without a caaare in the worrrld by the Dwarves. Pardon, was I too harsh?"

With the utmost joy, she worked to break the face of that statue—trolling as hard as she could.

"You had to downgrade them so that your long-ears could use them, didn't you? ♥"

"Fi?! That's a cheap shot! Don't get mad, please?!"

"...Why would I? A Flügel knows nothing of seals, useless should even one spirit particle be warped. Why, I'd never take to heart the words of one who hasn't the faintest idea what subtlety is, to say nothing of being able to use seal rites..."

"Are you sure you're sealing away your emotion?! Don't mock her back with that face, that voice!!"

With that commotion behind them, Sora and Shiro looked at the back of the little figure ahead of them.

...Til had talked about Dwarven craft as if it had nothing to do with her. They looked at the hammer on the back of that self-described *"grubby mole"*...

"...Yes, yes. I'm sure you've realized by now, you have..."

Without turning, Til nodded deeply and self-deprecatingly. All right. Dwarf had a crafting cheat. Got that. But when Til had repaired her spirit arm and the subterrane, the way she had done it defied even Sora's comprehension. That speed the eye couldn't follow, that inexplicable skill—but what was it...?

"...I can't make *anything* the way the others do."

Til turned with a grin as if revealing the secret to a cheap trick. She bashed her spirit arm into the ground, and it blossomed like a fan with thousands of slats, the slats unfolding into countless tools and measuring instruments.

"...I...don't have a bit...of that sensibility, I don't."

So she was saying... Even with tools, there was nothing she could do in that regard. Til sneered at herself to confirm Sora's thoughts and continued.

"...Whether it's this hammer or the subterrane, the best I can do is to fix things or patch them together, it is."

Til was supposed to be one of those Dwarves who "never failed." Sora now understood Jibril's consternation when Til had blown up her spirit arm.

"But even when I patch things together, I don't understand the meanings of the seals...so I fail, I do."

This civilization had passed down knowledge and experience by natural sensibility. Without that sensibility...*there was nothing that could be passed down.*

Sora noticed the way Dwarves looked at Til, her face hidden by her coat...

—*What are you doing here?* Their eyes asked her that warily.

"...So do you still need to ask...why I hate Hardenfell?"

Sora and Shiro, Chlammy, even Jibril, all found themselves silent. If what made a Dwarf a Dwarf was that gift—that god-given sensibility—then Til...

...of course wouldn't like it. Nor have a place.

——She *wasn't even a Dwarf*...from her point of view. She gently brought her face into sight to declare her inferiority——

"It's because I'm a grubby little mole, I am!! Do you understand now?!"

—and sang the triumph of *I told you so*—!!

......*Uhhh...?*

Her glorious mien paradoxically suggested pride. The rest uniformly were without words this time.

Til's heated discourse reminded one that this was the point she was after. But then she walked up to Sora with a smirk that made even Sora nervous and leery, and she went on—!!

"Sir?! I have heard that Immanity is a 'thinking reed'!!"

"Uh, yeah... Someone said that in this world, too, did—"

"But an *unthinking Immanity is not a reed*!! It's *just a moving reed*! A pestilent freak of nature just waiting to be blasted with weed killer. At least a real weed stays put, it does!!"

Til's furious invective didn't even give Sora time to acknowledge her statements. He couldn't breathe.

"An Immanity that *doesn't think*! A Werebeast that *doesn't have keen senses*! A Flügel that *can't fight*, a Siren that *can't attract*, an Ex Machina that *doesn't learn*—these are all cases of utter and irredeemable hopelessness, which I would to, here, as I said!!"

Til, so impassioned she was losing her command of the Immanity tongue, concluded!!

"There is nothing worse than a Dwarf who *doesn't have sensibility*!! This should be self-evident, it shouuuld!!"

Her words had an echo of thunder quite unlikely in an underground city.

......*Oh. Must be the factories*, Sora hazily realized. Fiel nodded with her Buddha-statue face, while everyone else was simply overwhelmed by the tide of her momentum—

"Oh. You weeds who *can't be eaten* and *can't be burned* should hurry up and rot down into fossil fuels before you start talking, you should. **Pft!** No, I won't apologize, I won't! I'll never apologize to a bloody Elf, I won't!!"

—*But, Elf. I'm not including you here.* Her motor-mouthing seemed to have led to Fiel weaving a spell, still with the Buddha-statue face.

"Heh! *You can try to destroy me*, but it's futile, it is; I'm not scared, I'm—waiiit! H-help me! Queen Shiro, please let me in; I was bluffing; I am sooo scared, I am!!"

Til tried to flee under Shiro's skirt again, but that wouldn't work a second time. She hurried to hide behind Sora and Shiro, where she quivered. Sora—and for some reason Jibril and Fiel, too—frowned at her quizzically.

* * *

"Uh…hey. But, Til…you *can* build spirit arms…can't you?"

Til had asserted her inferiority with a fervor going past humility all the way to pride. But…

"From our point of view, you're so skilled it's bullshit. We can't even see spir—"

Sora chose his words to probe out the identity of this unease that had arisen within him but was interrupted.

"Sir. Immanities cannot fly, they can't."

"………Well, yeah, we can't. Sure."

Til looked straight at Sora. Her next words, with her pale blue eyes, followed:

"So, then, do you resign yourselves to the fact you can't fly?"

——.

…*Oh… That's how it is…*

Sora fell silent. Heedless, Til once again took on again a triumphant visage and added, *That aside—!!*

"A bird that cannot fly is a chicken, it is! A farm animal! Good only to be cooked to a crisp and deliciously— Wait! I-if I cannot even be deliciously enjoyed, then am I even inferior to a farm animal?! I—I'm afraid I've insulted chickens, I have… B-but at any rate!!"

Til's speech, resounding ten thousand meters below the surface, seemed to be finally reaching its conclusion.

"I *have no sensibility*! I *can't build spirit arms*! I *can't even use magic*! And as such I'm *not even a Dwarf*!!"

Her endless stream of negatives sparked something in Sora. He thought he might be putting a finger on his unease—but then her conclusion crashed his thought process.

"Finally, I *have no hair*!! I'm as smooth as a dolphin!! And therefore: I'm a grubby little mole, I am!!"

"Hmm?! I find this a non sequitur! Please elaborate on the implications of this smoothness of yours!"

Sora turned toward Til so fast the air friction could have lit a match! And—

...*Yoink, yoink, yoink...*

—his little sister, eyes cold enough to freeze Hell itself, tugged at Til's suspenders.

"...Dolphins...have no hair...on their *bodies*...and are used, as an analogy...correspondingly..."

"Oh, Master? I mentioned that Dwarven females have less hair, but—"

And then, when Jibril added—

"—I only meant in comparison to the males. They *are* still hairy and bearded, you see."

"Oh, we're talking about beards?! Of course! I thought she just made a really dramatic revelation and—"

—the females in their party all peered at him as if to ask, *What did you think she meant?* But Sora said to himself, *That's not the issue here.* He looked around the city in a panic and shouted:

"Wait... Jibril—did you just say the *girls are hairy and bearded*? What? Where?!"

Out of nowhere, Jibril had seemed to hint that this Shambhala, its streets filled with brown Loli monster girls going this way and that, was secretly the abyss.

"The mithril hair of Dwarves is an excellent material for spirit amplification."

Oh!! So their hair isn't silver; it's mithril. Yeah, she mentioned that! And she said that caused the magic overload that meant they needed catalysts!! But—?!

Though Sora clung to hope, the answer that came was merciless— and yet, obvious, if you thought about it...

"It is used, of course, for catalysts, and also for spirit arms... In fact, it is used in most every machine produced by Dwarf. However, to use it, first one must harvest it... In other words, one must shave."

So, this city—this mechanical civilization so advanced…

…was a Naraka of beard hair… And on top of that…

"The amount of hair Dwarves have indicates the strength of their spiritual amplification and the amount of material they produce. Therefore, males intentionally leave some as a display of power, but since females have less to begin with, they generally shave it all. ♪"

So the dudes in this abyss were originally fluffballs of a whole different order of magnitude. While even the girls were just shaving their beards. Sora collapsed.

…Oh… Oh, god…

Ocain, god of the forge…Old Deus who did create this race of sensibility…verily, you have no sense at all…!! **Curse you…**

"But…dear me? If you lack hair, then would that not protect you from internal spirit overload due to the mithril and allow you to use magic without catalysts? Is it not advantageous in some ways?"

"It is *not*, it isn't!! I don't have the capability to use magic at *all* without boosts, I don't!!"

"Y-you mean you have not just less hair, but *no* hair… You can't even produce the minimum spiritual amplification required for magic?"

"I cannot, I can't! But I can accidentally blow up the spirit arms I use for boosting, I can! Without boosts, I can't use magic, because I have *zero* hair, I do! And at the same time, I have *zero* sensibility for making the spirit arms required for boosting, I do!! You may say I should have someone else make them for me, but we're talking about spirit arms for the hopelessly hairless—it's as incoherent a request as to make an underwater breathing apparatus for a fish, it is! No one will make such a thing, they won't!! In conclusion, I'm sunk every which way, I aaam!!"

Til was announcing checkmate on herself, while Sora meanwhile saw a light at the end of the tunnel.

…Hopeless? What were these numbskulls talking about? Til, ah, Til alone *was not hairy and bearded*—!! The One True Brown Legal

Loli Monster Girl, was she not?! Sora squinted and stared at the sparkle of hope down at the bottom of the deepest Naraka.

"…It's okay… If you, believe…it will grow… **Grow, growww!**"
…*Yoink, yoink, yoink*…

Then Sora heard Shiro chant a curse as she repeatedly stretched Til's suspenders: *Die, last hope.* However Til interpreted it, Til spoke resolutely with a face reddened by shame—!!

"Heh. From the time I was a child, I looked in the mirror saying, *It'll grow, it will; at least one hair will grow, it will!* I believed, I did, for more than seventy years—but not a single strand of peach fuzz grew, it didn't!! Belief's made a mockery of me, it has! If you don't believe me, I'll show you, I will!! Look at this smooth, hairless—"

"Heyyy, just to check, okay?! You are talking about your *beard*—righhht?!"

Til put her hands on her panties with vigor, and with equal enthusiasm, Sora jumped forward and closed up her coat.

—*What were you trying to do?! In public! D00d!!*

Sora's shoulders heaved, but…

"…Brother… I don't…have any hair…either…you know…!"

"Oh, Master? I don't—or rather, Flügel in general don't, either. ♥"

"…Why, even if Chlammy doesn't, I'll take you to the hereafter if you touch her, you knowww?"

"I—I have hair! At least on the peach-fuzz lev— Hey, Sora! I mean, Fi, how could you?!"

"S-Sir, are you one of those perverts who fancies them smooth and hairless?!"

"Look, we're talking about **BEARDS**, right?! I can see that with my own eyes, and obviously it's better if you don't have them!! Guys who are into bearded ladies at the very least aren't in the majority, right?! Why are you looking at me like that?!"

Sora tearfully defended himself against the gazes accusing him of being a pervert. But—

"…Sir. As you've seen, I've no place to go back to here, I've not."

—Til's eyes rested on the darkness of Sora's, uncertain, weak, afraid, and fragile. But with great conviction...of her inferiority. She asked:

"Is it really all right? For me to make my place...with you...?"

Those orichalcum eyes shimmering with pale blue flame asked, *Will you abandon me? I can't do anything. Is it worth anything to have me with you? Is there anything I can do for you?*

That was what Til's eyes were asking. Til herself probably didn't even know it as she looked to Sora with hope, and asked:

"Is it possible...for me to be something more than a chicken?"

"Sure it is, kid. You just gotta be *deliciously enjoyed*... *Hic!*"

It wasn't Sora who answered. The booming voice was that of another man, who spoke Immanity with an awful accent and a filthy delight.

"You get on a man and *beg*, and he'll blast right off... He'll send you so high you'll— Oh, but not that man. He's a virgin. And a *little flat-chested girl lover*, and a *sister-fancier*... Ya swine, you're a piece of work, ain'tcha?"

"Why are we using a *chicken* as a basis for comparison?! And why you gotta slander me with things that are half-true? It makes it really hard to argue with!"

Sora howled at the indecent proposal and the uncalled-for observation. Before him were the ashes of a smoking pipe, a bottle of booze...and a faint, particulate afterglow.

"Oh, you want me so much you're leapin' for it? Ya flatter me, Niecey."

"Nooooo! He's caught me, he haaas!! Sir, Ma'am, help meee!!"

The ironic laughter and the heartrending cry both came from *right in front* of Sora and Shiro.

They couldn't follow it with their eyes, but Jibril explained later: Til came sailing through the air toward Sora and Shiro and ended up against the chest of a man who'd cut her off with something called a demi-shift.

There was no need to ask who this Dwarf was, nor to even guess.

He grabbed the weeping, pleading Til with one hand and a large mechanical sword with the other.

"—'Welcome to Hardenfell...' I suppose that's what I'm supposed to say, at least? Ya *fockers*."

He talked down to them with a grin, making eye contact with just one orichalcum eye, dressed in the rags of a vagrant, covered in ratty gray hair... *Hic.* He rubbed Til with his cheek as he burbled drunkenly. That said it all.

"Yeah!! I'll make a woman of ya, Niecey!! Ho, I'll take you high—"

■■■

...He was a sex offender.

"Wha...? It's not like that... I just came to say hello to my fockin' niece, y'know?"

Regardless, he was still a sex offender. Nothing more, nothing less. So Jibril had posthaste severed the space to collect the testimony of this drifter they'd caught in the act. In the makeshift interrogation room, a stern-faced Sora questioned the trembling victim behind him.

"...Til? The perp claims to be your uncle. Is this true?"

"Eek...! I-I'm baffled, I am! He—just came out of nowhere... I don't know what's what anymore."

"Oy, none o' that shit, Niecey! I got no choice but to come t'you, or you'll run away, won't ye?!"

"Keep your voice down, pervert!! You want us to add an intimidation charge?!"

Sora shouted down the criminal who was protesting Til's teary and terrified claim not to know him. He listened as Jibril, who'd been at the side writing down the testimony of the gray hairball, gave her take.

"He says he *came to say hello*. This indicates that he was aware of the victim's movements... Master, does he not seem of the sort who might be deluded that he is her uncle? I would suggest looking into further charges… At the very least, there is a sound case for stalking—"

"Spit it out, asshole!! How did you know where Til would be?! Who are you really?!"

"I just had a hunch!! Who am I? Oy, Niecey! Didn't you give them the letter?!"

"Wh-what are you talking about? The chieftain should be in the Chieftain's Hall, he should. What head of state would greet guests looking like that?! It proves you're a perfect stranger, you aaare!!"

Hearing the incoherent argument Til cried out, Sora got the picture.

So, this drunken gray hairball, this would-be sexual assailant, is the agent plenipotentiary of Dwarf—the chieftain of Hardenfell.

And from the testimony, it appeared that he was also *Til's uncle.*

"…Hmm. Then let's just suppose, for the sake of argument, that you're the chieftain and Til's uncle."

"What do ye mean, suppose? I am, for fock's sake!!"

"Doesn't that just make it worse?! What kind of country do you have here? Is pressing your niece into carnal relations legal here?!"

"Oh… Ya see…I just got a little carried away by the booze… It was just a little joke, damn it—"

Chlammy and the other women eyed his defense piercingly:

"…I was drunk. It was a joke." The top two excuses of male scum.

"All right, then we'll return to the victim. Ms. Tilvilg, what is your uncle like?"

"I—I certainly don't remember being related to such a shabby hairball stinking of booze and smoke— Oh, Chieftain, you **reek**, you do!! You smell sooo bad, you do!!"

Prompted by Sora, Til went and admitted that he was the chieftain. It looked as though being repeatedly called stinky with such a pained and tear-stained face had a considerable impact on the chieftain, who slumped silently. Meanwhile, Shiro was lost in her own thoughts…

*　*　*

The uncle of the lowliest of Dwarves was the greatest of Dwarves. An embarrassing middle-aged ne'er-do-well who wouldn't leave alone the unwelcoming girl disappointment.

...*What if...?* Shiro started thinking. Til was a cheap and easy potential heroine who naturally stirred the desire to protect—the kind you'd see in a visual novel. She'd assumed her to be her rival for the little sister role, fearsome for her characteristic of falling as soon as she appeared. But what if......*she wasn't a potential...*

...*NPC pairing flag...? Yeah... Enough circumstantial evidence. But not there yet...!*

—*What if she fell to someone other than Brother?* Shiro shook her head, flustered. It was too early to make that call. A drunken hairball and a legal Loli—there were still some issues with the optics!

But, of course, no one else was aware of the new logical perspective Shiro had discovered.

"...Ahhh, ohhh... I remember nowww... I'm...faaake."

The chieftain was finally coming out of the shock—

"I'll go take a bath... Let's say I was just the messenger..."

—but he didn't seem quite to have recovered. He wobbled away.

—*The one you just called stinky wasn't me. Let's just leave it at that, please.* Sora and Shira nodded silently at the droopy hairball.

"Make sure you bring those guys to me—I mean, us. All right?"

"Sir! I was already doing that, I was!! Tell the chieftain there's no need to send some smelly, suspicious stranger. I'll have them at the Chieftain's Hall forthwith, I will!! Shoo, shoo! Pft, pft!!"

Til dismissed him, Jibril unsevered the space, and the dejected hairball swung his great sword, a spirit arm, whereupon the blade split into multiple parts—or rather, countless dazzling short swords.

"Ahh, ya fockers. If my fockin' niece runs off again, I'll have to go get her, so you'll have to wai—"

"Chieftain's Hall, Floor Five-oh-eight!! I'll take them with tears to the reception room right in front of the chieftain, I will!!"

As easily as breathing, the hairball saw right through Til's full intention to wait nearby.

"Okay, you're released. But what's your name, Chief?"

Sora peered at him keenly just as the teary-eyed Til was doing.

The man tutted and left just a few words with the faint light as he vanished into thin air.

"Veig Drauvnir. Move your arses, fockin' outsiders."

The Chieftain's Hall was a giant column piercing up through the city center. They stood in the elevator, heading up to Floor 508 to meet Veig.

"...Fi, I know it must be a strain on your magic to hold your emotions in check right now...but does that really calm you down?"

"*Breathe, breathe... Why, I won't frighten Chlammy... Breathe...*"

"Such an emotionally unstable long-ears. What is it you're giving birth to that requires Lamaze? ♥"

"S-Sir, Ma'am, p-p-please don't abandon me, please? You promised me, you did!"

Hearing the man's name had not helped the party's integrity. Til stood behind Sora and Shiro, gripping their clothes. They thought...

"Yeah, sure...but, Til, just to check: This is..."

"...the administrative center...of Hardenfell...right...?"

Through the window of the elevator, they watched the contents of the column fly by as they ascended.

Actually, they were looking at a particular, *familiar* object decorating the space.

"It's not a *military base*, with this *weapon of mass destruction*? I mean, **why are you still armed?!**"

Sora had seen this weapon in the Great War RTS. He wondered about that part of the Ten Covenants that claimed war was a thing of the past.

"Oh yes. No, Sir. That's a memorial to a great ancestor of our chieftain—it's only a decoration, it is."

...Decoration? Ancestor? Sora blinked. Til started—

"It is the legacy of the first chieftain of Hardenfell, Lóni Drauvnir, it **errrz?!**"

—but was interrupted by the explosion of Fiel's wrath.

"Fi?! What's wrong?! All right already, I'll do it with you! *Breaaathe!!*"

Chlammy was right there at ground zero, trying to get things under control. Jibril seemed to find this quite amusing. Since Til was busy clutching Sora's and Shiro's clothes and shivering in a huddled mass, Jibril took over her story.

"Lóni Drauvnir is a famous personage in Dwarven history, reputed as an unprecedented genius..."

Apparently, he was the Dwarven leader toward the end of the War. He'd *invented seal rites* and put together spirit arms. A revolutionary craftsman. Spirit arms—operated by synchronization with the cores of transforming machines built from countless catalysts. They allowed Dwarves to emulate the ability that *had* been exclusive to Elf—multi-casting. Along with the race's natural dexterity, they allowed Dwarves to compile extremely precise and complex rites that even outdid the Elves'. Moreover, it was said that this man had well-nigh created all of the other weapons from the final period of the War single-handedly.

"He was truly instrumental in making the Great War what it was. Even the Elves were forced to *imitate the seal rites* to defend themselves; I myself found his works useful when I went out to kill some dragons. ♥"

...In other words, he'd indirectly *made* the Elves use seal rites and create Áka Si Anse. Basically, one of the leading war criminals who'd contributed to the total devastation of the planet. Right, and...?

"I hope this is just an optical illusion—but are you saying *that* is there because he created it?"

Sora and Shiro together pointed to it, their faces pale and their knees trembling. No doubt about it, it was what they'd seen in the

Great War RTS... It hung there, exceedingly sloppily, without a modicum of thought. A *bomb*, just floating there like a cheap toy——

"Yes, Master. To detonate inactive essence... Truly, the E-bomb is a work of art. ♥"

"What are these guys doing just casually hanging a weapon here that would totally *blow nukes out of the water*?!"

Yes... Sora pointed to the E-bomb, capable of destroying a continent in one blast. He shrieked in condemnation of this armament so excessive for a world in which all violence was forbidden.

...Why all the fuss over a powerful bomb, you ask? What about Flügel or Ex Machina, who are essentially walking, flying, warping superweapons? Let me stop you right there. Why?! Because while the Ten Covenants may cancel acts of malice!!

...They don't cover mistakes—*accidents*!! And here was a bomb that could go off without malice should someone be *careless*——?

"It's a *bomb that could blow away a continent* by *accident*. Shouldn't you dispose of it, or at least store it under tight security?!"

So it was just unexploded ordnance. What were you doing just hanging it there?!

"Master, please be calm. The exhibits on display here—*no longer function*."

Jibril got down on one knee before the teary-eyed, screaming Sora and Shiro.

—*Ah*... They recalled the literature they had read regarding Ex Machina.

"Since the Covenants, all mechanisms, spells, and the like that would harm spirits have been rendered inoperable."

Ex Machina was said to have killed spirits as fuel to operate. But the Covenants had forbidden them from killing spirits—Elementals—so they'd switched to a new system or something... In other words, she was saying these weapons that continued to go by as the elevator rose were not unexploded ordnance, but basically just models. Sora and Shiro sighed in relief and followed Jibril's gaze upward. Then they all looked confused.

Up there was just one thing *they'd never seen before*. Til picked up on their bafflement.

"...Oh... Th-there is one...exception to what you were saying, there is...*that*..."

Looking up with them...Til explained calmly.

"...*That* is a work from after the war—Lóni Drauvnir's posthumous masterpiece, it is."

So—the final work of a genius unprecedented in the history of Dwarf. No—

"The ultimate spirit arm, which *they say* no one can ever outdo... it is."

—the be-all, end-all, a work no one had been able to equal in six thousand years.

—*Hmm... His masterpiece, even leaving the E-bomb behind?* Sora's face twitched as he laughed at the majesty of the giant humanoid machine before his eyes.

"...So, what... That giant robot is a spirit arm...?"

"Well, a spirit arm, essentially, is a single-operator machine, a system that integrates multiple catalytic seal rites implemented through synchronization with a core. It could be a hammer, or it could be like that. In principle, form and size are not at issue..."

Warped in shape, girded with black masses of metal, probably tens of meters tall. An imposingly hard and solid body covered in seal rites reminiscent of electronic circuits. Its shoulders carried what looked to be superheavy weapons off the charts even for the size of the frame. It was a giant robot clearly made for war—yet if it had been made after the war, then presumably it would *still work*...

"But I cannot think it possible that a Dwarf could possess enough spirits to operate a spirit arm of such a scale."

"Yes, yes. I certainly don't, and it's far beyond the ability of even a normal Dwarf to even turn on, it is..."

Sora was secretly relieved to learn that *no one could operate it,* apparently.

"So, what nefarious purpose was this giant humanoid robot made for?"

The ground wasn't enough? Now you're gonna bust up the heavens? When Til answered Sora's snark, Jibril was consequently rendered speechless, her expression wiped away like sand on a beach.

"The shoulder-mounted unit is a spirit arm for conceptual rewriting, it is."

......

"I'm told it's a conceptual rewrite machine, which repurposes inactive essence used in the E-bomb...the materialized fossil of a divine concept. It uses seal rites to alter the underlying concept. So it depends on false essence, it does..."

....

The response was silence. Sora and Shiro narrowed their eyes to speak for themselves—and for Chlammy and perhaps all Immanity, or perhaps everyone with common sense, while they were at it. Yes...

"Jibril... Around what level of holy shit is your holy-shit meter clocking in at?"

"...Is it at...holy shit...or holy fucking shit...or fuck this shit, I'm out?"

Ah, I see—that's some incomprehensible shit!!

So it altered the bullshit of the bullshit with some other bullshit... Well, then. That was about as boldly heartburn-inducing as putting meat inside meat inside meat and calling it a hamburger.

—So what you're saying is it's bullshit, said the vulgar two with world-weary eyes.

"Well said, Master. It is a sacred progenitor, sublime bearer, and superlative apotheosis of feces. ♥"

Jibril, representing those to whom common sense was foreign, laughed that *Til's brain was rather divinely shit.*

"If that were possible, then it should be equally possible to simply *make one's opponent lose conceptually.*"

Having finally got the concept, Sora and Shiro silently went, *Ah...*

—*Conceptually*—i.e., in fundamental meaning...

......you could rewrite your opponent's concepts......?

"Huh? What, so you're saying they could just rewrite you as the loser and then you'd lose unconditionally?"

It would just *become the case that you lost,* without regard for process, circumstance, or cause and effect...? No wonder Ms. Bullshit herself was calling it bullshit... I mean, what? D00d. That was already beyond the level of cheats or exploits. That was like you just ran any code you wanted. This shit wasn't even a game anymore, Sora suspected. But:

"*You are correct,* you are... It is without exaggeration a divine spirit arm, it is."

Til looked straight back at him and nodded. She continued regardless of Sora's dumbfounded shock.

"That said, it is a system to virtually revive inactive essence for conceptual rewrite with the target, it is. That means that, when it stops, all reverts to normal, it does—and it can only rewrite the concept specified in the false essence, it can."

And, most importantly... The elevator had gone past the giant humanoid robot, at which Til now looked far down...as she gave an empty smile and murmured flatly.

"That—is no great shakes, it's not."

"...Masters. It seems she was correct in describing herself as less than a mole. Please do not take her seriously..."

Jibril called Til out for acting so as to deceive her masters. Sora thought.

"To begin with, no one has ever been able to elucidate *what essence is.*"

...Indeed. Even Holou, an Old Deus herself, had agonized over it for hundreds of millions of years.

"And she says they *falsify* it...? I have never heard such presumptuous rubbish even in jest."

...Indeed. She was saying they'd already uncovered it six thousand years ago, even used it, and had kept even a rumor of it from reaching Jibril...while putting it on display so carelessly? Bullshit. That was impossible. Jibril was right, he thought...but—

"...You're right, you are. *We've not explained it*, we've not. Goes without saying, it does."

—Sora was sure that Til, speaking so plainly, wasn't lying, either.

"...It's a product of that divine realm only one...Lóni Drauvnir... ever laid eyes on, it is..."

In that case, there were two possibilities. Either Til was mistaken, and it was impossible...or......

"Oy, Niecey. Talkin' shit, are ye? Take that back."

The doors hummed open as the elevator stopped on the 508th floor. And from beyond, the man's booming voice spoke the truth. Yes, the atmosphere surrounding the man who loomed before them once again, now on a mechanical throne, his chin on his hand, spoke the truth. A different man from the drunkard they'd seen, now smiling with the brutal might of one at the top, spoke the truth. The orichalcum eye burning red-hot from within the messily cut, gray—no, mithril—hair, accompanied by the fitting raiment and the lethargic attitude of a man whose arrogance is well justified, spoke the truth:

"Only one ever laid eyes on that divine realm *before*—"

A genius *unprecedented* in the history of Dwarves had gotten there—but he *wasn't the last*. His greatsword leaning against the throne, the *current* chieftain of Hardenfell crossed his legs proudly. Veig Drauvnir spoke...

The alternative was——someone had *made the impossible possible*.

"Before *I* bust into this world. Fockin' pathetic. Tell 'em."

He spoke the truth—that he himself was the second, and that was all there was to it...

His countenance and his single eye made even the Flügel and the Elf, members of higher races, step in front of those they wished to protect and brace themselves silently.

...Which was only natural. Veig represented the pinnacle of Dwarves—a race that had built a civilization like this by pure sensibility. The epitome of the talent that made possible what had been inexplicably impossible, *without explaining it.*

His burning eyes seeing through everything from that throne. *I knew it,* Sora and Shiro each thought. *This is undeniably one of the naturally strong.*

It was unmistakable. That presence against which all manner of devices were contrived just to keep up, to respond, to explain. And yet...

"Fer fock's sake... In the rush I ended up shaving too much. Fock..."

Veig paid no attention to Jibril, Fiel, and Chlammy, who were rigid with tension and wariness, but instead pouted and complained.

"Who would ever need a bloody deodorizing seal? I'm almost surprised I was able to build one... But you know me."

He rubbed his chin and nervously sniffed at himself. Sora and Shiro thought:

...*It's* too late *by now for him to try to look cool.*

"Tiiil? Your uncle holds a grudge about being called smelly."

"Sir! Whatever do you speak of?! This is the first time today I've seen you, it is!!"

"...Useless, demigod... Embarrassing, middle-aged ne'er-do-well... OTP...?!"

An uncle who sexually harassed his niece for whatever reason and got super depressed when she told him she hated him...

It was too late to reverse his characterization as a sad papa shunned by his rebellious daughter.

"Bloody hell, ya don't get to say I'm smelly anymore, damn it. Here, c'mere."

And moreover—just as Til, now trembling and hiding behind Sora and Shiro and hurrying them along, said:

"S-S-Sora, sir!! P-please hurry and sell the customer your medicine and let's be on our wayyy!!"

…Yes, whatever Veig might be, it was *too late*. They were the dealers and he was the buyer—the winner was already settled. All that was left was for Veig to say the words *I'll pay for the medicine*.

All the Dwarves would come under Sora and Shiro's leadership. *They didn't have a choice.*

But——

"Mgh? Oh, right, that was the point… So let's do this. Hand over the drugs."

Still on the throne with his chin on his hand, the man waved the *missive*.

—*Hey, dumbasses, you need some help? How 'bout you thank us by giving us your whole damn country?*

Yes…the *national missive* they'd made Steph write and send. And that's all it said. It had certainly reached its destination, all right. Sora confirmed Veig's indication that he'd fallen into the trap.

"…So, can we assume you're paying us the entirety of Hardenfell, then?"

"……?"

It seemed that Chlammy still hadn't wrapped her head around it. She furrowed her brow dubiously. But Veig already had it all figured out. He just sneered, at which Sora smirked to himself. Yeah… But Veig wasn't just any old customer.

…He was a *tough* customer. "Tough" as in:

"Rrngh? *I'm not gonna pay.* Put it on my tab."

—*Yeah, no surprise…*

He'd "somehow" easily found Sora and Shiro, whom even Fiel and Chlammy couldn't find. Several days after sending Til, he'd "somehow" managed to greet them there. Those eyes of his.

—Those eyes said this: "Somehow," he'd been expecting them,

today, at this hour, at this place. Expecting Til, and Sora and Shiro, and the Flügel, and the Elf. Those eyes had shown *no surprise.* Learning that he was the chieftain had only confirmed Sora's suspicion.

"...Sorry, but we don't offer credit to new customers."

"Hey, hey, don't be like that. Why don't you pay your tab first?"

It fit that Veig would say that in return. Yes, that was no surprise, either... That was something Sora had been ready for ever since he'd read that brief "letter."

"Arright, I see. It ain't profitable fer you to give credit to someone who ain't even your friend, huh? And I ain't about to be friends with some little shits like you, anyway."

Yes...and Veig's next words, following a "No, not with..."

Also no surprise. The siblings already had their eyes averted. Only Chlammy, behind them, kept her eyes on the chieftain, the noise in her perception making her face wrench as she listened.

"...some fockin' losers who skipped out on the tab from their old world..."

......

....

The sound of Jibril's interrogation and everything else she could sense seemed distant. Chlammy's consciousness was overwhelmed by the flashback. The hallucination flashed so brightly it hurt. The memory couldn't have been hers.

"Good job. Ya didn't just poison me—ya poisoned damn near the whole world, didn'cha?"

—The sound of static...

Til was facing away, holding her breath, eyes shut tight, but that too was beyond Chlammy's consciousness. What was flashing in her brain were the memories of those who had left all their debts in the past—the *siblings who never lost*—in particular the man who had also never once *won*.

"I either give everything to you unconditionally, or I go down. Gotta choose one or the other."
—Buzzing, hissing...
What was flashing in her brain was the man's memory of being imprisoned in a tiny cage with his sister. The two of them alone... without any place for them in the world other than each other's side. And therefore without any world to go back to...

"...Nice. Ya got me good. The game's over. I lose."
—*Zsh, zshh...*
The hallucination flashing in Chlammy's increasingly agonized brain was...yes, Sora's memory—getting lost, worrying, stumbling, failing and running in the wrong direction over and over, and finally staining his hands crimson...

"But I ain't gonna be friends with ya crazy little shits—not even if ya beg on your knees, ya know?"
—*Zshh, zshhhh...* They'd been trapped, and still they managed to get lost...until they finally made it here. Leaving their sin, their past, their whole world behind. The man who'd fallen down the rabbit hole—the puppet—and the girl with him—the baby bird...
....
......

■■■

And at last: Sora and Shiro raised their heads, as if switching places with Chlammy, crouched over in torment. The eyes of flame that greeted them from the throne, the words that questioned them next—everything—
—was no surprise. Sora grinned as he listened.

* * *

All the countries were searching for " "'s true identity...and the answer to what their unbeatable trump card was. No one would believe the real answer—that they were nothing more than humans. But if Veig, knowing that they were otherworlders, was able to sense that it was true, then someone, surely, would have to ask these outsider siblings, these aliens who had challenged Tet—

"...If you can do that much—*why'd* ya pansies *run* from your world?"

—What were they doing here?

"If you've got the grit to skip out on yer tab, I'm gonna open a tab, too. And of course I'm never gonna pay it."

Veig looked at them, demanding they settle up. However.

"But if I'm mistaken, then: Ah. Sorry to test ya, *friends*. I'll make it up to ya—right, all that belongs to me belongs to my friends. I'll pay up in full."

Sora and Shiro naturally had no words to give in reply. So...

"...What you're saying is *you won't work with bastards you don't like*, huh?"

"Glad ya get it. And you know what men do to understand each other better, don't you?"

Sora took Shiro's hand, and Veig got up from the throne. They sneered at each other mightily. Indeed, they had no words to give in reply. In the first place, words were of no use in such circumstances. One was a lying swindler—Sora. The other was an intuition monster—Veig. If one were to *press the question*—there was only one method of answering.

...So yeah, no surprise. They'd known it. They all had. Shiro, Jibril, even Chlammy—each with their own thoughts, they got ready. Veig's single red-hot eye spoke likewise as his smile dug yet deeper into his face.

—Speak it to me. Speak your answer; speak your soul. Not with words—it's time for action!!

——Let the games beg—

"Rahh!! Let's beat some sense into each other, shall we, stranger?!"

"It's not a spirit-arms competition? Isn't that against the Covenants? Nooo, violence is baaad!!"

—Isn't the traditional Dwarven game the spirit-arms competition?

—Does combat sport count as a game if all parties consent?!

The very moment Veig grabbed his sword and roared, Sora waved that white flag hard without hesitation.

Sorry, but we'll fold unconditionally in the face of violence! That's what it means to be a gamer—!!

Veig cackled at Sora and Shiro's genuine terror.

"Well, I hear in the old days they settled things with their fists, but now we've got these damn Covenants—"

Oh, thank you, Ten Covenants! Sora and Shiro both offered their gratitude to Tet. But then…

"So—*we'll beat each other with spirit arms.*"

Veig deliberately thrust his sword into his throne.

"Spirit-arm expansion—connect. Arise, my frame!!"

The same moment he howled, the throne took his sword and abruptly *transformed*. Now in the form of a belt woven of steel, it spiraled about Veig and swallowed him up with a mechanical roar. Then the floor broke open, and it appeared like a four-legged beast arising.

That *thing* was a giant knight in silver armor, maybe fifteen meters tall. A giant humanoid robot of the same kind they'd seen on display from the elevator—or more precisely, a seemingly more advanced version… Holding a predictably off-the-charts giant sword aloft, the robot boasted a polished, streamlined form.

...To be straight about it, if the body they'd seen was the standard V-series type, this was more like a NEXT.

Anyway, it pointed at Sora and Shiro—

"We'll beat each other with these things—spirit arms synchronized with our souls. Simple, ain't it?"

As Veig's voice resounded through the speakers, Sora and Shiro agreed. No kidding, it was simple. So basically, Veig was proposing a game in which they got in giant robots and beat the shit out of each other.

—A *robot battle game...*

Sora and Shiro nodded with steely gazes at this glorious proposal that spoke to the dreams of every man-child.

"So you make the bold claim that a Gund*m Fight is not against the Covenants. Let's hear your argument."

"...If that's, okay...then you could just, have a war... I mean, it's *violence...*isn't it?"

They lingered on their doubts about the Covenants—doubts that had only been increasing lately, ever since they saw that E-bomb from earlier. Teary-eyed, the two declared with determination that depending on the rules they might say no.

■■■

Having accepted the game, the party left the Chieftain's Hall. Sora already had his mind full of furiously racing thoughts when Til shouted at him pleadingly.

"A-are you serious?! You can't possibly defeat the chieftain in a spirit-arms competition, you can't!"

She was saying the game was impossible for them to win. With a chuckle, Sora silently agreed: *Yeah, no kidding.* He went over the preceding events. In summary, the details of the game Veig proposed had been like this...

——......

* * *

A *mech action game* using spirit arms... It was basically a robot battle, but the damage to their spirit arms would *converge into the cores.* No matter what kinds of attacks landed, only the core would break, and the operator would not be injured. And the strength of the core would be *proportionate to that of the soul synchronized with it...* So, literally, they'd have to put their souls into bashing each other, and the one whose soul broke first would lose. It really was simple. How it worked was anyone's guess, but in any case, it was supposedly safe. However, Sora and Shiro lacked one of the minimum requirements for the game—a robot. And even if they had one, they couldn't manipulate spirits. Nor could they learn to. They couldn't operate this thing. So—

"*Then take someone with you. No magic other than spirit arms—seal rites. One core per person. I'll lend ya all my resources and facilities and personnel, so you go do it however seems best to you.*"

The game started from designing and building the machinery and selecting the pilots. But in another sense, the rules were very lenient: They could choose freely who would use what kind of machinery, who would build it, where and when, and all that stuff.

"*...Gimme all ya got. You can bring all the friends ya want.*"

The rules were so lenient because Veig, naturally, was confident he would win even against an Ex Machina or Old Deus. None of the Ixseeds could rival Dwarves when it came to seal rites and machine manufacturing. No one alive could build a spirit arm better than Veig could. The upshot being that this was a *game Veig was sure to win......*

———......

"Damn it, Til, you just don't get it, do you? This isn't a contest of whose spirit arm is better..."

Done reviewing, Sora slapped his forehead.

"It's a contest of our *souls*—!!"

"......Uh, all right, that— *What?*"

Ah, perhaps it is not possible for people to understand one another. Perhaps they just cannot get along.

"But even so, they can acknowledge each other—if their souls! Their feelings! Are true!!"

"…But he's got, zero interest…in acknowledging us, right…? He's only interested…in us, acknowledging him…right…?"

Next to Sora, Shiro sadly grasped at the air in front of her chest, longing for *that which she had lost.*

"Of course! 'Cos he's————*sick, right*?!"

As members of a civilized race, they carried the burden of educating him—wait. Or was it treating him?!

…Sora reflected on that which had just transpired in the Chieftain's Hall——

■■■

It was right after the rules had been explained and they'd mutually agreed. Suddenly, light surged forth from the giant sword of Veig's robot, and—

"……………………Hey, Til…?"

Sora didn't know what had just happened. He was half passed out. He asked about what he was just seeing.

"That…*thing* Veig's robot has—is it the same as that god-tier spirit arm you were talking about?"

"…Yes, sir. It is *history's second* false essence—conceptual resonance rewriter, it is."

—"And so their concepts were rewritten…"

Til confirmed it: That light-blasting giant sword Veig's robot had was the holy shit that could redefine you as the loser unconditionally, without regard for cause and effect. Til had the same hollow smile as they'd seen in the elevator.

Back when she'd said: *That—is no great shakes, it's not.*

…Ah, now Sora understood her true meaning. Once it had actually been used…and he'd seen the *results*, it was clear.

"Near the end of the War, it is said that a buxom woman fell in love with Chieftain Lóni Drauvnir, she did."

Sora attended quietly to Til's sudden narration.

"Her passionate courtship made the chieftain think, *Damn, it's tough being loved by all the ladies*, it did. He fell in love—and ever since, men of the Drauvnir line have *never been able to love a lady without big boobs*, they've not."

...I see... Sounds tough. By the way...

"*...Are* there Dwarves with big boobs?"

"Sir. Of course—*there aren't*."

Yeah, thought not. Dreams are dreams because they aren't real.

"You see, it's only a legend, it is. There's no such thing as a Dwarf with big boobs, there's not. It's unknown who the woman was or even if she existed, it is. But in any case—*because there's no such thing*, he *created* it, he did."

—"*So he* created *it.*"

Meaning, the shoulders of that machine on display and the giant sword of Veig's machine were actually never-before and never-after manifestations of that man-made dream both stupid geniuses sought! The pinnacle of talent squandered on the utterly pointless— yes!!! The truth indicated by Til as she nodded beet-red— specifically—!!

"It's a spirit arm using big boob essence to *conceptually give someone big boobs*, it is…!!"

...Jiggle...

As Til nodded, her ample bosom heaved to demonstrate. Veig came down from the giant machine and spoke with contentment and a dashing smile.

"Mm. Gotta give you the real stuff… That's my fockin' niece for ye, always trying to run away."

—Ah. So this was why Til didn't want to see Veig. He'd just gone and used it on her without warning—and apparently this was typical. No wonder she wanted to leave as soon as possible. Sora looked away awkwardly. An uncle who augmented his niece's boobs with such casual sexual harassment, panting lasciviously…

Yep, he's a sex offender. It seemed this country was a little lacking in the rule-of-law department. Even so—Sora nodded with heartfelt respect.

So what the two supreme geniuses sought with such fervor as to reach the divine realm of rewriting concepts…

…was *boobs*—!!

Ah, such sublime brilliance, such wondrous dumbassery. It merited respect—but!! Still.

"…I get that you gave Til big boobs, but…why'd you have to do it to *everyone*?"

Sora mumbled as he glanced around, not knowing where to look—and at the same moment, the cheers, tears, and shock of the females present filled the air.

"So this really isn't a dream?! I can't even see my feet past my boobs—is this real?! *Conceptually* big boobs are real big boobs, right?! Eegh… They're not going go *fshhh* and deflate this time, are they?! *Ngh… Sob…!!*"

"Is this actual conceptual rewriting…? Hmm, it seems I am unaffected…"

"What the hell?! You're trying to show off how perfect you were already?! …Heh, it doesn't matter. With a heart as big as the surface area of my chest, I can even forgive a devil like you. ♪"

"I haven't the slightest idea what you're saying, not that I have any interest, either— Oh! ♥ Lord Shiro, how daring! ♥"

"…You've, got bigger…too, Jibril…from the golden ratio, to the silver ratio…"

"Hey! They're so heavy when I lie down, I can hardly stand it! You can measure happiness in weight! Did you know that?!"

"By the way, Lady Shiro, are you dissatisfied with your bosom? What is it that troubles you?"

"……Calculating…whether this is a plus, or a minus…for a little sister character…"

"Oh, I have such incredible cleavage when I get down on all fours!

I'm going back to walking on four legs!! Hey, Fi, look! Come on, look at my boobs! Come on, how long are you going to keep up that enlightened expression?!"

—The conceptual rewrite had affected all of the ladies present. Ah…from big-breasted Lolis to proper racks—this was a place abounding with boobies and dreams. And there was approximately one individual who'd become so soft in the head as to announce her regression from humanity, but at any rate—

—still, somehow…*something seemed off.* Sora furrowed his brow, while Shiro nervously brought her boobs close to him.

"…Brother, I'm guessing…my boobs…still don't—get it up, do they?"

"Still don't *what*?! Get *what* up? Between a brother and sister?!"

"Heh, too bad for you. It must be hell to be a lolicon and be surrounded by huge boobs, huh?"

"The hell is with you, getting all stuck-up the moment you get fake boobs?! You're a class act!"

Sora shouted back at Chlammy, who looked positively triumphant as she crawled, letting gravity take hold of her boobs.

"Oh my. Master, I didn't realize you objected to large-breasted Lolis."

"…I don't, know… The statistics…don't give, a clear picture…!"

"Hey… Hey! Can you all stop debating with each other on the premise that I'm a lolicon?!"

This time, he shouted tearfully at Shiro and Jibril, who were whispering to each other. Meanwhile—Fiel, who had taken a step back from the ruckus, remarked with her Buddha voice.

"Why, it's a known fact that the *two* of you are lolicons. The only debate is over whether you lust over children with breasts. Either way, the fact remains that you're perverrrts…"

Her eyes, with their four diamond shapes, were directed toward Sora and one other—Veig.

If a Dwarf desired large breasts, it followed necessarily that he favored large-breasted Lolis. So their argument was just over whether Lolis should have big boobs or not. They were pretty much perverts of the same level either way, she was saying. Sora was shocked. He tried to rebut her assertion when—

——suddenly, gravity increased. Or at least there was a tension in the air that gave that illusion. Sora turned to see Veig standing there wide-eyed. A bit late, he'd finally realized Fiel was there.

—Fiel *Nirvalen*, who needed magic to suppress her urge to kill.

—Veig *Drauvnir* stepped forth with piercing eyes and light feet.

And then…Veig, as he'd been sworn to do from the moment he was born—no, bound to do since a time far before his birth—so serenely, so inevitably, so naturally that nobody, not Tet nor the Covenants could question it… Ah, as naturally as Mother Nature makes the streams flow, he extended his hand…

…and grabbed Fiel's boobs.

Placidly. Appallingly. Quite resolutely, he squeezed her boobs…

Everyone froze. Time itself seemed to get distracted and forget to flow in the silence. While they were all stuck there, one man alone demonstrated his ability yet to move! *Foof, foof…! Gwish, gwish! Fa-foof, boink! Ba-bounce—!!* Boob-squishing sound effects couldn't even capture the nimbleness of his handiwork.

"Ab-absurd… What is this?! How can its shape, firmness, and weight all conform *exactly to my ideal*?!"

—Indeed…there had been no need to use the big boob essence, conceptual rewriting. He had to admit it: This bust had been the ideal itself from the very beginning. He shivered. His eyes opened wide. He became short of breath!!

—He'd called it absurd. So shaken he forgot that nothing could be more absurd than he was himself, this god-tier pervert gave the voluptuous bosom a feel with his still-trembling fingers—and came to a halt. Then his red eye glinted, and he sneered with uproarious derision, and he continued thus:

"Heh… My blood screams forth—that *this is not the answer*… It's not the real thing, only raw material."

—*Crik.*

"Ho, come here, fake friend. I'll work you over till you're the real thing. Ya better be grateful."

——*Cr-crikk*—

"Everything—especially tits!—exists to be forged, by me, into something bigger! These natural tits are unrefined, just swollen up with no artifice. But they're a material worth the challenge to work!!"

There couldn't actually be something loudly creaking, but it seemed as if there was.

".......Why, could it be you're talking to me...?"

Fiel's question was as emotionless as the sound of a machine. But Veig—

"*Who the hell are you?!* Don'cha know it's scary for the soil your crop's growin' on to start talkin' at you all of a sudden?!"

—was just shocked to notice, now for the first time, something beyond the boobs.

———Sora finally could hear something break, and he understood...

"Oh—I get it. I knew something was off..."

—It went back to the Dwarven philosophy: *Everything exists to be forged...*

An unpolished diamond was just a rock. Unprocessed iron was just sand. The boobs honed by that divine spirit arm were the ultimate. Everything else was just material—unfinished, Veig was saying.

"To touch them in spite of the Covenants—is this *proof of goodwill*?"

"Th-that's right, this man of goodwill has saved me!! S-so, Fi, hold back, please?!"

Jibril sounded impressed. Chlammy tried to soothe Fiel. Sora barely heard either of them as he ruminated on his conclusion...

Til said that Veig could only love big boobs—but *that wasn't it.* Veig, that bastard asshole son of a *bitch*, had a deeper problem.

*   *   *

——He could only *acknowledge* big boobs——‼

And so—at last—Sora put his finger on what that sound was, what had broken *inside him*—and, that moment…

"Pardon me, Master? You seem deep in thought—what is it that——?!"

…Jibril's voice caught in her throat as her wings trembled. She hadn't felt like this for thousands of years. She'd never expected to feel this sort of impact from her master, from an Immanity—the surety that she was about to be killed.

"You wanna throw down over our tastes? Our souls? All right, let's have at it."

Veig was questioning him—true to his first words when they first met.

—*A little flat-chested girl lover, and a sister-fancier… Ya swine, you're a piece of work, ain'tcha?*

I ain't gonna be friends with ya crazy little shits, he said, side-eyeing his taste from above.

—*I ain't gonna be friends with some sick focks like you*, he said—‼

In other words—Veig was questioning not only Sora's past—but also his present.

————He was questioning…Sora's taste in boobs——!

Then bring it on. Sora's roiling soul flared from his eyes. He laid down the gauntlet.

"—I'll show you who's got shit taste, Veig Drauvnir."

■■■

—And so, leading the party through the Central Industrial District, Sora breathed a sigh of relief at the boobs that had returned to normal thanks to the deactivation of the conceptual rewrite—Shiro's in particular. Ah, let us respect the freedom of the individual in matters of thought, philosophy, taste, and preferences. However—!!

"If he's gonna *push* his shit on us, saying *only his taste is right*, then we're gonna have to exercise our individual liberties, too, aren't we?!"

Yes, namely—!

"Our freedom to tell him: Shut up! Eat shit! You get me?!"

"—Sir... Yes, sir!! Certainly, sir!!"

Til saluted, looking deeply impressed. Chlammy sneered.

"...Heh... Freedom to be a lolicon... I wonder who you're calling sick...?"

"Hey! Why you gotta label me like that? I object to the boobular fascism currently in vogue!"

"But it's true, isn't it? You've got a thing for your sister, and you like them smooth and hairless... What's your excuse?"

"I said it's not like that!! And for the millionth time, we are talking about **BEARDS** ☆, aren't we?!"

Unperturbed by Sora's outburst, Shiro rubbed her chest, in apparent lamentation of things come and gone.

"...Jibril...what are you...doing...?"

"Oh yes. I was just cataloguing the immediate reactions my master has given to those he met for the first time..."

Shiro sadly inquired to Jibril, who was groaning as she wrote something in a book, and Jibril answered.

"The ones to whom he has responded in a clearly favorable manner are the little doggie, the pretender mosquito, Holou, and this new one here... Oh!"

It seemed a revelation had caused her body and voice to tremble.

"C—c-c—conversely...those to whom he has not reacted with particular favor are the long-ears, the Shrine Maiden, the Siren and her queen, Elder Azril, that Ex Machina...and—and I... Oh—Master!!"

At last she fell to her knees, folding her wings, begging forgiveness.

"Please, forgive my abject failure to realize until now! I shall at once—"

She was momentarily bathed in light.

...Dink.

Shrunken to look like a child, Jibril made as if to pray.

"—serve you in a more proper juvenile form. I would that you might *use* me..."

"Are you assholes really that desperate for me to be a lolicon?! Look, you can think what you want. But if you try to push it on me, I'm gonna have to push back, so keep it to yourself from now on— D00d, I said it's not like that!!"

Sora's screams were met by snickering that caused him to turn and rip at his hair.

"——Look, you! How long are you gonna keep admiring your fugly fake boobs, anyway?!"

"Fake? I agree with some of the things he said. If it's greater than nature—it's better than the real thing!"

Chlammy was decisive as she gazed at her massive rack.

Just one of them had wept to be spared the deactivation of the conceptual rewrite, and she continued in high spirits.

"I remember a line from a game in your memory—*nothing says a fake can't rival the real thing*!!"

"Is that the best time you could find to use that quote?! You're really gonna quote that looking all smug with your fake boobs flopping around?!"

Even if you surpassed the real thing, fake was fake.

—You're inferior because you can't tell the difference—!!

But before the words could even come out of Sora's mouth—

"Chlammy, you shouldn't talk like *that* to a frieeend. ♥"

—a voice warm as the sun filled the air...and brought silence.

——.

"Wha...? F-friend...? Sora and I? Fi, are—are you all right?!"

Not a trace was left of the murderous glares and Buddha faces. Fiel was her normal warm self, so normal it was disturbing. What she'd said made Chlammy doubt her ears and fearfully check her

best friend's sanity. Chlammy's eyes filled with tears for the thought that she might have *broken* her best friend by telling her to tolerate the outrage inflicted on her by Veig. But—

"Whaaat? Why, I thought we were all bosom buddies, for all the time we've spent naked together. *Arrren't weee?*"

—her pure, warm smile won Sora's confirmation. Yeah. "*Bring all you got at me.* You can bring all the friends ya want..." Those were the rules. Any kind of mecha would do, and they could take as many friends as they wanted. There should be no question that Fiel was invited. And, after all—

"Heh, why you gotta ask? We have to work together to beat Veig, *bosom buddy.* ♪"

"Why, yesss. We'll do all we can to help you win, since you're our *beeest* friends. ♪"

——*Friends forever...*

Seeing Sora's and Fiel's implausibly sunny smiles flashing back and forth...

...*Ah.* Even Chlammy got it.

"Why, to Sora and Shiro! Let's form a team and get those seal rites designed!"

Fiel walked off with graceful power, and Chlammy followed.

But as she left, Chlammy took a reflexive look back at Sora and Shiro.

Knowing Sora's past, her eyes held a feeling hard to explain. But they also asked—*Is it okay to say? Can I even ask?*

"*...You're okay, right?*"

Without indicating in what way regarding what, Chlammy's eyes just said:

"......"

Nodding faintly at Sora's and Shiro's smirks, she didn't once look back again.

"...I hesitate to inquire, but, Masters, are you certain about this?"

It seemed she'd watched and waited for them to disappear. Jibril knelt, still looking like a little girl, not seeming to notice Sora's squint.

"I recognize that that long-ears' cooperation is essential to this game—but *I am fairly certain she will betray us.*"

"*Of course she will.* She just basically swore that she'll uphold the rules and betray us. ♪"

Sora shot right back with a smile, more than adequately aware of and ready for such basic matters.

—Indeed, the rules said you lost if your core, your soul broke. So Veig would win if he broke anyone's core besides his own... But if anyone else broke Veig's core, *then who would win...?* No question about it—*the one who broke the core.* In other words—*the one who beat Veig.* So:

"With this game, we're gonna give Veig the medicine whether we win or lose."

"...The only question, is...whether he'll...pay up...with his, whole country..."

"So if Fiel and Chlammy beat Veig before we do, it's no-risk, full-return for them. Betraying us is a deal too good for them to pass up. ♪"

...What was it that Fiel hoped to do with Veig's country, though...? That was a little worrisome—enough for a few drops of cold sweat. But anyway.

"That's fine. *They're not gonna be able to win.* They just gotta cooperate with us just like we asked 'em. ♪"

Sora dismissed the threat with a devilish smile, and Jibril nodded.

"...It is as you say. The only ones capable of handling seal rites are the Dwarves and the Elves, who are a lower-grade model of the same thing. In addition, only the Dwarves can build spirit arms—and they cannot be trusted. Victory is impossible."

Yes. This game required, at a minimum, a seal-rite machine and a spirit arm. Supposedly, they had access to all of the personnel and materials they wanted—Dwarven personnel, that is. There was no reason to trust them. Therefore, Jibril concluded that it was impossible for Fiel and Chlammy to beat Veig.

"Hmm. Is it my imagination, or are you saying that we don't have a chance, either?"

"To be candid...*I am*. I'm afraid I am not blessed with the vision to perceive just how we might prevail."

Jibril took Sora's snark with apologetic reverence as she further shrunk her juvenile self.

Veig was the chieftain of Hardenfell because he was the greatest craftsman of spirit arms. He was Dwarf's agent plenipotentiary because no one could outdo him in the field. So Jibril took it upon herself to speak, with a sense of apology for her presumption in assuming that her masters were doomed.

"Why did you accept a game...your enemy is certain to win...?"

That's right—in the first place, it was Sora and Shiro who had been challenged and therefore had the right to decide the game, by the Covenants. Besides, Sora and Shiro had the drugs—yes, just as Veig had admitted. Drugs so undeniable they could compel Veig to offer up Hardenfell to them. There seemed to be no reason for Sora and Shiro to accept his challenge, much less on his terms. So why? At Jibril's question, Sora and Shiro looked down for a second.

"He has a point that it's unfair for us to deny him credit when we haven't paid ours."

Sora murmured as his ambiguous expression clouded over—which then transformed into an indomitable smile.

"But hey! You're asking why we accepted? Isn't it obvious?"

The trick to never losing was never playing a game you couldn't win... So—

"—It's because we *do have a chance to win*. And Veig's game isn't unbeatable. ♪"

"...And Veig isn't...the best person...to build spirit arms. ♥"

That's right... He was a tough customer—but a customer nonetheless. It would be more trouble than usual, yet still they'd win, just as they planned. And just as they planned, they'd get Hardenfell.

"Y-you say there is someone better than the chieftain, you do?! J-just who—"

Who in the world could it be? Til shouted in consternation.

Then she felt their eyes boring a hole in her. She looked around behind her to find who they were staring at.

"Sir. Where is this person...? —Um, huh? ...You're joking, of course?"

But their eyes continued boring in.

At last, she realized who they were looking at. But—

"Th-th-th-that doesn't make any sense, it doesn't!! I-I'm a grubby little mole, I am!"

As she screamed that she didn't know what they were after, her fragile eyes, nervous and weak and brimming with tears—yet also *boldly convinced* of her inferiority—

"Yeah. That's why you can do it. Or rather—*only* you can do it."

————opened wide as Sora's words took her breath away.

And then......her fearful orichalcum eyes, flickering with pale blue flame as they looked straight into Sora's blackness, seemed to say that she had no value and could do nothing. *Seemed.*

"...I'm worth less than a chicken... What can I do...?"

It seemed she didn't know herself as she looked to the *sky.* Sora and Shiro answered her.

"...With the power...of foreshadowing...! ...The tropes...will rise again...!!"

"The self-described loser and the invincible foe! The comeback ending is already set in stone!"

Til's eyes immediately filled with tears of despair, and she sprinted away...

☉ Chapter 3: Formula Front
Generalization

*F*inding no way forward, time passed.
The cage closed in on them, until at last...
...the baby bird's end drew near...

"Let's leave this cage right now.
Break me apart,"
the puppet's trickery claimed.
And the cage broke just like that.
But the crimson-stained puppet's efforts only
earned the words
"You liar"...
...along with the baby bird's tears,
and the despair up above.

There was no sky in that world.

Beyond the cage they'd broken
was yet another cage.
These two were one —
leaving the chick alone,
tricking the baby bird —
these two were one.
What will I do now that the
cage is broken?

The sky was accusing, and yet
what else could they have done...?

The capital of Hardenfell, full of the sounds of Dwarves at work, as usual. Already two days had gone by since their meeting with Veig. Now, sheets of paper were raining over the underground city. Posted here and there, flying through the air, they showed a photograph of a blushing girl with her suspenders being tugged on, along with the following caption in the Dwarven tongue:

LOST MOLE
Til   Age 84 Girl
Smooth as a dolphin
If you see her, contact " ", bitches

■■■

"So yeah… Til somehow managed to *successfully run from Jibril*, so we're looking for her."

"…Anyone…have an, idea…where she…might be?"

"………………………Errr… Why, you can't be serious?"

Yes—to run from Jibril, despite Jibril chasing at full speed… She was truly an epic gamer to beat such a punishing game. Fiel couldn't believe her long ears when she heard Sora and Shiro ask where Til was. Just how did one run from a Flügel, who could shift position at will? Fiel was dumbstruck, which was of no concern to Jibril.

"... I do apologize, my masters. I have made an inexcusable lapse... I should have anticipated it."

Jibril was hanging her head, her fists and voice similarly trembling. She wept as she expressed her contrition.

"I cannot follow her to the afterlife!! I did not intend to drive her to such...!! Now I have allowed your precious resource for spirit arms to escape and obstructed your victory... H-how can I ever atone for this...?"

"Yeah, you're jibbing up what to apologize for as always... And by the way, *she's not dead*!!"

I—I think... No, definitely! Sora reassured himself as he thought back two days. Yes...when the self-described grubby little mole... the *flightless bird had flown—*

"I—I should have known—I don't have any home at all, I dooooon't!!"

As Jibril gave chase, Til cried out, and light poured from her hammer. The end of the hammer struck the ground, and the next moment—Til flew...

Yes...she truly flew... Flew, or rather... Well—

————*Got blown away...*

The blast shook the capital... She left nothing behind but that great explosion and the remnants of her totaled hammer. Not even a trace of spirits——

"That wasn't an act of self-destruction... Til wouldn't do something like that."

"...Which means...mission successful... She gets...the platinum trophy..."

Jibril was sure she was dead, while Sora and Shiro only became *even more sure that she was alive.* Which necessarily also backed up a certain *conjecture* they had—but leaving that aside, they'd known from the start that Fiel wouldn't know. If even Jibril had concluded there was no trace of her spirits—*then she wasn't in the capital anymore.*

"So that's why we've been asking around, you know. For someone who might have some idea where she went…"

And that's what had brought them *here*. Looking from the control room, they figured they'd ask the Dwarves down there building the "humanoid machine"—but first, Sora squinted back at the Elf girl sitting on a chair.

Fiel was capable of using seal rites, in the Elven style, at least. So she was able to take up Veig on his promise, borrow materials and personnel, and give the staff design drawings for seal rites and have them build a unit accordingly.

…The thing was, the personnel seemed a little too loyal. Sora brought up a salient example.

"…Maybe I should ask first whether I can ask questions—say, to *that chair* for now?"

Sora pointed to the Dwarf on whom Fiel was leisurely sitting, her legs crossed.

"～～～～～！ ～～, ～～!!"

"Mmm? Why, Mr. Chair…who permitted you to speaaak? ♥"

The chair spoke what probably was Dwarven. Sora and Shiro didn't understand, but they winced to see Fiel kick her underling. It was true Veig had said he would lend them personnel—make them help in other words, but…

"Isn't that…past the bounds of asking for help?"

…he hadn't said he'd *give* them to them, had he? And hey, she just kicked the Dwarf. Wasn't that against the Covenants?

"Asking for help? Me, of these moles? Why, your jokes are so haaarsh. ♥"

Fiel answered with a smile as bright as the midday sun—the scorching desert sun.

"Why, this thing licked the floor and swore by the Covenants, 'I'll do anything to make up to you my sin in being born, Lady Fiel.' So

I just haaad to *allowww him to help.* Look at him choke on his tears of joy. ♪"

She again dug her heel into the chair who was crying, reportedly, for joy.

Loosely translated: *I used a game to make him pledge himself into bondage.*

Uh, okay, that was pretty messed up, but if it was a game then it was the Dwarf's fault for losing. And it did have the advantage that this way she could force the Dwarves to apply their crafting sensibility in a loyal fashion. Only Dwarves could process the material for spirit arms, but the Dwarves couldn't be trusted—it made sense. On the other hand, not to disparage Fiel, but would it really be so easy to sucker those savvy Dwarves?

"—Why, it was simple…for the *twooo* of us. ♥"

Sora's confusion was ultimately dispelled not by Fiel…

—*Clack, clack…*

"…? Ohh, if it isn't Sora… I haven't seen you in two days… Heh-heh…"

…but by Chlammy, whose heels shrilly echoed as she entered. Or to be more precise—

"You're here to observe the work—is that your excuse? Whatever you say, I know what you're really here for. Very well. If you get on your hands and knees and beg, I'll be nice and let you *look* at least… *Mwah!* ♥"

—by the hip-swaying, Marilyn Monroe–inspired strut of the fake-boobed abomination blowing a kiss.

…She's this uppity just from getting big boobs…

Contemplating the factors that would lead to this reaction, Sora almost cried. Conversely…

"…B-Brother… Can having boobs…really give you…that much… confidence…?"

—*Maybe I shouldn't have deactivated it, either…* Shiro fought back tears of regret. Sora smiled warmly and rubbed her head.

* * *

"So, Chlammy. Can you do—*that* thing?"

He took out his phone.

…But that was all he did. He didn't even hold it out to her. However, Chlammy grinned imperiously, snatched it from his hand—and, without hesitation, with a once-in-a-century, shit-eating grin—placed the phone on top of her bust…

"You see, my sister? *Nothing has changed.* Her confidence is as fake as her tits."

"Wh-whaaat?! The way I remember from your memory, if you ask someone with big boobs if they can do 'it,' you're referring to *this*, right?!"

Sora's smirk and the snap of Shiro's camera ripped off any and all pretense instantaneously.

"*Hfff…* Listen well, Queen of Boards."

"—Heh… What is it now, *little boy*?"

"Don't react to that… You do know, don't you…? Listen."

And as Chlammy scrambled to put her gilded pretense back on, Sora preached the truth.

"Someone with big boobs doesn't assume that '*that* thing' is *specifically something to do with her boobs*!!!"

"——*Gurgh!!*"

"I mean, all I did was take out my phone! You didn't think I might be trying to take a picture or something?! I could have been asking for a sexy pose or any number of other things, right?! You didn't even hesitate! You're so desperate, I feel bad calling you out. **Sorry, okay?!**"

"……I-I'm, sorry…! I kind of, feel like it's…my fault…!"

"Why are you two crying?! I mean—it—it's not like that! A-ahem!"

Sora's apology broke the dam on the tears long held back. Shiro and Chlammy both started crying—and then.

"—*Huff.* All right. With magnanimity as deep as my cleavage, I'll accept your constructive criticism…"

As Chlammy assumed the pretense once more, Sora and Shiro

thought: *I see. It would have been difficult for Fiel to sucker a Dwarf alone. But the two of them*—Fiel and Chlammy together—*shouldn't have had any problem.*

"Before, I was flat-chested... You're right, there's no sense in denying the past..."

After all, look at Chlammy—sticking out her chest, one hand on her hip, the other flaring out her hair, like a hot babe full of confidence. Just the way a comedian would play it. And she refused to even recognize this. Those discerning Dwarves would surely spot right away that her confidence was as devoid of reality as her chest. And for that very reason—

"But a real woman doesn't let her past drag her down... You see now, kid?"

—Sora, watching as Chlammy desperately maintained the seductress act, became all the more sure.

All Fiel had to do was make the Dwarves think their opponent was this weirdo to lower their guard and get them into the game. Then if the *real player was Fiel*—talk about a sucker punch. Sora and Shiro could see how Fiel could have captured swarms of Dwarves easily.

"All right... I get it already. Let's end this sad world where everyone just gets hurt."

"...I accept it... You have...big boobs... Okay?"

"Would you stop it with those tender gazes?! What did you even come here for, anyway? God!!"

As Chlammy's tears reappeared from beneath the gilded veneer, Sora and Shiro left her with their sympathy. Looking back at the Elven girl still sitting on her chair, Sora asked:

"Hey, Fiel, do you still think you can steal a march on us to beat Veig?"

"Whaaat? ...Why, how could you accuse me of such a thing...? I'm so hurrrt. ♥"

Fiel professed her brokenheartedness with a smile so over the top you could practically feel the sarcasm oozing from it. She continued:

"After alll I've done to help my friends succeed, my goodness."

"Fine, so you need to save face. Then, okay, if we win, we want to do something for you, as friends. What do you want?"

Sora indirectly asked what Fiel wanted if she won. She must have been asked this by Chlammy many times already, from the uneasy way she listened.

"Dooon't worry. I'm done with seeking death and destruction."

Fiel seemed focused on reassuring Chlammy.

"Why, that *thing* crossed three lines that should never be crossed…"

However, her words that followed, with an evil smile, were not very reassuring at all.

"I can't kill him nowww. Why, I *must keep him alive.* ♥"

"—By the way, what are those three lines?"

"Being booorn…and touching *two* things he shouldn't have. ♪"

Things he shouldn't have touched… Sora cast his eyes upon *those two things*, plump and heaving. It occurred to him that Fiel's gaze spoke eloquently as to the manner in which she wished to win.

—But Sora was surprised that she'd failed to notice *that other thing* for two whole days. He repeated what he'd said two days ago.

"I mean, *you have to cooperate with us to beat Veig,* so I hope you'll give this some thought."

"—Whaaat?"

He clearly implied that Fiel could not beat Veig by herself. Fiel looked at him to ask what basis he had for his assertion. Sora answered cheerily.

"Yeah, look—*you're already relying on Dwarves to build this for you, which proves you can't do it yourself,* right?"

"_____."

That instant——the atmosphere froze hard enough to crack.

"…? Huh, what? What are you talking about?"

Chlammy looked quizzically as Fiel winced with displeasure.

—*Thunk.* Fiel's heel dug into the chair—and an argument began.

"~~~, ~~~, ~~~, ♥"

"〰〰〰!! 〰〰!! 〰〰?!"

"…That's Dwarven, right? Jibril, can you interpret?"

Beside Sora, the trusty weapon supporting seven hundred languages bowed reverently and answered.

"First, the long-ears demanded, 'Tell me where Til is.' The chair answered, 'I really have no idea,' pleading for its life… Oh, and the long-ears said, 'Tell me even if you don't know. I'll be the judge of whether you have any idea.' The chair's will seems to have been broken. ♪"

And so the elderly chair, pathetic tears about to fall, complied with the order to cough up anything and everything, mumbling this and that.

"*No one can find her now…even the chieftain, who was so* fond *of her.*"

Jibril transitioned to simultaneous interpretation, and Sora and Shiro listened sympathetically.

"*Way back when, she used to chase after the chieftain everywhere, sayin' she'd surpass him and become his wife—*"

"**…Hooooold up…!!**"

But Jibril was paused by a sudden cry.

"…Jibril… Play back, that last part… More, detail…!"

Shiro pounced with a horrifying glare, seeming to take even Jibril aback. The Dwarf, confused, replied:

"*Mm, mrg? The* promise they'd marry if she built a better spirit arm than him?"

Shiro thrust both her arms into the air. Without exceeding her usual whispery volume range, she shouted—*Huzzahh!!* Her pose was so epic you expected big letters to appear behind her.

"…Brother, *the route's been set*! Pairing is complete! …Childhood friends for the win!"

Shiro looked like she was hearing UC music in her head. Sora grinned and nodded.

"Yeah, even your brother can see that now… No going back from here, all right…"

Thinking of *those eyes* of Til, together with *Veig's intent*, they could only say, *Oh, yeah...*

—*A promise of marriage in their early days.*

After which one shrunk away for shame at low specs and failure. They were totally the one true pairing... If they were to say anything about it—

"Hrrm. But, Shiro...is uncle x niece okay? 'Specially when the uncle's a hairy old bastard and the niece looks like a kid... Kinda pushing it, don't you think? Whether in terms of ethics or optics, it kinda looks like a situation where one would get the police involved, doesn't it?"

"...Brother? It's not okay...to impose, our views, on other cultures..."

"Well, fair enough! But a global commonwealth ought to have a certain amount of cultural exchange, don't you think?!"

"...I welcome...the uncle x niece tradition... *It benefits me...* We should adopt it."

"Oh, Masters. The Dwarf seems to be carrying on without you... What shall I do?"

"—Huh? Oh, uh, sorry... Keep interpreting, please."

Sora and Shiro's worries had slipped past the ending. Jibril bowed once more.

"Errr... To summarize—they used to be very close, long ago—"

Yeah, so they liked each other. To a pairing level. Sora and Shiro nodded, everything starting to make sense—only to be overturned.

"*But then it fled.*"

The cold words of the continuing Dwarf lowered the temperature of their gazes.

"*It threw away its passion, closed off its possibilities, and became that* thing *unable to become anything.*"

"Hmm? You're quite a proud little thing to be judging others, aren't ya?"

That fluff-face, trembling on all fours under the weight of Fiel's behind—pretty clever of him to manage to look down at his nose at anybody from that position, Sora thought snarkily.

"It ain't no shame."

The prostrate chair clarified.

"It's just a loss. Why should you be ashamed of the road to the ideal, when it ain't even your destination? Why should you be afeard?"

Free of doubt, the chair looked right at Sora and told him:

"Dwarves live to forge. Every victory and every loss is just one more strike of the hammer."

He spoke of the Dwarf race, the way of being of the naturally strong,

—Picture your ideal self. To the very limits of your imagination. Then forge it. Don't be ashamed. Don't get lost. Don't break down. Not until you reach that ideal. Once you're there—then it's time to realize that those weren't your limits after all. Time to picture a yet more ideal self and forge it! Without limit, without end!! Everything in this world exists to be forged—the self first among all. Keep pounding. Keep grinding. Keep refining. Keep creating the self you imagine—for ever and ever, till the day you die—

"That tireless forging lifestyle is itself our one destination as Dwarf, children of the god of the forge."

The corners of the chair-man's lips, buried in hair, drew up with pride.

"It's true, our chieftain creates things none of us can even imagine. It ain't gonna be easy to catch up with him."

His eyes likewise buried in silver hair flashed coldly as he continued.

"He's got an unrivaled talent. Might be that, that thing *aside, none of us will ever be able to catch up with the chieftain."*

Then the Dwarf's eyes lit up with anger as he spoke.

"But it might be that someone can! The only thing that's closed off that possibility—is that thing fleein' by itself."

—Veig had reached a level of peerless talent no one could reach. *But how could you conclude you couldn't if you didn't try?* the Dwarf asked. Sora thought:

—*Yeah, his argument's sound. So sound it's annoying.*

"Perhaps you can't catch up to him. Could be all your forging will never get you there... But if you run and do nothing, of course you'll never get there."

This indeed, this was why Dwarf was a monster of sensibility.

"Whatcha gonna get from runnin', lookin' for a reason you can't get there? You ain't gonna find victory. You ain't even gonna find defeat."

In his eyes were the downcast eyes of the black-and-white siblings.

"You should be ashamed to run! At that rate, that thing's *only goin' one place—the dump."*

The chair had been consistently referring to Til as a thing.

"It's not even alive anymore... It's just a—"

"Hey, douchebag chair!! Sorry to interrupt, but what do you think of this?!"

Sora wasn't about to let him finish.

"——Huh?! Uh—wha—what?!"

Chlammy's eyes filled with rage as Sora grabbed her arm and thrust her forward. Quite abruptly interrupted indeed, the old Dwarf instantly opened his eyes wide, and—

"...Nmm. That's the chieftain's work, all right—it's perfect. One of the reasons I'm here lettin' myself be used as a chair, ain't it? Gotta say, I'm gettin' sold on the merits of big—"

"**Is that so?!** Then I dismiss everything else you have to say!! Have fun as a chair!!"

Sora cut down the Dwarf's reply with one mighty swing and turned away.

"The hell. Race of sensibility, my ass. Veig and this guy, hopeless!!"

...Yeah, he'd actually realized a long time ago. Look, in the first place, their "Big Papa" had the sense as cataclysmic as Ragnarok to create hairy, bearded girls, you know?! What did you expect from his kids? More like *nonsense*, amirite?!

"Perfect?! If that's the kind of perfection you're after, forget the chest; just make her whole body into one big ball. You got it, asshat?!"

Sora gave the chair a good glare and launched his final barb.

"It's 'cos you're satisfied with mere perfection that this is where you're still stuck!!"

————Silence. Everyone looked at him to ask what he meant. But, taking no note, Sora tromped off. Shiro scrambled to follow, as did one other.

"Jibril, fix the dictionary! Dwarves are the perfect example of the *opposite* of sensibility!! If one of these assholes ever tells you that the world is round, take another look!! It's one hundred percent *not round*!!"

The logic? It should go without saying. If they were a race that never erred—

—*If they were also never right*, then that made their opinions ideal for reference, didn't it?

"Y-yes, Master! I—I shall amend it at once!!"

Jibril followed Sora, scribbling in her book, as they left the plant. *I'll give you one proof to start*, Sora thought as he sneered.

—*They said there's no place for Til, and no one could find her, right? See?* ——*They were wrong!!*

"Jibril, *I know where Til is now*. Take us into the air *right above* the capital!!"

"Y-yes, Master!! I—I shall prepare—p-please wait just a moment!!"

As he waited as Jibril busily shut her book and prepared a shift—

"Hey, Chair. Try using your brain for thinking once in a while, okay? In exchange, I'll give you a bit of industrial knowledge from another world."

—Sora addressed the dumbstruck Dwarf as if he had a whole bouquet of sarcasm to give him. Grinding? Forging? *Ha!* He called bullshit on their claim to be a race skilled in manufacturing.

"It was very amusing listening to your description of a *so-called life based on nothing but effort*. There's also welding—"

And you might want to know—Sora continued, as he and Shiro left only the afterimage of their middle fingers—

"—there's also casting, which you do after you *melt everything down*. Bet you've never heard of that, huh?!"

—as with Jibril they vanished from the space.

■■■

All that remained there was Chlammy, Fiel, and silence. Even the chair had been tastefully removed, once it had been found out that he was ecstatic to be sat on. Surrounded by the sonic void of the room they two inhabited alone, Chlammy went on thinking about many things:

…About what the chair had said, and about boobs.

…About the cryptic words of Sora, and about boobs.

About the universe, and about boobs… In short, she agonized predominantly about boobs. Yes, about those who had stormed in to deny her boobs—

"Fi…I have big boobs, don't I?! They're real; this is the real me, right?!"

—and about her identity, now as wobbly as her chest.

What do you mean, "mere perfection"? Perfection is good!!

She had big boobs. Conceptually big boobs. If they were big boobs by definition, then how could you say they were not big boobs?! She cried out to her big-boobed friend for help, who smiled placidly in response—

"No matter what you look like, you're the *real Chlammy*, the Chlammy I love."

—But Fiel wasn't the Fiel Chlammy loved… With a smile she didn't know—had never seen—stained with tears and despair—

"——Hey—…F-Fi?!"

—Fiel buried her face in Chlammy's chest, rubbing her cheeks against it and breathing heavily. She was an *erof.* Chlammy was bewildered to see her bosom buddy taking in her bosom—but even more—

"…Why, just as Mr. Sora says—I cannot win this game."

—Chlammy gaped to hear her *admit she couldn't win.* She'd never before seen her friend *give up.*

"It's a seal-rites-only game…a game made for Dwarves… Of course I cannot win."

"Well, yes—but Sora and Shiro accepted it… There should be a chance for us, too, don't you think?"

Indeed—Veig seemed to have this game in the bag however you looked at it. But if Sora and Shiro accepted it, there must be a way to win. Which meant that the win condition *wasn't* to build a better spirit arm than Veig, since Fiel couldn't build such a thing—*no one* could. In that case—what was this path to victory Sora and Shiro were counting on?

There could be only one thing. It was that over which Sora and Shiro had been questioned—their *souls.* Sora and Shiro could be questioned about and answer whatever; it was irrelevant as far as snatching their victory went. The point was, what they had to do was bash Veig's soul and smash his core. That's all there was to it. So, what they had was Fiel's soul, her resolute will to reject Dwarf in its every aspect. They just had to build a decent frame, even if it didn't compete with Veig's, and bash him with it. That was the idea…presumably, but—

"Heh… Effort? Why, it is the idle prattle of mere moles, simply the self-delusion of pitiful beasts…"

—as Fiel played with Chlammy's breasts, she dismissed Dwarf's philosophy in one breath.

"No matter how you try…you can never overcome the difference in natural talent…"

—*You can never do what you can't do…* It was a self-evident truth Immanity knew better than anyone. After all—

—*no matter how they tried, Immanity couldn't use magic…*

* * *

But then, as it finally sank into her bones, Fiel bellowed.

"No matter how you struggle! You—you can never overcome…the difference in gifts…!!"

Listening as her breasts were squeezed, clutched, and swung, Chlammy looked down—and thought.

"…All right… Yes. I understand that it must have *hurt*…but…Fi?"

…Only Dwarves could process the materials required for spirit arms. But Fiel had asserted that there was no need to rely on Dwarves as long as they had the tools and the Holy Forge. *Why, we'll see who's better, won't we?* So she'd asked Chlammy, and she lifted a giant hammer she needed to multi-cast to be able to lift at all.

"You *shattered your bone*. Is that really a matter of gifts? As opposed to you just being clumsy."

"Why, the race of Elves is not one who uses tools! …Oh, how it hurrrt…"

Chlammy had almost fainted when she'd seen the outcome of Fiel's literally crushing failure. At any rate, Fi insisted that it was a matter of her race and not a personal flub.

"W-well, that's why we got the Dwarves to do it. How do you conclude from that that we can't—"

Healing magic had made it good as new, but at this rate, someone was going to die before the game began. That was why Chlammy had assisted on the condition that there be no exchange of lives—but now Chlammy halted midsentence, widened her eyes, and gasped.

…*How could I have missed such a thing?!* Finally she grasped Sora's words: *You're already relying on Dwarves to build this for you, which proves you can't do it yourself.*

—Given all this, how was Fi supposed to pilot the thing?!!

…You could go off all you wanted about how it wasn't about the machine's performance, but a "battle of souls." But you had to bash him with your soul—which meant you had to hit him.

…Or else you'd just get pummeled until the game was over…

Oh, what a ridiculous oversight; it's not like you, Fi—no, such blame could not be given. For Chlammy herself, even with Sora's memories, had overlooked it; it was impossible in this world.

——For this was a *physical fight*...

And " " had accepted the game—that was the evidence for assuming they could win. But, in that case...could Sora beat Veig in a fight? No. He'd fold unconditionally in the face of violence... That was who he was, and their conditions were the same......

——.

In the silence that fell, there was only one sound: the *boiiing, boiiing* of Fiel playing with Chlammy's breasts as she sobbed with her face nestled between them. Chlammy condemned herself for allowing their hopes to crumble over such a ridiculous oversight—such a misreading. She was left at the mercy of Fi, whose heart had been broken by the nightmare of being panted over by the Dwarven chair.

"...B-but, then...just how does Sora plan to win...?"

At last, Chlammy was really running out of ideas—when there came a flash and an ache in her head, in which a male voice answered:

——*Me? Of course I can't win.*

"—!! —Ah...!"

"...? Chlammy...?"

Chlammy clutched her throbbing head, her newly tangled thoughts, as she answered herself.

—*Sora? ...Of course he can't win.*

Indeed...if this game wasn't about the machine's performance, but a "battle of souls"—

—then all the more it should be *fatally impossible for Sora and Shiro to win*...

Besides, they *wouldn't be able to answer* Veig's questioning, Veig's soul.

—Of course they wouldn't... They could never...settle up—with this flashing...memory—this past————!!

"Chlammy?! Chlammy! Answer me! Chlammy?!"

Fiel's voice, even the feeling of her body being shaken seemed somehow far away... But Chlammy thought, certain there was something in there she ought to hold on to, struggling to reel it in.

...In that case, did Sora accept a challenge he couldn't overcome? That couldn't be the case.

"Ya got me good. The game's over. I lose."

...That's right. He never played a game he couldn't win. Just as in those memories, in which he ran from one challenge after the other. He'd never lost...but, in exchange, he'd never won either.

"Some fockin' losers who skipped out on the tab from their old world..."

...That's right. If he'd accepted the game despite it calling into question his past, with which he could never settle—that meant he could win. The way he always did—yes...definitely. Just the way he always did. On a high-risk tightrope, like a cotton string stretched across a valley. One wrong step and it was straight to the bottom. Which left only the option not to make a wrong step... That...was how he'd win—

"If you can do that much—why'd ya pansies run from your world?"

——Be quiet... I'm not thinking about why he *wanted* to play this game, only how he *intended*—

"But it might be that someone can! The only thing that's closed off that possibility—"

——Be quiet. Be quiet, be quiet!! Don't look at me like you understand. Don't talk to me like you know!!

"You should be ashamed to run! At that rate, that thing's only goin' one place—"

——Then what about you? Aren't you *running from your own shame*?!!

An enraged voice boomed inside her. She wasn't even sure whose emotion it was. But something felt like it linked up—and with that, Chlammy was out like a light...

*　*　*

————.

—And the next thing she knew...she was in darkness. She could see the sky, in a world with no sky. She could feel someone's hand in hers, in a world with no one.

—*Pop...*

Just a bit of the sky appeared, like a spotlight. Lit by the blue sky, a red-haired girl came into view. Then, again. The blue sky opened further, and she saw a girl with wings and a halo. Three, four... As the sky opened, she saw a girl with long ears and a tail, and a bewitching fox-lady. Five, six, and so on—as the sky opened, she saw someone new each time. A Dhampir, a Flügel, Sirens, an Old Deus—and Ex Machinas... As they all looked up to the blue sky, she thought, *Ah...* The blue sky had opened above her head, too, and it illuminated her. Realizing that the hand she held was that of her warmly smiling best friend, Chlammy also smiled. Oh...these were those whom Sora and Shiro had beaten—including her.

Then, that lone figure still looking up at the blind darkness... She could only glimpse the silhouette of the man and the white-haired girl huddled together in the shadow.

—Yes, they alone...could still not see the sky. They, more than anyone else, admired the superior. They, more than anyone else, took pride in being inferior. There was no place for them—so they hoped to create one. They spoke with confidence—in their utter helplessness. Eyes wavering nervously—afraid—fragile—but.

—Always watching the black sky, dreaming of the blue...

The girl...with *pale blue eyes*——

...

.........?

.........Pale...blue eyes...?

No. It was supposed to be a girl with red eyes and a man with dark ones… Chlammy raised her gaze from *them*—the two figures seeming to overlap—and took a look up at what everyone else was looking at…

—And she chuckled to see why everything felt as if it had connected. *Oh—why didn't I realize… I see, no wonder Shiro is desperate to ship them.*

——*They look just like them…these guys…*

——……

"……mmy……lammy!"

A voice called to her. Chlammy's consciousness floated upward like a bubble seeking the water's surface as she thought.

—Ah… Those *weren't* the people Sora and Shiro had beaten—they were the *very factors by which Sora and Shiro had won*… It was simple. When, after all, had Sora and Shiro ever won through their own power…? All these people, including herself, had always just…*gone and lost on their own.*

Her best friend called her, tears marring her blanched face. Chlammy answered with a smile, remembering the blue sky that had been gradually pried open, and the white bird. Chlammy told Fi where Sora and Shiro's chance lay…by murmuring this:

"…Basically, all they have to do…*is win as usual.*"

Yes, as usual…that is, with fraud and bluster…

They were in a cramped little hole deep in the dark ground, the clanging of metal the only sound that filled the air. The hole was crowded with pieces of metal, but it was more than spacious enough for a little figure swinging a hammer alone. Suddenly the sound stopped, and through the hole now full of silence a vacant voice intoned:

"…How did you know to find me here?"

The little figure—Til—uttered a dry inquiry as she turned. The young man pointed to the ceiling of the dim, narrow cave—a hole

through which a little of the blue sky could be seen, and through which sunlight flowed in. It was Sora, with his sister and their servant. His eyes were like that sky as he answered with a smile.

"The *sky*—It bothered you not being able to see it, right?"

……

"…I like the sky, I do… I like…to see the birds fly, I do."

As if to say she didn't want to run anymore—no, had no place to run anymore…

"I like to fantasize about what those birds see, I do—swimming through the air, doing what I can't as if there were nothing to it. I'd like to be able at least to dream… *If only I could fly…*"

…Til glanced with eyes of resignation at the *dark sky and white bird*, and then turned back.

"…It's time for a demonstration of some simple and easy spirit-arm manufacturing, in the style of a *grubby mole who can't do anything*…it is."

She self-mockingly referred to the lesson she'd given before about what any Dwarf could do. That had been two days ago. Her mumbling now indicated that she would show them with actions rather than words.

"First…you do your best to rifle through a heap of junk for existing seal rites…and collect what you find, you do."

Indeed, here in this hole echoing with the strikes of Til's lone hammer, they were at a corner of Hardenfell's greatest dump site.

"Next…you desperately try to figure out what the seals mean and what you can make, you do…"

Junk covered the bottom of the hole in the ground, visible from the sky above. Til held some of it, decorated with seals whose meaning they couldn't sense. She beheld it with a defeated gaze.

"Then, as always, you moan that you *can't make head or tails of it*, and, one by one…"

Belying her words, she flashed about her tools with speed beyond what Sora's and Shiro's vision could follow—

"...you muck about with them, thinking, *No, not like this, nor like this*...and that's all, it is. So this is all you get, it is."

—and—smirking—she indicated that, in this pile of junk filling the hole, there was now *one new piece of junk.*

"Then you just continue until you get something that *happens* to work... See? It's simple, isn't it?"

Punctuating the irony of her words, she tossed the item she'd just finished. So—here, she fished through the existing seal rites...the scrap...cobbled it together...

She made her own mountain of junk, building her own geological stratum—right here.

Born to a race that never erred—then erring constantly.

Of a race that forged ever ahead—yet unable to follow.

Doused in shame and frustration and failure, she'd fled her homeland, fled her country, fled her talented uncle. She'd fled and fled and fled. And this is where they ended up, those who'd fled from it all. As the chair had said, this was the destination—for those no one needed, those not even alive...

"Welcome to my home, if you will... What brings you here?"

Til smiled weakly, in that deep, dark dungeon—that desolate nonplace for those with no place at all—and asked:

"Having seen this...do you still want me to make something for you?"

"......"

Til's back continued to tremble. Sora silently took just one step forward.

"Live without shame, without running away? That's hogwash, it is. If it's so possible to surpass a genius with effort, then why doesn't *someone go prove it already*?! No one can do it—well they claim it's their destination, they do!!"

Another step. And another. Til seemed frightened of Sora's approach.

"Th-they can go toil. I've had enough, I have! Taking pride in failure? That's insane, it is! I just don't see any sense in going to try and fail when you can't win, I dooon't!!"

She didn't turn. She couldn't. Til just kept shaking as she piled on the excuses. But…

"Effort will be rewarded?! Talk of dreams is all well and good. But they're *just dreams*, they aaare!!"

Thus she finally shrieked as she felt Sora get right behind her. The next moment, she practically leaped up into the air as Sora *nodded dramatically* and roared—!

"Damn straiiiiiiiight!!!"

……

"I'll spell it right out!! *Effort's not rewarded, and you can't overcome talent. That's reality!!"*

"…………Sir. Um, uh… That's right, it…is?"

Til turned with fear, dumbfounded at Sora's unexpected agreement. Her round orichalcum eyes got even rounder in her bewilderment, which Sora elegantly trampled right over!

"Back in our old world, characters in games and comics are always saying, 'Effort pays off,' 'Effort can outdo talent.' And why?! Because they're **fiction**!! *Because they're telling a story of something that doesn't exist!!"*

Sora grew impassioned, vehement! He raised his arms triumphantly. His fists, his voice shook as he spelled it out article by article—yes!!

"And thus it is clear! 'People can understand one another.' 'All people are equal'! All those lines they spout out in entertainment, they're *all fiction*!! They're dreams we wish for 'cos we ain't got 'em. That's entertainment, right?!"

—Anything they showed in entertainment could be expected to be fiction! If it were obvious reality, *it wouldn't make for entertainment*. For example!!

* * *

...*People get sleepy.* Is there a work of entertainment in which the main characters argue passionately for this? Probably not. Why? *Because it's obvious.* It's a reality more familiar to us than our pillows at home. We know, stupid. Give us back our money! What kind of idiot wants some idiot to argue in detail for some reality that goes without saying?!

If it's depicted *thus* in entertainment—it's proof that it's *otherwise* in reality, and so—!!

"'True friendship'! 'True love'! 'The guy all the girls go for'!! All of these are inherently fiction. This should be self-evident!!"

"......Uh. Well...I'm not, sure...about, that...?"

Shiro interrupted, evincing residual attachment to hope, but Sora mercilessly cut her down!

"*It's fiction!!* Friendship breaks down. True love turns into a mess! The guy all the girls go for gets stabbed. That's reality. I mean, you gotta make a choice here, either retreat into fiction or get stabbed and step off the stage of reality. But anyway—!!"

He cleaved hope in two, and again looked Til in the eye—

"Til, you are absolutely right. Make an effort at a game you can't win? *Hogwash.* Any sane person would run."

—and affirmed what she had said.

"Beat the greatest Dwarf by effort alone? *As the worst Dwarf?* Yeah, right."

"......! ...Sir. It's as you say, it is."

Her pale blue eyes agreed in confusion, fire waving in them fragilely—eyes Sora knew well. Til didn't seem to realize they'd clouded due to Sora's affirmation...

"If effort's enough for the lowest to beat the geniuses—then the geniuses can just make an effort and kick your ass, can't they?!"

"Sir! That's it exactly, it is!! It's impossible to catch up with a genius who makes an effort, it is!!"

She nodded furiously at Sora's continued address.

But she didn't seem to realize the fire flickering in her eyes as she looked up at her sky, or the spark of hope roaring to life inside her...

"Can you train your body to beat a Werebeast at arm wrestling?! Can you train your eyes to see spirits?! If you really think that kind of effort will pay off—go train your muscles and outgrip a gorilla!! *We're all just human*, you say? With all due respect, that is a fallacy!! No human is *just* a human! If you think that kind of twaddle will get you anywhere, look, *we're all just living things*, okay? So you make that effort and evolve so you can shine light out of your ass like a firefly!!"

"Yes, yes!! Shine that light—sparkle, sparkle!! It even sounds a bit cute, it does!"

"If you're gonna hold us up to the same standards as the powerful, all we have to say is, *Fuck you!!*"

"Yes, yes! *Fa-kew!* …What does *fa-kew* mean?!"

Til saluted, weeping with the grand emotion of Sora's speech. But *fwip*, Sora turned his back. Only Shiro and Jibril saw his face, wrenched into an evil smile. And by now it was no surprise…

—Overcome the naturally strong by effort? —*Hogwash.*

No matter how hard he tried—he could never become like his sister. He knew that better than anyone—*and that was why* he'd lived looking down at such conventional strategies, more than anyone… They knew him, and so they knew. The fundamental question was this:

——*Why did you have to win through your own power…?*

They knew that was what that savage smile meant. They kept quiet and watched Sora's farce unfold. So, Sora whipped around to face Til again, and initiated a dialogue!!

"I ask you, Til! Can you defeat a Werebeast in magic-less combat?!"

"I cannot, I can't! Not by any means!! I cannot, I can't!!"

"And I ask you, Til! Can you beat an Ex Machina at chess?!"

"No, sir! No, no, no, sir!!"

"Then let me ask you, Til! Can you overcome Veig, the greatest master of spirit arms?!"

"*Semper fi!* Do or die! Hell no!! Hell no!!"

Til answered Sora's questioning passionately, complete with a martial salute!

...Yoink, yoink, yoink...

"Let's see, your score is... ☆ Zero. ♪ And what's the penalty for the *smartasses* who get those questions wrong?"

"...Sexual harassment...courtesy of, Shiro...plus...a photo..."

Til was greeted by the obnoxious smiles of the easygoing Sora and Shiro, looking like kids who'd pulled off a prank. Til stood there, even forgetting to blush at the harassment she'd previously endured three days before. But Sora's next words—

"The correct answer to all the questions is *yes*... It's just reality. It's just fact."

"————!!!"

—made Til remember, whether she liked it or not, just *who* those two pairs of eyes that pierced her now belonged to. She stood shivering as though she'd been struck by lightning. Yes... They'd *always overcome and trounced higher races*—those talents insurmountable by effort. Now they promised to defeat Veig. No, just as they had with their previous victories, they boasted that they'd *already won*. They were Sora and Shiro—" "...mere humans, who embodied the fact that it was possible to utterly destroy those with greater gifts—even the divine.

"Til... Do you realize who you're speaking to when you *claim* to be the most inferior of all?"

"...We're never-before-seen...literal *unprecedented* scum... That's, us..."

The dignity of their (inexplicable) godly presence as they took Til to task made Til and Jibril gulp, feeling as if they heard the subtext audibly...

—Know your place, O strong ones. Stretch. Swagger.

—Know, too, that however you may crawl or squirm, you will never reach our depths.

"*You can beat a gorilla, right?!* You can see spirits, and in the first place—!!"

…Yes, looking up at everything farther down their noses than anyone else, the two crowed mightily!

"You can go out alone and talk to people alone!! That alone makes you far, far stronger than us. Don't get full of yourself!!"

"…We can barely, breathe by ourselves, and you think you're worse…? You've got something to learn, missy…"

"A-as you say, it is, but, uh, um! I—I am eighty-four years old—so I am your elder—"

"Gaaah!! I'm not going to take it easy on you just 'cos you're exactly my type!! Why do I have to set someone else's heroine's flags? It doesn't make any sense! We're going Spartan on your ass now. You ready?!"

Sora declared on his own that he would not accept any rebuttal from Til. They belonged to the weakest and most inferior race. And of them, they were the select bottom of the bottom of the bottom.

"Perhaps you'd like to know how we, ' ', the true claimants of the title of most inferior, prevail and continue to prevail… If you are so determined to boast of weakness rivaling ours, if you intend to go to the extreme—then very well. Prick up your ears, listen, and learn…"

Sora smiled wickedly, ready to enlighten Til as to what constituted the real thing, what it really meant to be the weakest. Ready to reveal the culmination of the abyss, the secret to defeating talents that could never be overcome with effort alone. He stuck his elbows at his sides and raised his palms, prophesying in the manner of a conqueror. He said——!!!

"——You beat them by cheating…!"

……

"That's right!! You stab 'em in the back, hit them when they're not looking, make them shoot their friends, poison them, undermine them, and trick them into traps!!"

Ah, fiction tells us Evil never prevails... *However, sadly enough, in reality,* evil always prevails!!

"You analyze the strong, study them, exploit them, copy them—*it doesn't matter what you do as long as you win.* You got it?!"

"............Uh... I suppose, I...do..."

Sora concluded his speech with his face twisted in a wicked smile that, in entertainment terms, looked like that of a demon lord destined to be slain. Til was confused to hear evil's praises sung so gallantly, but Sora proceeded to pass right by her.

"That's right, you cheat. If I must grace it with a word—"

Sora picked up one item from the heap of junk and turned. Now smiling serenely, he exalted the epitome of evil he had just sung. You might call it...*wisdom.* Or perhaps *calculation.* Or *learning.* Or *deliberation.*

—Or, in the final analysis, *theory.* That academic system, the grandfather of all manner of tactics and strategy—

"......It's called...*ingenuity*..."

Indeed—that was the nature of human weakness. That was how humans lived, and it was just that which the self-described grubby mole, likewise proud of her inferiority, had stacked up all this time. Yes—it was impossible to overcome the naturally strong by pure effort. And that was why just as exemplified by that which Sora now held, described as one of many failures, and its *clearly strange engraving*:

"You win by piling up trick after trick, just like you've done."

Groping in the dark. You considered, inferred, observed, patched together the principles of the strong. Grasping at straws. You failed and suffered until you had amassed a mountain. Sora knew where it led—to victory. And so he spoke with a grin.

Fundamentally—to begin with:

—*Why did you have to win through your own power...?*

If you were to overcome absolute talent—to win against a Flügel:

"The way you've *relied on others* to *escape Jibril*, for example. ♪"

"*Oh.* Oh, ohh—uh, um! I-i-it wasn't l-like that, it wasn't!!"

Sora threw Jibril the object he held, and Til seemed to finally realize what it was. She leaped desperately to snatch it from the air but ended up in a futile dive.

"Oh my…? Is this not…an Elven seal rite?"

"Noooo!! Please, no, I beg you, don't look, oh pleaaase!!"

Jibril simply shifted to catch it first, regardless of the supplication of Til, now stuck headfirst in the pile of metal.

…She just cobbled together existing seals. All right, that sounded plausible enough. Cobbling together seals more complex than integrated circuits in machines more precise than a mechanical watch?

Objects built by sensibility alone?

Without a shred of theory?

"I see… So you *used the theoretical framework of the Elves*, even though you despise them so…"

"Aaah, I can't hear you, I caaan't. I want to di—just kidding, I don't want to die, I dooon't."

Right. She just had to patch in Elven seal rites, which did have a theoretical system. That would explain how Til had known enough to detect Fiel's magic before it fired. But Jibril's eyes still asked how she'd been able to escape her.

"Hey, Jibril. If she's gonna use Elven rites…"

"…there's no…reason, she wouldn't…use others', right…?"

Magic wasn't Sora and Shiro's specialty… They couldn't even understand that shit. But in this case, things were especially easy to piece together from the circumstantial evidence. They both smirked. After all, there weren't that many ways to flee from Jibril other than through the afterlife. Of them, one could again be *a rite Til had seen through before it was used*. And the only time she could have engraved the rite was when they were on the subterrane—yes…

"For example, the shift rite you first wove to go above the capital of Hardenfell, Jibril. ♪"

That was why they'd commanded her to shift there, they were saying. But then that meant—!

Jibril's eyes opened wide at the revelation.

Til had fled by engraving a Flügel rite onto her hammer and using it to shift...

"Inconceivable! One does not merely transcribe—no, in the first place, to perform a nonvirtual shift—even if it could be expressed as a seal, it would not operate with the amount of spirits a Dwarf has—it's meaningless!"

"Yes. That's what boosting is for, right? *Til can't use a single spell without boosting. ♪"*

Jibril caught Sora's subtext, and now was truly lost for words.

True, for a normal Dwarf, it would likely be meaningless and impossible.

But for Til, who was not a normal Dwarf, it was both a given and entirely possible.

"And it's quite a meaningful trick to use against *us,* since we're not normal either, right?"

Sora called affectionately to the rear end growing from the pile of junk.

"Hey, grubby little mole who's so proud of her conviction she can't do anything."

To defeat the greatest of all Dwarves—Veig—they needed the lowest of all Dwarves—Til. That's right...

She boasted with overflowing confidence that *she couldn't do anything without cheap tricks.* She ran from pointless effort—and yet...

"Despite all that—why'd you *build your spirit arm looking up at the sky?"*

"_____!!"

The rear end jumped with a gasp. Hesitantly, Til produced her face from the junk. Then, waffling and wavering, fretting and frowning, she looked directly into Sora's eyes. Her own eyes were the same as two days before; the same stare. And she asked in the same way:

"...Is it, all right, for me...to go, with you...?"

Indeed—

"I'm...a grubby little mole, I am. I can't do anything without staining my hands with the terrible, horrible crime of using Elven rites. I've no sense nor courage nor guts—nor a speck of hair, baby-bald mole that I am."

—when Til's eyes had rested on the darkness of Sora's, uncertain, weak, afraid, and fragile—but with great conviction...of her inferiority—she'd asked:

"Despite it all...is it—*possible for me to fly like you...?*"

Orichalcum eyes shimmering with pale blue flame—they didn't ask, *Will you abandon me?* Nor: *Is it worth anything to have me with you?* It was: *Is there anything I can do?*

That was what it looked like they were asking. Til herself didn't even know it as she looked to the *sky* with hope, and asked:

"Is it possible—for me to be something more than a chicken...?"

The chieftain; her uncle; her natural gifts; spirit arms—promises...

Could she face all that she'd run away from, everything she'd turned her back on—and *win*?

—Could she believe that she could be like Sora and Shiro?

——Could she be a flightless bird yet able to fly...?

The fire in her pale blue eyes, flickering a hotter temperature than red, roared: *I won't accept it*—and *I won't surrender.* Sora recalled how Veig had interrupted things that day and chuckled.

—*Sure it is, kid. You just got to be deliciously enjoyed.*

Beg, and you'll blast off so high...

"Yeah, Dwarven opinions are perfect negative examples. After all...*they're only half-right.*"

And with a smarmy grin, Sora adopted Veig's vernacular for his answer.

"No way it ain't, kid."

The hope in Til's eyes instantly clouded with disappointment, but—

"I mean, *we can't, either.* A chicken is a chicken. No matter how we cheat to fly, we can't become birds. However…"

Sora smiled gently, offered his hand, and continued.

"…If you beg to win, we'll help blast you up with us, *higher than the birds.*"

Til's eyes wavered, her hands trembling from fear and admiration, hope and unease. She looked back and forth between Sora's darkness and the literal sky's blue. Finally, she made up her mind and took hold of the dark sky, in fine spirits. She had no more hesitation.

"Very well, then!! Um, I can't vouch for my deliciousness, but **I'll gladly blast off with you, I will!!**"

"Okay, I worded that poorly!! Veig was right, you shouldn't do it with a virgin, so stop stripping. Hey, being 'deliciously enjoyed' isn't part of it, okay—**d00d, she's strong!** Someone help me stop her, will ya?!"

Ready? Here's my cherry. Take it, bitch—!! Crimson-faced, Til started ripping off her clothes without a second thought, so Sora had to call in the reinforcements. However—

"…It's okay… The pairing's already set… Cockblocking is inevitable… In the worst case…it'll be just the tip…and then…there will be, a precedent…which…suits me… I can live with that…"

"If so saith Lord Shiro, then all I've to do is to stand by in diminutive form… Geh-heh, geh-heh-hehhh…"

—he was heartlessly abandoned by the eagle-eyed little strategists, already focused on the next battle.

■■■

——……

"A-are you really going to remove *this*?! It's a historic property, it is!"

"Hnh? Don'cha mean a historic burden? The rules say we can borrow *anything in this city,* don't they?"

"...Which means...we can also borrow, *this* and *that*...nooo problem..."

"We'll make good use of it to defeat Veig! And while we're at it we can *dispose* of it! Two birds with one stone, right?!"

"Then you're not borrowing it, are you?! If you don't intend to return it, that's borrowing as a euphemism for stealing, it iiis!!"

"And now, Master, we can shift all of this to the plant where the long-ears awaits—"

——......

□□□

——And then...since when had it been like this?

Sora suddenly felt a pleasant warmth and heard Shiro's voice from seemingly far away...

"...Brother...I thought about it, so long...and finally...I found... the answer."

—Had he been asleep? Or was he still asleep...?

In the darkness, his senses drifted through indistinct conscious-ness as Shiro continued...

"...The Veig x Til...flag...has already been set...right...?"

...and Sora slowly, reluctantly accepted the facts: *Ah. But.*

"...Brother x Shiro...must progress... But the content guide-lines...were tricky."

Shiro's voice sounded joyful—and somehow, something con-nected that made Sora tense.

"...But Til, gave me...a hint... I found...the answer!"

Then——Sora abruptly—

"...If I do *this*...you can, see!! You can touch... And it's acceptable... right?!"

"What, am I inside Shiro's skirt?! It's dark; I can't see anything; d00d, what's going on?!"

—*Gwish. Gwwish...!*

The warmth was of her stomach, which pressed him. Sora rushed

to pull his face out. But even after he escaped the darkness, things still looked bleary, unsteady—

"......Eh-hehhh... Brother... How'd...you like that? Did it turn you...on——?"

"—Shiro?! ...Whoa, don't tell me, is this alcohol...? We're both underage..."

Shiro suddenly conked out, and Sora scrambled to grab the clearly drunk, red-faced Shiro before she fell.

—*Seriously, what's going on?* he meant to scream, but amidst the haze in his head, the best he could do was to groan it.

...He looked around to see what appeared to be the inside of a tavern. It seemed Shiro had stood on the bar to put her skirt over him. There were two glasses of a frothy liquid that looked for all the world like beer—maybe ale, if we were talking about Dwarves? Dwarves made merry in this scene straight out of some fantasy game with steampunk elements. But all the ruckus and the sights felt terribly far away... A voice answered his foggy head—

"*Don't worry, this spirit oil is my own brew. I'd never cut it with such swill as alcohol.*"

It came up from an unfamiliar old man who sat next to him and downed his own glass.

He was a man such as you might see anywhere, yet one you'd never see anywhere. Still, somehow, Sora *felt he had seen his eyes before*. His suspicion deepened.

—Who was this guy? Or rather...

"*Looks like it's a little too spiritual for a human like you. But it's good, ain't it?*"

Nothing seemed real, except Shiro asleep on his chest...

...What was this......?

"*So? How 'bout the rest of the story? Aren'cha gonna tell me?*"

...The rest...of what story...? I mean...what...am I even......doing here......?

"*The story of your world. Ain't there more?*"

............Oh yeah... That's right... I was talking about that, I think...

Sora felt his doubt washing away with his grip on reality, and somehow it seemed to make sense. He took a swig.

"Aaagh... Ahh, where was I...? Did I tell you about how it sucked?"

"Ya did. Heard that part."

"Did I tell you about how it was a nightmarish dystopia full of idiots like me?"

"Heard that part three times or so."

"Oh, okay. Then *that's the story.* That's all there is to it... Damn, this is good... More, please."

Sora concluded that those two statements summed up that world. The man poured the "spirit oil" or whatever into his empty glass and said—

"Ya said, 'But they've got more hope than these guys, at least.' Where was that goin'?"

——*I went there? Me...? I must really be drunk... This has gotta be booze...* A suspicion surfaced in his dozing mind, but—

"...Aaah... That's righhht, they're all idiots. All they do is fail. If only they'd say they were choosing the wrong paths on purpose at least... It's a world of rules set by a lost cause..."

—once he chugged his glass, it washed right out. Leaving it at that, Sora collapsed on the counter. Still nothing was clear to him except the heat of Shiro on his chest. Aimlessly, he thought...

...Yeah. A race of fools, making one mistake after another.

That dear old world of mine, built of failure and error and wrongdoing.

They made so many mistakes, to the point that they grew to fear making mistakes...

...and made the worst mistake of all:

To learn that they should never make a mistake again...

It was a bad joke.

It might be a mistake, they said, so
  what might not be a mistake, you had to
eradicate before you even knew it was a *mistake.*

* * *

—What was a mistake…? If we knew that, we wouldn't make mistakes in the first place…would we?

"Oh…but yeah. *For that reason*…they might still have more hope than you guys," Sora felt, grinning as he lifted his head from the counter.

"…At the very least, I don't think they'd hole themselves up in a place like this."

These guys had built flying battleships way back in the Great War, along with bombs that could smash entire continents.

—And six thousand years later, *this was all they'd managed*…

It's quite ironic, but there's such a thing as being too clever for your own good. Just using your sensibility to create exactly what you imagine—see…the thing with that was—

——*you'd never go past your own imagination*, you know——?

"…*Didn't you say…it was a turd of a world?*"

The man frowned at his smile of hope and conviction.

"Mmm? Oh… Yeah, that world and its *rules* can kiss my ass… But I'm just talking about the *world*, you know? Can't you see what's written herrre?! …*Hic*…"

The spirit-drunkard displayed his shirt, which read, *I ♥ PPL*.

"'*I love people*'… *Don't it embarrass you to walk around shoutin' out your love like that?*"

…*It is kinda embarrassing when you point it out, so knock it off.* Sora smirked as he answered, then awkwardly blushed and looked away.

"Humans never change. They're just gonna keep making mistakes… They'll keep messing with the world, keep messing up the rules."

He imagined as much, though he figured it would happen in a manner as ugly as ever.

…His old world. Earth—six thousand years later…

Past 8000 CE…the eighty-first century… Hmm…

That was so far away he couldn't even imagine it. Well, anyway. That world wasn't going to get shelved as science fiction by any means. It was either going to be a space opera or a spectacle of the rebuilding of civilization too outrageous to even be described as postapocalyptic.

…And…well, knowing humans, the latter seemed more likely. But like the humans *here*—Immanity—they wouldn't give up the ghost so easily. So. Sora thought back to those distant humans, and he announced one of their possibilities loudly, with a smile.

"They might blow up their home planet, maybe even the solar system—or actually, perhaps even destroy the universe over some *silly mistake.*"

And then they'd grudgingly go looking for new pastures—like Disboard.

"And then come here by 'intermundane travel,' like—*Hi, guys* ♥ …Ha-ha!! I can see it. ♪"

They'd leave all the races of Disboard far behind. For better or worse, they'd be someplace no one—not even humans themselves— could ever imagine. Riding on his confident laugh…Sora started to drift away……and another laugh…seemed to follow him——

"*Gah-ha-ha-haaaa!! You think big, kid. That's stark ravin' mad. I like it.*"

……Seeing the man disappearing, hearing him, Sora thought—

"*It's like you say. Ya can just run through your world like a spend-thrift with a fortune. Smash it, melt it, use it as fuel, process it.*"

—*Who is this…?* Correction:

What *was this…?*

"*I don't know what your papa was thinking, but it's the duty of a kid to outdo his parents. You're gonna smash up space. Fantastic. Ya gotta be a good kid and hand it back reshaped into a form they never imagined.*"

A man such as you might see anywhere, yet one you'd never see anywhere—*and not a man.* Still, somehow, Sora felt he had seen his eyes before…and now he remembered where.

—The Holy Forge...

His eyes were like that divine pillar of fire... No—he *was* its very existence. And he continued—

"So. Whaddaya got to do to bring kids up like that? Won'cha give me a little hint how to raise my kids?"

——Ha. Ah-ha-ha-haa!! How should I know...?

It's because you're so well-behaved as to go and ask that that your kids end up like that, isn't it, "Papa"——?

☐ ☐ ☐

——And then...since when had it been like this?

"......ter... Master?! Please, answer—Please! Master!!"

Sora suddenly recognized the plaintive voice calling him and opened his eyes...

"Oh, Master, you are safe! I acted quickly to seal off the *explosion*, but I feared the worst!!"

Amber eyes containing crosses and tears broke into a smile of relief. Sora wondered:

...Hmm... What just happened? Where am I...?

Gradually his consciousness stabilized, but even so he could not escape his confusion. He looked around.

It was a terrible spectacle.

"...Ohhh, *I* see... So that's a *near-death experience*... That's not something you see every day..."

Shiro likewise woke up and looked around, and they held each other. Finally, they remembered everything. They broke out in a cold sweat—and strained smiles.

It was the plant they'd viewed from Fiel's control room—*Was.* Apparently, Jibril's protection had allowed it to *merely get blown away without a trace.* They'd cheated—that being the very foundation of science. This was the result of one little experiment Sora and Shiro had done. That's right:

"I *told* you so, I did!! It was *such* a failure, it was!!"

Til had performed the experiment at Sora and Shiro's behest. The experiment was—to extract the essence from the E-bomb on display and engrave *exactly the same seal* as used for Lóni Drauvnir's "big boob essence."

...The base essence was of a different concept. Voices flew at them from all directions telling them it was pointless to apply the same false seal. But they boldly ignored them. You never know until you try, and all that. Sora and Shiro obeyed their instincts, and the result—

"Failure? You calling this a failure? This was an epic success!! Ha-haaa!"

"...Just as we imagined...the result, was like *nothing we imagined... Good...*"

"If you call this a success, then I've done nothing but succeed my whole life, I have!"

Sora and Shiro answered with cheery grins, while Til shot back with tears.

"*That's right.* Til, you've just opened the door to the divine realm only two others have ever seen before."

Yes—Sora grinned not at the ruinous result neither Fiel nor Chlammy nor even Jibril, who'd regained her composure, could believe as they gaped, but at the *side effect.*

Someone once said failure is what leads to success... Yeah, *whatever.* Though a race that never failed would probably never even have heard of that.

"All the failures of your life, Til—now, just at this moment, have turned into success."

Success was just a byproduct of wandering. Just a fancy name to dress up failure with.

"No one can say what was wrong...and what was a failure."

Yes, no one could say:

Was it really wrong? Was it really a failure?

Were they really even...fleeing...?

"Dwarf is the race that thinks they know. That's why *Veig's lost.*"

Sora's declaration was bold, and then suddenly he added:

"—Alll right. We gotta work together to beat Veig, don't we, *dear friends?*"

Having revealed their chance of victory by empirical proof, Sora turned back to the two with the same words he'd said two days before—with the most sarcastic smile imaginable.

"............Chlammy?"

"It's just as Sora says, Fi. We can't win by ourselves. *Even Sora and Shiro can't.*"

Fiel turned her eyes to Chlammy with a bitterly forced smile, but Chlammy smirked back with a trace of enlightenment. They nodded to each other reluctantly.

"Why, that's quite all right... We'll do all we can to help you win, since you're our *beeest* friends. ♪"

"In exchange, if we win, we hope to receive a token of appreciation...as *friends*, you know?"

They quoted claims from two days ago, including Sora's, to tell him the *deal* was on. Sora nodded back contentedly.

"Okay, Jibril. Why don't you just *jaunt* on over to Veig and tell him the schedule?"

Jibril greeted Sora's savage sneer with a bow and vanished. In other words...

"—It starts at noon four days from now. The venue, units, and participants...*are a secret until ten minutes before.* ♪"

...there was no sense in playing a game otherwise than on their turf.

—You'll regret allowing us to take the initiative, Veig...

■■■

...Meanwhile...at a rest stop far northwest of the capital, beyond the door of a little medicine shop with a sign that read Business Suspended. Inside, a red-haired girl approached a clerk with a smile from across the counter... Yes.

"Come. Lead me to Sora. ♥"

It was Steph, who in less than three days had tracked down the apothecary of Sora and Shiro's that Chlammy and Fiel hadn't managed to find in three weeks of searching. Her smiling visage inched closer to Emir-Eins...

"...Query: Coordinate identification method unknown... How did you find us?"

Even an Ex Machina was intimidated by the something she detected in that insistent grin. So Emir-Eins inquired, but Steph's smile only deepened as she answered.

"Oh, it was simple. I only had to tell on you to that department of government known universally to be the *most able of all.*"

Indeed. That administrative agency where somehow the most competent personnel inevitably pool... Namely:

"I told the *tax office* banknotes were being used by an unlicensed business...and learned the location of this shop the *next day.* ♪"

And that was that. All there remained afterward was the paperwork and carriage travel time. The girl spoke with a smile that was nothing but mild and genial. Emir-Eins—

"——Qu-Query: Reason for focus on banknotes unknown."

—involuntarily took a step back and queried over and over in her head, which buzzed with errors and alerts.

"Paper currency was printed less than one week after the coup d'état. And in less than two weeks it went into circulation? *That's absurd.*"

Steph answered immediately and conclusively, still smiling, that you only had to stop and look at it for a second to see. And she expounded:

"It was as if they'd been thinking of it since before the coup. Or perhaps it would be better to say: They'd been *made to think of it* by Sora and Shiro's massive publicity for the printing press with their glamour shots of Holou. ♪"

At last Emir-Eins had nothing to say, but Steph went on, with a different tack.

* * *

"However—*I know Sora and Shiro have no interest in money.*"

She wiped the smile off her face but kept her definitive tone of voice, which said that she knew the two better than anyone. Gradually that tone grew more heated—

"So, what they're collecting is *banknotes.* The banknotes issued by the Commercial Confederation, which Sora and Shiro themselves *caused* to stage a coup. They must represent a code only readable by Shiro—or, indeed, you! A crib subject to a time limit up until competitors crowd the market—but possible to gather in one place by those who pounce on the currency first!!"

Then, her tack changed once more.

"That is what is really behind the medicine. And you'll of course explain to me the details. ♥"

Definitive as ever, she smiled again. Emir-Eins swallowed, feeling as if her mouth was full of saliva, not that an Ex Machina was capable of secreting it.

Emir-Eins now realized a little late the weight of what had been entrusted to this person—the *entire government*—by none other than her master and his sister. She deemed the smiling visage before her as a *threat.* When it came, in particular, to politics and economics, this woman of unknown name was unmistakably the cream of the crop—the *real thing*—no…

Correction: Logically evident fact. Serious error occurred in unit's analysis. That is all.

Indeed, this very woman had been trusted to manage the unprecedented scheme of a multiracial commonwealth almost single-handedly. She was the backbone of "   " themselves. There could be no doubt: She was a player…!!

Error: Fails sanity test. How is this possible?! Contradicts appearance! Unexpected value for unnamed entity!

Steph seemed unconcerned with the struggle of Emir-Eins to resolve the inconsistencies swarming her head with errors.

* * *

"I'll say it just once more: Lead me to Sora. ♥"

She was smiling—but her eyes didn't move.

"...Negative acknowledgment: This unit assigned by Master to remain in Master's absence. Executing duty of wife. Frau of master... Blush."

But Emir-Eins silenced her thoughts warning her of a threat and resisted. First of all, her master's commands were absolute. She would execute them to completion. And second:

"That was not a request, but an order. Will you please not force me to use my *last resort*?"

"Ridicule: Methods of woman of unknown name to force this unit to act: None. Taunt: Go right ahead—"

Emir-Eins had announced as much with certainty—but Steph's continuation revealed to her why her heart had defined this woman as a threat:

"I'll accept that I love Sora! How do you like thaaat?!"

"Cancellation/correction/contrition/capitulation: Command acknowledged. Directing to master. Executing now. Deactivating safe mode. Lösen: *Shurapokryphen*... Entreaty: Please... Don't."

Emir-Eins had no evidence, but she knew that the heart needed no such thing. Recognizing this declaration as an ultimatum, she surrendered unconditionally. She still didn't know why—but she felt that this rival, who lied to herself, would be insurmountable *the moment she stopped lying.*

Foreseeing a premonition of the fall of her master, and even his sister, Emir-Eins at last took her formidable rival across space.

Then:
 The empty puppet and the white bird
who could not fly
ran hand-in-hand from all that worked
to pull them apart,
and looked up at the sky.

The sky let them believe they could
go anywhere.
That sky the chick's wings could not reach.
But if they could, what would they gain?
the puppet wondered.

It was the day they had first met.
When the chick had spoken
the puppet's name.
A title shunned for meanings two
and a name sworn in three.

I am the sky. The empty sky. Your sky.

The puppet vowed on its name
to bring that sky to life.
To break and smash every cage.
To forever defy that which held
them down.

So—where do you want to go?

The puppet asked the bird,
who implored…

It was the appointed day...only an hour until the game was set to start. All Sora could perceive clearly in the darkness was the hard seat and the feeling of Shiro in his lap. Behind him—

"Spirit-arm expansion...connected! I'm launching it, I am...!"

—he heard Til shout as she swung down her hammer. It struck at their feet with a boom.

Everyone was silently praying: *Please, start up okay.* Then spirit light raced through the seals and lit the small space, the cockpit that enclosed the three of them. Next, the unit's field of vision was displayed across the whole surface of the cockpit.

They were situated amidst long-abandoned underground city ruins. It was a waste disposal site, metal refuse filling the remains of plants where everything had stopped except the eternal Holy Flame. This was the place where the unneeded scrap came to rest—in other words, their promised place. There stood their giant humanoid machine, heavy Gatling gun in both its hands. From the Demon Stance, it twisted back its left hand and fired in the eight-o'clock direction.

"Yuhh! It works, Til! Shiro, how's it lookin'?!"

"...All systems, green... Leave the shooting...to me..."

Sora and Shiro shared a single seat in the cramped cockpit, checking the grip on the joysticks on either side. Sora held the right and Shiro the left, catalysts they held with orichalcum gloves while willing their body to move. They nodded with satisfaction as the unit took just the "cool pose" they imagined. They moved it like their own bodies—no, like one body, two in one. Both smiling, they controlled it more nimbly than their own bodies. Meanwhile, behind them...

"They're not green, they're nottt... Despite all that, the screen is all red, it iiis."

Til whined in the second seat, clutching her hammer. The screen had gone red, alerting them of errors even in the startup process, even in the initial diagnostics.

"Are you truly sure about this?! Sir and Ma'am, you intend to confront the chieftain—with me, you do? In a four-day rush job like this? I can't guarantee it went well, I can't! I couldn't even if we'd had forty years, I couldn't! I—I don't want to dieee..."

Yes... Combat through spirit arms. All damage would converge into their cores, which meant they'd lose the game if Sora's and Shiro's joysticks and Til's hammer broke. It was a very safe battle game in which it was impossible to break each other's frame. However...

Damage unrelated to the collision of their spirit arms, such as, oh, accidental explosions and other forms of *self-induced damage* were outside the warranty. So, they were all glad it had *started up okay*, sparing them a "dead end" before the game started, but Til's point was that they'd have little room to complain should they die in a sea of flames any moment now.

«—*Is this really going to go all right without Jibril?*»

The voice chimed in from far beyond the vision of Sora, Shiro, and Til's unit. It was a signal from the unit lying in wait at the top of an abandoned factory. They could just make out its silhouette at maximum zoom, but it was clearly distinct in style from the others: an iron golem that looked well-suited to be the boss of the end of some ruins.

Its simple yet refined form was decorated with flowers, and several lines of spirit light glowed on it. This was Chlammy and Fiel's unit.

"Yeah…Jibril *can't participate* in this game. We knew it."

Sora answered with a grin that everything was as planned. After all, differences in gifts were absolute—including burdensome gifts. As in the case of bullshit gifts that *vaporized* orichalcum upon synchronization due to excessive spiritual energy. Poor Jibril, unable to fulfill the game's basic requirements, was left to sulk at Til's hideout.

"What I'm more worried about is…are you guys sure you can do this with *Chlammy as pilot*…?"

Sora brought up another "gift" with a solicitous smirk.

In unit testing, Fiel had said she'd give piloting a try. Then she'd pushed all the limbs of her unit forward at once, fallen, and gotten its head stuck in the ground. She was unimaginably gifted when it came to being clumsy.

… How did you manage to do that with a unit that was supposed to move according to your will like your own body? Sora started to suspect that it was less a gift and more a curse that forbade the race from using tools, but—

«…*We knew how it would be, too. I'm at least better suited than Fi.*»

«*Why, I'll be providing support back here. There's a proper place for each of us.* ♪»

The voice indicated the bizarre, insanely big cannon mounted on the unit's back, which was apparently made of wood. So Chlammy was piloting and Fiel was shooting. Then again—

«… *Just checking one last time. You're fine if we go for the win for real, right?*»

«*Why, we're more worried about you two. Can you really* hold up your end of the bargain…?»

—" " were only human, too, after all. Chlammy gave a somewhat complicated reminder, while Fi prodded sharply.

"Not to worry. When we play—we intend to have fun. ♪"

"…Trust us…we'll *play*…until, we're satisfied… ♪"

But Sora and Shiro replied with irreverence, as carefree as could be. Sora also muttered:

"I doubt no one but Blank could take on Veig."

Until our tricks *come to light*—that bit he kept to himself. Sora and Shiro cast aside their doubts and closed their eyes in anticipation of the start.

...Orichalcum gloves gripping their joysticks, Sora and Shiro—and Til—synchronized their souls, their three cores connected... and they moved as one unit. At the sense of their feelings lining up, as if they were holding hands with their hearts, Sora felt—

—it wasn't bad... It was kind of like when Shiro would fall asleep on his lap. Their heartbeats, their breathing, even their emotions gently overlapping...it was, in other words, as usual. Sora and Shiro didn't even need to connect through catalysts for their comfortable tension and pulsations to sync up. There was just Til, who was supposed to sync up likewise.

"...It's six hundred seconds...to the start of the game...it is."

As if in response to Til's uneasy murmur, a device shot up before them.

It split into many pieces that attached themselves to the ceiling: countless cameras and shift anchors. They themselves had stipulated that the venue and their units would all remain secret until ten minutes before the start. The equipment Til had launched had been supplied by Veig for the purpose of broadcasting the game throughout Hardenfell. They felt the gazes of Dwarves on every monitor in this country, the second largest in the world.

Sora, Shiro, and Til. And Chlammy and Fiel. Two units, five people—they waited in the silence disturbed only by the burning of the Holy Forge, waited for the start of the game, the arrival of their opponent. And in the end—

"Let's paaaaaartyyyyyyyyy!!!"

* * *

That didn't come over the comm system; rather, it boomed from the external speakers. This thing appeared in the air over the venue, the blue particulate light of its demi-shift through the anchor following in its wake. Its flowing silver body landed kicking up a storm of scrap and rubble like a cannonball. This was the unit they'd seen six days ago, with just *one* difference, but still—

"*We're live!! Ya got the theme song goin'?! Ready to break down the highlights after I win?!*"

Its left hand drew the ridiculously large sword from its back and brandished it at the countless cameras. It was ready to declare victory to all of Hardenfell.

No Dwarf could need to ask why. For indeed—

"*It's me—the mothafockin' chieftain of Hardenfell!!!*"

—it was, in fact, the greatest of all Dwarves, a talent unrivaled in this age…and his masterpiece.

……

Sora and the rest had no way of knowing what kind of cheers and music were going on at the other end, but—

«……*Mmm? So, this is the place, is it…? Well, I suppose anyplace will do, eh…?*»

—on-site, these words were echoing emptily, while those present said nothing. Looking slightly peevish, he switched to the comm system—directing the head of his unit into the distance—and switched gears.

«*You really think you can beat me with that sort of rubbish? Are you fockin' with me?*»

As Veig's deeply disappointed blame came through, everyone there had to admit:

—*Yeah…it sure looks that way…*

Face-to-face with Veig's machine, even Fiel was forced to chuckle at the inferiority of her own. And then there was the one controlled by Sora, Shiro, and Til.

«*…And even you can't do better than borrowin' some shit? If you're mockin' me, I'm gonna have to crush you.*»

Indeed…it was "borrowed."

The machine of Lóni Drauvnir, from six thousand years ago, which had been displayed at the Chieftain's Hall. A relic of the past. Already an antique. Moreover, they had removed the offensive equipment from the shoulders. It was no wonder that Veig looked at them with spite and disillusionment. No one could refute that their unit was inferior to Veig's. No, they couldn't refute it…they couldn't do that. However!

"Who the *hell* are you to talk?! You think *we're* the ones fucking around?!"

They could *rebut* it!!

Sora spoke for Shiro and Til in the cockpit with him—as well as Chlammy and Fiel at the venue—and probably even Jibril, who was watching:

"You don't even care if it's alive now?! Why are you talking shit to us from a *big-tittied robot*? Are you out of your mind?!"

…Bwoing…

There swaying in an annoyingly healthy manner was the *one difference* from the unit they'd seen the other day. The faces of all twisted in disgust at the big boobs that looked as though they had simply been bolted on. However—

«Hff… Inspired by those lovely raw tits, I found a way to reach even loftier heights, and you still can't appreciate it…? What's wrong with you? Are you one of those? Some pipsqueak who doesn't know art when they see it?»

"You think jiggly boobs are art?! Hey, stop pushing them up! Stop pushing them forward! Stop twisting around!!"

Undeterred, Veig exhibited his mighty mammaries. Unable to take it, Sora clutched his head.

"…Look. It's like game genres. When you specialize like that, you're limiting the audience… And when you're so specialized that what you're looking at is narrower than the head of a pin, you really gotta expand your viewpoint and think like the man on the street— **At least shape the whole mech like a woman, will ya?!**"

As for what was pissing him off: It would be one thing if we are talking about a female robot as in Virtual-*n, but this was just a bouncy lump of metal with huge boobs attached to a sleek frame.

…What was with the bouncing? Even liquid metal shouldn't bounce like that!!

«*Whaddaya want from me, kid? I gotta fight with this thing! You don't get to rebuild it. That's against the rules! The specs can tolerate minor cosmetic modifications like this—so I ripped my heart out settling for what I could, ya know?!*»

"Rip all your guts out!! Why'd you have to stick those on something you were gonna fight with in the first place?!"

Their exchange continued across the communication line, unbearable to listen to. But on an entirely unrelated note—

"… It's sixty seconds…before the game starts…it is…"

—Til mumbled, growing more and more uneasy, and, concurrently…

…the sound of steam from the Holy Forge filled the venue, heralding noon.

«*…Arright, then—no changes to the rules or chips—*»

Whomever he was responding to, Veig raised his mech's hand and continued.

«*It's over if I break all your cores, or if you break mine… By the way, is this all the players? If you wanna allow new challengers, you gotta say so now.*»

Veig asked high-handedly, *somehow* recognizing that Jibril wasn't there. But Sora, Shiro, and Til likewise raised their mech's hand and answered.

"Well, you know, we don't have that many friends. The ones here are everyone. We'll keep it closed to new challengers."

"…No magic, other than, spirit arms and seal rites… Can't use it anyway… No problem."

«*Why, we're such good friends, I'll let that sliiide even though it's quite a problem. ♪*»

Fiel's agreement was dripping with discontent as Veig gave a little smirk. The twist in his lips could be heard in his voice as he laid out the main point with resounding weight.

"Arright, ready to rumble? See if you can make me accept your soul."

And so the three mechs and the six people in the cockpits each raised their hands and boomed out in chorus:

—Aschente—

«Ha! Niecey, you're in this, too...? Ain't got nowhere left to run, huh?»

"......"

Veig, who'd heard Til's reedy voice, went on with a jolly laugh.

«Just so you know: I keep my promises. Don't be expectin' any mercy from me.»

—...Grk...

Through the catalysts, Til's feeling as she tremulously gripped her hammer made its way faintly to Sora and Shiro.

...It was the natural feeling of one who looked to the sky despite not being able to fly. The trembling of her hands was that of *throwing one-self into it*—a mixture of fear and unease. However, when she realized they shared her feelings, the trembling subsided slightly. Yes...they felt the fear as it honed their focus to the max. Til likewise felt the unease...*and for that very reason*, felt herself filling with hope.

«...Ho, fockers. Let me add another chip. You got to tell me where you poked to turn on my fockin' niece's motivation, arright? You can do it after you lose and come to.»

Veig's savage sneer was answered by the fire and brimstone that signaled noon—the horn of the Holy Forge, announcing the start of the game. Simultaneously, the clumps of metal, amalgamations of truth and falsehood, collided and produced an explosion louder than the Forge itself.

■ ■ ■

No sooner did the Holy Flame erupt to mark the start of the game than Chlammy and Fiel's golem turned tail and disappeared into the ruins. The unit controlled by Sora and Shiro also fled without a moment's hesitation. Veig's specs were unknown, but clearly superior to theirs. And on top of that, the pilot was Veig. Close-quarters combat was out of the question. Therefore, Sora and Shiro went for the tactic of firing projectiles from mid- to long range—but.

«*Mmm... Arright, I'm gonna check...*whether you're really playing me for a fool. *You can dodge this, can't you?*»
The voice came through the unit leisurely watching them from four hundred meters away.
And then—*something* flew in front of their eyes, while before their brains could even process it, Sora and Shiro, and even Til...just perceived one thing. It was as incoherent as if several seconds had been lost from their memory. It was too sudden. Veig's unit was supposed to have been four hundred meters away—and now it was *before their eyes*, raising its giant sword overflowing with light. All they perceived was the *chill*, the goose bumps rising on their skin with the knowledge that their unit was about to be cleft head to toe...
——.
...Sora's understanding just managed to catch up: Veig had hurled his sword and used it as an anchor to demi-shift before them...as Veig grabbed its hilt in his unit's left hand. But understanding it wasn't enough to evade it. Sora couldn't even move. He just sat there watching the blade come down with literally all Veig's spirits, his entire soul... A flash sufficient to take down their mech and reap their souls with it... It should have spelled instant death. But true to the Covenants and the rules, the damage converged into Sora's, Shiro's, and Til's cores—yes—
"Agh———aaaaaaaaaaaaaaaaaaghhhhh?!"
The blow assaulted their synchronized cores, and they screamed——

——......

The next thing Sora knew, he was on a hill, where a pleasant breeze was blowing.
"... Master. Why—why is it...you choose to flee...?"

Jibril stood before him, the mountainous peaks of her chest swaying.

"My flesh is yours...and yet you have never once sunk in your hands."

—*Wha...? Um, it's not so much fleeing as desperately holding back.*

"Why is that, Master? Is my flesh not worthy of your use?"

—*Uh...why? B-because my sister—Shiro's here, and...*

His eyes wandered in search of an excuse not to cup the massive boobs of the teary-eyed Jibril...but what they found was the big-boobed Loli Shiro smiling beside him, giving him the go sign with her upturned thumb.

"Is it because you lack confidence as a man that you flee from my bounty?"

—*Wha... Uh? Have I...been...fleeing...?*

"Master...*titties* are not threatening. Please summon your courage and overcome your fear..."

—*Oh... Okay, I guess maybe I have been fleeing; I mean...*

Sora extended his arm to answer her prayer that he knead her ample bosom. After all, to refuse such a plea under these circumstances would be a boy's shame. If his big-boobed sister, Shiro, said it was okay, then he shouldn't have any motive to hold back!! And so, ah...if happiness had form, it could only be the form of this sensation!

"*...Brother... The boobs...are fake... Wake...up!*"

As Sora massaged his unnaturally soft happiness, he heard a distant voice. Yes...from somewhere far away—*a voice not of the fake sister beside him*—!

—*..........*

That's right—fake is fake... It could never compare to the real *Shiro—!!*

With firm resolve, Sora escaped from the *illusion* and returned his awareness to the cockpit where the real Shiro awaited...

"Wha—?! Heyyy, Shiro! For a brother to squeeze the huge boobs

of his eleven-year-old sister, isn't that cause for a unanimous guilty verdict—?"

...and lamented his crime, realizing that the illusory happiness he'd experienced was the feeling of the *mammillary augmented* Shiro on his lap. Sora pulled away in a panic, but— *No you don't!!* Shiro swiftly clenched his hand tight. Kneading her large breast with Sora's hand as if she wanted to add to his sentence, she told him.

"...*Fake boobs are superior!* Fake boobs...are pads...!! Which means...you can touch them and squish them...you can do anything...and it's okay! Is there, something wrong...with touching...a balloon, stuffed in the chest?!"

......

......*Huh? Now that you mention it...*

Just as Sora was starting to be convinced—

"......Mm. ♥"

"S-sir... Ma'am!! Th-the control... W-we're out of synchronization, we aaare!!"

—Til, likewise thoracically enhanced, yelled over Shiro's moan, for which Sora was thankful.

"Come to your senses, Shiro!! A brother who sticks a balloon into his little sister's chest and squeezes it saying, 'It's oookayyy, it's just a balloon, gweh-heh-heh' is seriously fucked in the head! And in any case, people aren't gonna look kindly on it, you know?!"

Sora gripped the deeply *cracked* joystick and screamed as a sight filled his newly reclaimed vision—the sight left behind by Veig, *now far away*. Shiro and Til, too, blanched and swallowed.

Veig's blade had just *started* to sink into the chest of Sora and Shiro's unit, whereupon they'd shaken it off. His blow had activated the "big boob essence" within the sword—its conceptual rewriter—and broken through the junk pile around them. But it wasn't its raw force at which they shivered. It was Veig himself, who'd produced this spectacle. Statues rolling at Veig's feet, even statues of little girls that looked to have been cast aside, all showed prominent breasts. He was a pervert.

«Tch, you refuse my ideal tits. Picky, picky... Who do you think you are, virgin?»

"I know who *you* are if you're fussing that *even statues all have to have big boobs.* You're a pervert!"

Sora howled on behalf of everyone, aghast at Veig. Then—

—all three shivered: *It's as expected, but what a fearsome game.*

...The damage converged into the cores—yes, *the cores that synchronized their souls* with orichalcum. So, they literally smashed their souls together, and if his soul overcame theirs, it would infringe on theirs as it had just done. And if their hearts broke, just as their joysticks were cracking now, their cores would crumble... Ah... Indeed it was a collision of souls...!! The frame was safe; it wouldn't break. But one wrong step, and big boobs would reign supreme, statues and all!!

... They had to think a little about whether they'd rather cross that line or die...!!

«...Hff... Who would have thought...?»

Sora and Shiro's unit was bracing itself with unconcealed terror. But Veig, facing them, seemed more interested in that unthinkable last moment, which he recounted with heartfelt pleasure. Yes—

«First of all, for my fockin' niece to be about as full of spirits as me... Who woulda thought?»

Yes—Sora and Shiro's unit was a masterpiece of a past talent and Veig's only rival, Lóni Drauvnir. Even without the "big boob essence," no one should have been able to move it but Veig. Moreover:

«And ya demi-shifted that great big thing—and that firepower! Who woulda thought?»

Indeed, just as Veig had done a brief while ago, they too had used a demi-shift to dodge behind him. And immediately afterward, the Gatling gun in their unit's arms had unleashed a torrent of suppressive fire that cut through the ruins in the way, pierced Veig's mech, and stopped him in his tracks. Such a powerful barrage should have been impossible without spirits similar in magnitude to Veig's.

«*But what I* really *never woulda thought*—»

Veig named the yet more unthinkable, his voice tinged with both glee and ferocity.

«—*is that you'd* dodge me without being able to react, *and* cut off *my pursuit. How'd ya fockin' do that?*»

Indeed. Neither Sora nor Shiro, nor even Til were able to react to Veig's maneuvers. On top of that, they'd failed to dodge his strike completely and had lost themselves to an illusion for several seconds. So looking at that whole series of events—

—what was their trick to *pulling that off without being able to react or even be aware*, the voice asked?

"Ha-ha, something impossible in a game? Gotta be somebody cheating, obviously. ♪"

"…If you can find…the *trick*…then try…to find it… ♪"

"Uh, um! Should I not point out that both of you are dripping with cold sweat?!"

Til quite needlessly ruined Sora and Shiro's tough-guy act.

«*Ha!! Game's on… You'd better not let the cat out of the bag too easy and let me down.*»

Veig took a fighting stance following this bold statement, and the atmosphere grew tense once more.

Indeed…among the things Veig "had never thought"—

—*wasn't* that they'd be able to dodge at all…

The new tension made it clear: As he'd said, that was just a test run. Of course they should be able to dodge that. Now things would get real. Veig lunged at them again—

«*But first…*»

—or so he made it look, while without the slightest hesitation—

«*Did you think I wouldn't figure it out, ya unworked titwad? You think I'm stupid?! Do ya?!*»

—he swung his mech's left fist around with the full weight of the unit, roaring out of the blue. How *could* he figure it out?

The projectile came from over seven thousand meters away at a magical speed close to that of light, from the mighty cannon hauled on the back of the unit of Chlammy and Fiel, who'd hidden immediately after the game began. They'd used that oversized bazooka to snipe at him the moment he let his guard down. There was no way he should have been able to sense their magic bullet. But somehow, he must have had a hunch. Seeing its trajectory as plain as day, he took it down with his fist.

Iron fist intercepting ammunition. A collision—a flash. A roaring shock wave. Having laid waste to all the ruins around him, Veig stood calmly rooted to the spot—

«...Oh, I see... This whole time...I was *a rubbish-eater not worth living...*»

—and let such melancholic words spill across the comm line... But that was only momentary.

«—*Hey, damn you, titwad! The hell are you doing? You almost made me depressed there for a second. The hell?!*»

He pulled himself together just in time to dodge the second shot. Another voice answered Veig's clear cry of fear and distress.

«*What am I doiiing? Why, I'm merely striking you with my soul—expressing my proclivities just as intended.* ♥»

Fiel's transmission as her unit once more disappeared brought another chill down Sora's, Shiro's, and Til's spines.

Yes—this...this fearsome game... It was truly a clash of souls. And so...!!

What Fiel was expressing, as she momentarily dragged Veig deep down into the dumps—

«*I simply cannot abide you moles.* ♥ *You just* rub me the wrong way! ♪»

—was a deep-seated, 100-percent-pure, utter rejection—an instinctive revulsion... What specifically had Veig seen and thought? They didn't know.

«*Aren't yer tastes a little out of line, witch?! If I lose, it looks like I'm gonna* have a mental breakdown!»

«Why, that would be wonderful. I was planning to commaaand you to do so after my victory anywayyy. ♥»

But Veig quaked and howled at the soul so intense it had sunk him into self-loathing until...

...suddenly, he glanced around and looked up.

«...Huh. Well—suppose I should have expected it.»

Sora, Shiro, and Til's mech had vanished, while Fiel, on the other hand, still knew where Veig was.

«...I did say you could come at me with as many of whatever kinds of machines you wanted—and I never said you couldn't meddle with the venue, either, did I...? So if you say the venue's a secret until just before, then yeah...»

Sora, Shiro, and Til all got the chills to hear Veig put his finger on the edge of their scheme so easily.

Yes, they'd been able to dodge his first attack because *they'd planted demi-shift anchors in advance*. For the time being, they reloaded with ammo they'd likewise planted.

«I should assume the stage itself is your machine—your hunting grounds, eh? Ha...»

But they'd been well aware he had the intuition to read that far. So they got the chills not just because he'd revealed one of their tricks...

«...You're in way over your head—callin' me prey...»

...It was because they'd had the clear illusion of seeing his fang-toothed sneer as he spoke.

■■■

Indeed—there was no rule that said you couldn't prep the battlefield. Nor was there any dictating that players at leisure in their cockpit, like Chlammy and Fiel, couldn't watch the broadcast that so helpfully relayed throughout Hardenfell their enemy's movements. And so Chlammy and Fiel observed as the fight of Sora, Shiro, and Til versus Veig ratcheted up. The golem lay concealed in the shadows of the ruins, its propulsion deactivated to forestall spirit detection. But its residents frowned.

They could never stand a chance in terms of machine specs or combat ability. So, when engraving rites on their machine, they hadn't bothered with the specs at all. They'd put everything into one over-the-top weapon—a *sniper rifle* specialized in raw projectile power. A *magicannon*: a cannon whose seal rites Fiel put all her spirits into so it could fire with the greatest force possible. Combined with her undying hatred, Fiel knew her potent soul was enough to overpower Veig. These two trump cards proved successful in impinging on Veig. Yes, just as set out in their *deal* with Sora and Shiro, they had plenty of chances to win. It was all going according to plan. And for that very reason, Chlammy and Fiel cursed at the screen silently:

——*You nonsensical little* shits...

This was bullshit. It was absurdity they could predict but not comprehend. For instance—

«*Ha!! That's a powerful shot ya got there—but your soul's light as a feather!!*»

—there was Veig, demi-shifting using the sword he'd struck into the ceiling like lightning as an anchor. Then transforming his giant sword into countless curved blades that traced innumerable arcs through the air. Demi-shifting all over the place as they flew through every nook and cranny of the ruins. Bullshit.

Or, for instance—

«*You can scratch my frame, but you ain't touchin' me!! I can't hear your soul!*»

—there was Sora and Shiro, dodging the countless blades flying too fast for the eye to follow. Veig used blades as anchors to demi-shift, and although Sora and Shiro shouldn't have been able to identify which anchor or how to even react—

«*Well yeah, if you're gonna be screaming about how you'll only accept uniformly huge boobs, we can't help but joke around!*»

«...Brother...! Before, you joke around...shift...!»

—they somehow identified it and somehow reacted. Howling a ferocious battle cry, they rained bullets on their opponent as if they'd known he'd appear behind them.

How did such absolute bullshit manage to hit him? Even the near-light-speed magic bullet of Chlammy and Fiel's sniping, while it had hit him when he let his guard down, was dodged the second time—

«Did ya know?! Your taste in tits corresponds to the size of your self-confidence, ya mewling kitten!!»

«Is that so? Then you're one overconfident bitch!! Learn a little humility, little man!!»

«Ngrah! Hey, I ain't small! I'm packin'!! You're the one who's small!!»

«I meant little as in small-minded! Are you saying my thing is small?! Th-th-that's not even true!»

They easily picked out the positions and moments in which Veig wouldn't be able to dodge. Veig ended up coming up behind the building at Sora and Shiro's back and slicing it in two.

«Ha!! Only a small man can't answer with "It's big"!!»

«...Brother...! ...Even, if...he's right...don't listen to him!»

«Hey, Shiro, knock off the friendly fire!! He doesn't know what your brother is capable of—not that we want him to!»

How did they dodge that? They couldn't have seen it. They couldn't have reacted to it. Even Sora and Shiro were just humans—!! Chlammy at last let out a gasp—Most incomprehensible was that which Sora uttered as Veig's fist burst out through the crumbling building—an instant too late to feasibly evade—and Sora's unit shifted just as it connected.

«—Pshhh, no sweat!! Get outta here, ya big-boob fascist!!»

«I—I, too! A-am not done yet, I'm not... I'm fine, I aaam!!»

—How can they endure it? How can they remain so steadfast in their rejection of big boobs—?! My core would have crumbled into dust with the very first strike!!

Their resolute resistance against Veig's soul was the greatest bullshit against which Chlammy shrieked internally.

It's inconceivable. It's bizarre. And these are mere Immanities? Mere humans?! They couldn't be human. Normal humans——

«…*Brother… Why, do you deny, my boobs…?*»
«——*Come again? What was that, Shiro?*»
—Yes…normal humans should behave like this. The sad voice of Shiro, who had buckled under Veig's whispers, echoed in Chlammy's mind.

—*Oh…I almost forgot.* Chlammy smiled as Fi restarted their unit at the same moment. *That's right…Sora and Shiro are just humans. Mere humans, who go astray and fail.* Chlammy was thus relieved to hear Shiro confronting her brother with the ultimate question.

«…*Brother, you're a, lolicon… You like them, smooth and flat… But* when I grow up and grow boobs…*will you, not like me anymore? Will you…abandon me…?!*»
The question of: *What will you do when she's not a Loli anymore?* Yes, the lolicon's fateful question. The ultimate question. However…

«*How many times do I have to say it?! I'm not a lolicon! Besides!! You can grow big boobs, or get old and wrinkly, or even turn into a man!! Nothing could make your big brother not like you! …**Hey, are you crying?!***»
…unlike the flustered Sora, Chlammy understood what was in Shiro's heart as if it were her own.

Yes, Shiro had been hit by Veig's soul and was just temporarily conditioned by it. Her words were not her own., and yet *neither were they entirely insincere…* Sora was alarmed because he sensed that. Furthermore—

«*Uh, excuse me—th-the chieftain! The chieftain's coming, he iiiis!*»
—Chlammy got Veig in the crosshairs so they could follow up on the attack of the out-of-sorts Sora and Shiro. That's right…fake was fake. Whatever you did, it was the same as pads.

However they might try, the weak could never become the strong...*and that was why*: If it was impossible to wipe away this feeling of inferiority—if one's essence would be the same regardless of whether one had big boobs——!!!

"Then obviously it's *better to have boobs*, isn't it?!"

As she pulled the trigger, Chlammy, having momentarily understood Shiro, was beyond Sora's own understanding.

From 820 meters, the unit that had cloaked itself even from spirit detection fired a shot that ripped through buildings. At almost light speed, the unknowable, unavoidable magic bullet rushed onward. But yet again—

«—Ha!! You think that'll work twice?! Ya dozy titwad!!»

—just one other than Chlammy understood—or rather, probably just intuited. Veig, having known the trajectory before the shot was fired, leaped before the trigger went down...and escaped. Evaded the unevadable. But Fiel answered without surprise at his paradoxical transmission:

«*Why*, yesss. *After allll, that was ooonce.* ♥»

Not having known the unknowable, Veig sneered back, while at the same time—

«*Aaargh! Who gave you permission to enter our lebensraum?! Begone, black devil!*»

«*...Eegh?! Qu-quick, I need a newspaper...or a slipper—or—or bug spray...!*»

«*I knew it, I diiid! The chieftain is more disgusting than a cockroach, he iiiis!!*»

—his evasion let Fiel's soul blaze on right into Sora, Shiro, and Til, infringing on theirs in an instant. They screeched as their Gatling gun roared.

...Their thoughts temporarily drenched in Fiel's soul, the three of them rained bullets on Veig. He cried out with the same amount of terror as Fiel's blast, but more critically—

«*Biiitch! Ya damn bloody titwad! Just how much do ya hate me?!*»
—he cried out from the heartbreak of being called worse than one of those black beasts by his niece. Undaunted, Chlammy ignored him and turned to go lurk in the darkness once more.

What sort of trickery were Sora and Shiro using to compete with Veig? Whatever it was, Chlammy and Fiel couldn't imitate it. So it didn't matter. If Sora and Shiro were going to act according to their *deal*, Chlammy and Fiel just had to live up to their end. In other words: *exploit it and win!*

"*We shall take the best and leave the rest!* You shall be the sacrifice for my sizable dreams, Sora…!!"

■■■

At the bottom of a dim hole a small distance from the venue, there was a girl calmly watching via broadcast as Chlammy disappeared into the darkness of the ruins, her voice tinged with tragic sobs.

"…Um… So basically… Let me go over this, all right?"
It was Steph, in Til's hideout, where Jibril was watching the monitor, hugging her knees. Emir-Eins had brought Steph here just after the game began, and Jibril had explained the foregoing events. Emir-Eins hungrily fixed her eyes on the monitor, but Steph went on.
"Sora and Shiro created a drug that would make another country sell itself for it—a poison, in other words."
"You archaeological artifact! You can't even follow so simple a command from your master as to stay home, can you?"
"So they were offered a game they had absolutely no need to play… and they accepted. Am I correct?"
"Lament: Threatened by woman of unknown name. Critical. Top

priority of this unit is *securement of master.* Therefore, evaded threat. Precedence over command. Flügel should agree… It's not my fault."

"—Excuse me, are you listening?! And I do have a name!"

Steph raised her voice at the two who seemed entirely uninterested in her recapitulation. Mumbling *TL;DR* to herself, she got straight to the main points, screaming as she went over the reasons why they were playing this unnecessary game:

"Because they say they'll only let friends run a tab?! And he said that he wouldn't be friends with someone who didn't like large breasts?! And this game is about whether women should have large breasts—?! That's the most ridiculous thing I've ever heard!"

…If the people of Elkia got word of this, it would be past time for a coup d'état and they would be well on the road to a revolution. The people be damned—Steph had half a mind to start one herself! But Jibril and Emir-Eins just looked at her pityingly.

"You are as reliable as ever, little Dora, in failing to see past the surfaces of things…"

"Enigma: Woman of unknown name competent in politics and economics, extremely incompetent in similar games. Unsolvable. Fallback: Lack of comprehension of master identified. Not eligible for love. Resignation recommended."

"I—I will do no such thing—and I said I have a name! It's S—"

Steph tried to change the subject, but Jibril interrupted her with a claim that made her gasp.

"My masters have been called upon to settle with the tab of their *old world.*"

"_____!!"

Sora and Shiro's past; their old world, before they came to Disboard. Steph couldn't say she'd never thought about it. After all, how would she feel if she were suddenly thrown into another world…?

…She'd want to go home. At the very least, she'd feel regret and homesickness. But those two showed no such signs—they never spoke of it all. So Steph always wanted to ask about it. Those two-in-one siblings, who had even toyed with a god… And surely, this past they never spoke of, that of these two who could accomplish *anything* if they tried...

"Of all things, he asked them *a most foolish question*: Why did they flee? They simply took that as a challenge."

"—A...a most foolish question?"

Steph was grateful to Jibril for cutting off her impertinent conjectures, but she did ask what was supposed to be so obvious. Jibril answered as if that very question were absurd.

"In the first place, under what conditions can one say that one has 'reconciled one's past'?"

"Truth: Our debts. Our sin. *To reconcile*. Does not change *past events*... Cannot."

"The past in which we killed each other, all the things which may have been wrong...all led to this day."

"Acknowledgment: Accept past. Proceed. Lesson of Master to Ex Machina."

Yes...Steph listened to those placid words, desperately holding back tears as she felt something well up in her chest.

These two were members of Flügel and Ex Machina...who, in fact, had each lost something irreplaceable at the other's hands. A past too enormous for Steph, born after the Covenants, to presume to understand... Still feuding, still at odds, even so, here they accepted the past, acknowledged it—and allowed for it... They shared that same hope.

"And then to ask why my masters fled their past? It is as foolish as a question can be."

"Conclusion: Masters *accept their loss*. Redundant explanation. Calculation probability—*zero*."

So. Hopefully. The two servants continued together.

"Just as I can now accept my past as *all for the sake of meeting my masters*..."

"Vow: Masters *fled in order to meet this unit*. Past assigned meaning. Unit will assign."

Their words were like prayers. At last a tear ran down Steph's cheek. Then Jibril once more gestured to the monitor.

"From this perspective, the significance of this game is great indeed."

«*Enough of your bloody claptrap! You're runnin' from tits 'cos you ain't got confidence, ain't it?! Ain't it that right?!*»

«*Shut up!! You scrubs who think any game that's not a triple-A sucks can kiss my ass!!*»

".......This...argument is over whether they like large bosoms...?"

The sentimentality-destroying repartee made short work of her tearful emotions. However:

"Sigh: Explanation. Central point of contention of masters in this game *is not value of large breasts.*"

"Oh, little Dora? Has my master ever said that he rejects large bosoms?"

Hearing the two, Steph looked back at the screen—*That's right!*

The reactions of those invaded by the souls of Veig and Fiel were easy to recognize. However—what was the reaction from Sora's and Shiro's souls? Wait, in the first place...!

"You're right...!! In the first place—it's *not the case that Sora despises large breasts!*"

Yes, Sora was a lolicon. This was more indubitable than the existence of Tet. But Steph herself had almost forgotten that unforgettable day on which she had first met Sora—!!

"**He, uh, um...groped mine!**"

Steph interpreted the racing of her heart and the heat in her cheeks as anger as she screamed out. Yes...Steph knew what kind of man he was: a virgin who would *take what he could get*, who would boldly announce that he was recording the goings-on in the bath for his own, shall we say, self-gratification! In that case, what, in the end, was his contention? Steph asked with a look. But—

*　*　*

"……Goodness? That is news to me, Dora."

"Confirmation: Inferred to be boast regarding size of own chest. Also—"

—right then, two voices continued emotionlessly and instantly rendered Steph's reddened face white.

"You intend to advertise that *you have been used* by my master, do you? ♥"

"Command: Disclose context of humblebrag immediately. Rejection not recommended. It will hurt."

—*When he hasn't even used me…?*

Steph felt as if their words and gazes were physically stabbing her and almost passed out.

"Reserved: Matter at hand has priority. Master rarely speaks of own past."

"And thus, this game has greater significance in terms of my master's present."

Behind their words, Steph felt just as if she could hear what their eyes were telling her.

…Has it really not occurred to you, Stephanie Dola? Look at that Sora—that virginal young man surrounded by so many women. But in only one case has he spontaneously, voluntarily, of his own will…

…groped someone's boobs.

——Yours, bitch!!!!

"I had taken it to mean that he preferred little girls and wondered only about his position on breasts, but…"

"Recalculation: Irregular data added. Master preferences. Mature body observed as compatible in one instance. Reanalyzing."

Jibril started scribbling in her book, while Emir-Eins's head made scratching noises. *I see…* Steph swallowed. If Sora really would go for any female, then why hadn't he touched any of them? No, why was it that, even as of now—he'd only touched Steph? It was, indeed, a question of his present situation, his preferences!!

"In any case, this is a test of my master's ideals. His soul will speak to them. The answer is at hand."

"Critical: Remaining Ex Machina cluster attempted to identify master *preferences*, failed. Revelation imminent."

If he liked small boobs, they would remake themselves at once with small boobs.

If it was confirmed that he liked little girls, they would remain little girls for eternity, they vowed resolutely.

Yes—for a future that would prove the past all to have been to bring them together—! Today, they would prepare for that day of reckoning, they declared with conviction.

Steph had her own thoughts on the matter:

—*I doubt that revelation will come...*

Actually, as Steph summed it all up in her brain, her suspicion turned to conviction. Sora, indeed, would *go for anything*. Or, put more simply—he *didn't even really care*.

But in that case—if it was impossible to make peace with the past, if it was unacceptable even to justify it—if, just as these two had declared, the past would be proven to exist for the sake of their meeting—then what about the present? What sort of answer would those two offer for their victory...?

Steph swallowed quietly and followed the others' lead in staring at the screen seriously.

—Why, in fact, had only her breasts been squeezed? Not even realizing that that was where her attention lay, alas...she watched in perfect earnest......

■■■

However, on the other side of the screen—in the cockpit, responsible for controlling the mech as it raced across the stage—Til, more than anyone, was wheezing with questions. The backs of the two competing neck and neck with Veig seemed distant. *How?*

…She wondered at ways of using a spirit arm she'd never even imagined…

«*Heh, I'm finally startin' to see it…! The secret of how you do the* impossible*!!*»

His strident laughter filled the cockpit… Ah… How could a grubby little mole like Til, with neither the spiritual amplitude of Veig nor the rite-compiling chops of Fiel, accomplish this? These bullets fast enough to catch Veig, this curtain fire solid enough to stop him—

«*I know how you get that* impossible *firepower. It's by intentionally overloading catalysts and discarding them, ain't it?!*»

Yes—under the storm of Sora and Shiro's Gatling gun, Veig had seen through this.

"What, you're talking about that?! D00d, that should go without saying. Of course we'd do that!!"

"…Using magic to accelerate bullets… Laughing…at Newton's, third law of motion…"

Smiling, they declared it the basic principle of otherworldly artillery.

…Til had lamented the fact that she didn't have the spirits to pull off a single spell without spirit-arm boosting, nor could she control a booster sufficiently to prevent explosion.

Sora and Shiro had laughed.

—Why bother controlling it?

—It's gonna blow up? Excellent. *Blow it the hell up.*

And so their projectiles fired from their cartridges by means of intentional failure and runaway. They careened toward Veig at twenty-four times the speed of sound, difficult even for him to follow. However…

«*Oh, sorry 'bout that. Okay—the* really impossible *part.*»

…just as Veig's ironic voice boomed through, their bullets, which had been striking him with relentless accuracy, whiffed for the first time. And Veig's slash flashed with movement even Til couldn't follow:

* * *

«*Can ya own up to your trick for* responding without reacting?»

Sora and Shiro's mech demi-shifted to evade and open up the distance with ease. Veig darted through their immediate return fire. The wild cycle of evasion and engagement continued.

Feeling Sora's and Shiro's backs grow ever farther away, Til pondered, her expression growing increasingly gloomy.

—*How did they dodge these attacks?*

—*How did they land these shots?*

They couldn't see what was going on. They couldn't even react. Even Sora and Shiro were just humans. But Til could answer her own question. She knew all the answers.

—*They weren't dodging. They just weren't where Veig would attack.*

—*They weren't landing shots. Veig just happened to be where their bullets would fly.*

It was more or less sophistry, playing with words—but that was the nature of their trick. They couldn't act or react fast enough. So Til had fulfilled their order.

«—*Damn you... You're movin' before you move, aren't ya?*»

Yes—a paradoxical feeling had led that arrogant voice to point it right out.

Til had built them joysticks that let them input commands in advance. So how had they evaded Veig's first strike?

Veig had announced he'd attack. As of the moment before that, they'd already performed the input to shift out of the way, turn to where Veig would be, and fire... That was all. But even now, they remained toe-to-toe with the strong, continuing to anticipate the future again and again. They saw a different future from that which Veig saw only as a hunch, a superior future. No, they didn't just see it—they *remade it* every time.

Was that just a trick? Were they just weak humans...? She couldn't see what they saw. She couldn't even imagine it. Most of all—

«*In that case, all I have to do is* move with the assumption you'll read me, *yeah?!*»

"Spoken like an OP scrub, all right!! Damn it—shit's gonna get real now. You ready, Shiro?!"

"...Mm...! Cancel that move...! Brother, use...your adrenaline dodge!"

—their input queues drew on Shiro's calculation and Sora's finesse, prediction and leading, tactics and strategy. With all of these working together, they were just barely able to stay ahead of the game. But now that the cat was out of the bag, if they ever lost the initiative...it would be too late for them to do anything. But Til most of all found herself unable to understand the emotions of Sora and Shiro that came through the catalysts as she gazed at their backs...

In the midst of the utmost tension and panic, they seemed to be having the time of their lives. Their hearts burned with a joy that was above all that, *played on top of all that.*

...Suddenly, Til felt their backs getting away from her. And there, in what was supposed to be a small cockpit—

—she saw it...the high, blue sky. That very sky...she'd seen as a child. That...very sky...she'd stopped seeing, at some point... At that sky...where the two in the same cockpit, with the same cores, controlling the same machine were not...Til finally looked down... with a smile of resignation...and grasped it.

Just as Sora said, she wasn't even the lowest... Those two really had flown... That white-winged bird in that black sky. If to be able to do such things, to be able to reach such heights was what it meant to be weak, then it was true that natural gifts could never be overcome... including the *natural gift of being weak.*

She grasped that the top and the bottom alike...lay far, far away from her...

«Well—*that leaves just one more* impossible, *don't it...?*»

The resounding transmission continued, and the feeling of the crack running through her core, too, felt far away...as did the mech which, hit by the iron fist that had finally caught up with Sora and Shiro's piloting, fell to the ground.

"Aaagh... Neverrr... I'll never accept your boobular fascismmm!!"

"…B-Brother…I—I…really…can't have…boobs?!"

As did the voices of Sora and Shiro, resisting Veig's glandular ideology. Everything, even the cockpit screen showing Veig's machine looking down at them, even the question he asked…seemed far away…

«…*If you can do that much…why'd ya run…?*»

…His question was clear-cut, free of rebuke or blame or even despair. But Til certainly couldn't answer that, nor could anyone else—

Then.

«*Damn you… We were havin' a moment there. Ain'cha ever heard of tact, ya bloody…*»

Again with a hunch—Veig anticipated the blast that hurtled forth at almost light speed. Grumbling at that soul which made him depressed just to remember it, that soul which therefore had to be dodged, he slid one small, unruffled step to the side.

«*Anyway, you ain't even got anything to do with this… I get what you're trying to say— Wha…?!*»

Or he tried, but it came anyway, leaving behind sound, light, everything. Undeniable—*infinite in speed*—it transcended space and arrived with a shock wave that flattened the surroundings. It was a direct hit, right in his mech's chest, knocking him hundreds of meters—

«*…Oh. ♥ I see, a demi-shift shot… Right, an* Elf *can demi-shift without an anchor… Yeah, a grub like me could never come up with ideas like— Hey, whaaa…?!*»

—and yet it didn't seem to be enough to break his core, his spirit.

«*Damn bitches, gimme a break, will ya?! I'll beat ya to a pulp, ya* shiiits!»

Veig recovered from his depression in a moment and dodged the second shot. He blew his top high enough to bust through the ceiling, and then glanced at Sora and Shiro's machine, which had managed to get up in the brief interval.

«……*Oh… That's how it is…?* You *bitches are a decoy…*»

His voice—

«*Guess I gotta go crush them before I listen to your soul, huh?*»

—sounded as if he had seen through everything. He scoffed.

«*All right. You can play with these babies. I'll be back in a minute.*»

Leaving behind countless curved blades to attack Sora, Shiro, and Til as well as blue light, Veig leaped away.

■■■

And far, far, away, the golem decorated with countless flowers by now was not bothering to hide. The Holy Forge that pierced the skyless heavens at her back, the pilot, Chlammy, tutted once and pondered.

The demi-shift shot… That had been their third trump card—and a *very risky one*, the kind that had to finish the opponent off if one were to survive afterward. Of course. The moment the opponent knew they had a shot that was more or less undodgeable, they themselves would become the top-priority target… And then—

—this is what would happen. Just as the blades flew, the sleek silver frame appeared from thin air, an enemy superior to them in both specs and technique.

«*…Ho there, fockin' titwads. I got a promise to be back in a minute, so, sorry*—die right here, right now.»

Chlammy chuckled to her backseat companion.

"…Fi? If we go head-to-head with that thing…how much chance do we stand?"

"Why, it's not even a conteeest. We're trapped, *true to the deal…*"

They'd rather it not be the case, but it was a cold, hard fact. Fi answered despondently, and Chlammy nodded back. Yes—trapped. Checkmate. They'd known: That silver frame, that monster—was some bullshit that spelled doom if they let it close. That was why Sora and Shiro had agreed to provide a diversion until they lost…

That was the condition of cooperation. That was the deal. And Sora and Shiro, believe it or not, had actually followed through.

Now Chlammy and Fiel's chance had crumbled. They had lost. And that was what would lead to Sora and Shiro's victory...!!

......But—

"Fi... It's all right... I won't lie to myself anymore..."

—Chlammy uttered something so contrary to reason. Yes—the two who had said they could go for the win had made it so much fun...

All right then. With that, they had no regrets——!!

"I won't make you lie anymore, either. From now on—I won't fear you, Fi..."

Yes—after all, Fi had told her that any Chlammy was the *real Chlammy* whom she loved.

"*Any Fi...is the Fi I love!!* So—answer with your heart!!"

Fi opened her eyes wide and smiled from ear to ear. It wasn't too late——

"**——If we go at it with all we've got—we're not done yet, are weeee?!**"

"**Why, of—course—nottt! It's the showdown—let's see what we have!**"

They called a little early—as their fourth trump card raced through their bodies.

...Yes...Fi released the power from the *two rites she'd been expending* on sealing off her emotions so as not to scare Chlammy—

«——?!»

—and right then, from the machine before Veig's eyes, Fi's feelings expanded in the manner of a detonation. That instant, Veig lost his composure and reflexively jumped backward into a defensive stance.

...Meanwhile, link tattoos glowed all over Chlammy's and Fiel's bodies. They sped up time within their bodies so that Veig's movement felt to them terribly slow as their golem positioned its sniper cannon at its hip.

The feeling unleashed like a vortex was not malice, not bloodlust, and certainly not malignance. It went over a line that should not be

crossed—a third line, which should never be crossed. It was a pure offering, gushing forth from every corner of Fiel's heart.

Knowing now that it would not easily break, Chlammy gripped her soul firmly and thought. Ah, she had known all along… He had only been lying about the true nature of her soul… In other words…

…what is it that makes boobs real?

…If it was true that any fat or air she could stuff in them would just be pads—fake boobs—then what was contained in real boob? Authentic big boobs? What was it that her small boobs lacked, for which even conceptual stuffing could not compensate? It was simple. Even Sora had never said you couldn't get big boobs. Rather, he had declared without compunction that if you only took his medicine every day, you too could have big boobs. You could. You could have big boobs. *Big, fake boobs.* If you weren't to take pride in that—

"—This humble chest of mine…is filled with my soul…!"

Indeed…her boobs were a vessel for her very self: Her dreams. Her ambitions. Her journey, as she struggled in the pursuit of the ultimate boobs. Her will, and her pride—!! Chlammy bellowed it without reserve, and Fi nodded with a bright and shining smile. Yes—by now…even Chlammy could see. When the conceptual rewriter—when the "big boob essence" had given everyone big boobs…

…what had made Sora rage so fiercely…

…was simply—

"How dare you alter my Chlammy without permission and then *call her fake…"*

—What would they do? It was simple—defined by their mutual vortex of feeling.

They weren't going to kill him. Why would they kill him? They needed him alive.

"… Why, if you've no awareness of the crime you've committed… we shall have to teach you…"

What he needed was not death. It was *understanding.*

"...Then you'll learn just what you've meddled with—and *repeeent*."

—Get on your knees and apologize. You hear me? Do it, bitch.—

So the overwhelming form exhorted Veig. He still couldn't grasp its meaning.

But when the golem turned red as the light bent from the vast number of spirits—an amount greater than Fiel's own—Veig merely had a hunch he should lower his stance—

«*...Ho there, looks like I ain't gonna be able to make it in a minute... Sorry, I'll be late.*»

—and he gave Sora and Shiro a heads-up. His intuition told him he'd better respond with all his spirits as well, so he poised himself at full attention.

Ah... One race unrivaled in seal rites, another in spirit arms: the Dwarf, Veig Drauvnir, indeed a peerless talent, the greatest of his age—but let it not be forgotten who was unrivaled in compilation of sophisticated rites. The Elf, Fiel Nirvalen, likewise. Though she might not stand at the top, she was one of the few who could stand as his foe.

Two machines facing each other in a vortex of spirits and pleasure. Staking their fates, their cards, their blood—staking that which lay deep in their souls—they stood poised for battle. In fulfillment of distant vows from long ago, destruction raged like a storm, under the protection of the Covenants.

■ ■ ■

Meanwhile, apart from that barrel-blazing dystopia, Sora's consciousness floated, singing the praises of love and peace, in utopia.

Ah...they all called him: Shiro, Til, Jibril, Emir-Eins, and Steph of course, and even Izuna and Holou. They bashfully begged him to massage their plump breasts. Yes...in this indisputable utopia, the amplebosomed beauties all asked him in the same sweet whisper:

Oh, what more do you want?

More? What more could I ask? he answered without a moment's hesitation.

Enveloped in titular bliss, he knew he had everything... For a great chest is a great thing. It should go without saying. It felt good to squeeze. It was erotically appealing—such basic, selfevident truths did not merit discussion. Who would not clutch his head to ask, *Why is chocolate delicious?* and be answered, *Because it's sweet?* Do you then assert that dark chocolate is not delicious? If all you want is sweetness, then go eat some sugar. If one were to ask where lay the appeal of large bosoms and insist on one simple answer, Sora's would be this: *It lay in their symbolism.* Indeed, big boobs are symbolic... To be frank: Don't they give you the sense that you could *squeeze them and get away with it?* To gird this theory, let us imagine what sorts of onomatopoeia we might use to describe the act of squeezing large breasts.

—*Bwoing. Jiggle. Floof.* Listen to your intuition: No harm no foul, right?

Now let us imagine the sorts of onomatopoeia we might use for small breasts.

—*Boop. Plink. Bwip.* Have you any doubt that this is a crime?

Therefore: What more could he ask for?! Embraced by a legion of voluptuous beauties, Sora was sure: *I mean—I'll say this once and say it again...I love...boobs......?*

————..........

"Eeyaagh?! Uh, huh-wha...?! Wh-what was that? I've no idea, I've nottt!"

Sora was roughly brought back to reality by the shock that abruptly shook the whole stage. To be more precise, it was Til—to be yet more plain, Til's *almost stark-naked abdomen*—her highly elastic tummy slapping against his back that brought Sora back at the speed of sound—

"—Whoaaaaaa?! Hey—shhhiiiiiiiiiit!!!"

—as the curved blades came at similar speeds. He just barely managed to dodge that one that had grazed him. And—*shit*—he clucked as its path curved above his head.

Veig's parting gifts turned in the air like boomerangs to attack him. It was as if they had some homing ability. They were easier to deal with than Veig himself, but—

"...Ah...if I had, big boobs...and it was an accident—then you could get away with it...with me..."

Shiro mumbled, her eyes bereft of light. Her joystick looked like it was about to break into pieces. You could see what that little scratch had done to her. She asked as if in a trance:

"...I'll pretend not to like it, okay? Brother...are you that against... big-boobed Shiro...?"

Sora could see ever clearer that if they took a direct hit, her core—her heart would break. He held her on his lap and did his best to speak gently.

"Shiro. I'll tell you once and tell you again... Your brother loves you no matter how you look."

Shiro was still caught in the illusion. Her cheeks flushed. Yet Sora continued:

"But if we submit to Veig's way of thinking, I'll end up *rejecting any Shiro that isn't big boobed*!!"

"———Uh. Wha...? ...Uh, ee...eegh?!"

That knocked her to her senses. White-faced, struggling against despair, she took hold of her joystick once more.

That's right... A big-boobed Shiro? Truth be told, he had no problem with that. She was fundamentally a perfect, flawless beauty. The materials were just too good; it was obvious. But that son of a bitch. He messed with Shiro based on his own shit taste. And on top of that, he called everyone without big boobs fake. And he rejected all that had come before, the past and the present—

—Veig had rejected his actual sister.

——He'd rejected Shiro *in her entirety*——!!!

Who the hell was going to break? *Not me! Not until I make you understand who's got the shit taste, asshole!!* The Gatling gun and the siblings flared at another blade curving at them.

"...I—I...can't take...any more, I can't...!"

But amidst the roar of their muzzle as they took the blade down, even more than Sora and Shiro—

"...The unit, my hammer, and I are at their limits, they are..."

—the unit, the hammer, and Til whined together that they were about to break.

...To begin with, it was a miracle that their mech even worked. It wouldn't have been surprising for it to break down at any time, or even to explode right at the start.

"...I knew it, you two flew, you did... You were birds, you were..."

But Til sounded even closer to breaking, having *already broken* into tears.

"If you only had a better machine, you could have...won...even... against the chieftain—"

And she went on: *There never was a place for junk like me...*

But.

——*Boom...*

The boom of their Gatling gun as it took down another blade, along with the explosion of their left arm, drowning her out.

"Ha-haa! Six left!! ...Uh, sorry, Til, I wasn't listening. What did you say?!"

"...She said...it's her fault, you...became, a big-boobs fascist..."

"The hell?! How could that be? Her tummy just totally made me into a loli—ow!"

Sora goofed around, and Shiro elbowed him. Their grins implied...

...that they hadn't heard her. Til's eyes lolled about.

"Hey, Til, you overworked?! Humans can't fly, you know?! We're cheating, that's all it is. We're cheating!!"

Indeed, in the first place, they were mere humans, mere

weaklings—mere cheaters. You could dress it up with words like *ingenuity*, but:

"Even if an airplane flies, it's not a human, but an airplane that's flying, you know?!"
"...And...*we're not even, the ones*...who built—the airplanes, you know...?!"
——.

What made Til gasp? Was it the sound suggesting that the Gatling gun in their right arm which had felled the blade was about to break? Or was it a recognition of the irony in the savage sneers of Sora and Shiro?

Indeed, these were the black arts of the weak, those who had to resort to such measures to win. The numerous tricks Sora and Shiro had shuffled out to compete with Veig—their strategies, their tactics; mathematical prediction, informed inducement, far-ranging academic disciplines and theoretical frameworks—all of it.

"All we're doing is patching together *stuff we've borrowed from others*!!"

The proud weak, the lovable fools—humans had endlessly maintained a way of life antithetical to the forging of Dwarves. The human way was a process of failure and error which continued pathetically on and on...while *even so* going on struggling, flailing in the dark.

Until something just happened to fit together. Until *something was born from a mistake*—a miraculous byproduct of wandering lost. It was by patching things together that they drove that forward. But *still*, they cried out—!!

"Still, that's not enough to win—so...!"

"...Gotta, collect, more...!"

The limited legacy of Dwarf. The stubborn theory of Elf. And—
Til's eyes opened wide.

What was reflected in those pale blue eyes, most likely, was the ultimate despair engendered by five curved blades. Their silver traces carved the air, coming at them faster than sound, their trajectories fatal. The Gatling gun and the right arm that held it were smashed up. Their frame was on its last legs, unlikely to be able to make it through another demi-shift. *But that was why*, Sora and Shiro savagely sneered. They were echoed by a roaring explosion. The next moment—

"We're flying on *the wings we borrowed from your way of life*."

"———Ah…"

…Til gaped again at the frame that soared high into the sky, and at Sora's laugh—but a feeling different from that of a moment ago coursed through the catalysts.

—It'll go out of control and blow up? Excellent—*blow it the hell up*.

The explosion of their legs propelled them so now they were way up looking down at those five blades. Her feeling was directed toward those two, who aligned their sights with those blades, and toward herself, who looked to the high, blue sky within that cockpit…

She looked up with confusion, worry, and even resignation.

High and blue… It was the sky…

The mountain of failure and error she'd piled up from the things she'd found haphazardly, not even knowing what value they had…

It all came together as if someone had made a mistake. She'd seen that sky as a child, and then it had gone from her—and now here she was. The heights *she'd never even imagined*…the place she'd longed for. Now—the three of them together had *leaped there*—at last Til realized.

"Come on… How long are you going to hold back?"

Sora pulled up the corners of his mouth and howled at Til over the roar of his fire piercing the blades below.

"———*Smile*!!!

"Isn't this the ultimate moment you thought you'd only see in your dreams?! Here you are in the sky!! Beyond the limits you thought imaginable—so how does it feel?!"

……*Gasp…* Til chuckled ambiguously as the machine fell——

* * *

——And then, the clunky mech, reduced to an immobile heap of metal by the devastation of its limbs, collapsed onto the ground.

«......*Hff... Oh, good God! Ah well, I suppose we've had our fun!*»

Chlammy's surly tone came through the comm system of the once-humanoid machine that was now a pile of scrap.

«*Go do as you like, as per the deal!! Waaah! Fiii, I can't staaand iiit!*»

...Ha-ha... Looks like Chlammy and Fiel really hung in there, too...

Sora and Shiro smirked together in the cockpit.

"Yeah... I'd say we've had our fun, too. Didn't think we'd make it this far. ♪"

"...Mm... Now...from here, on...it's, your turn to play...Til. ♪"

"............Uh. Um? I... What?"

They turned to Til as if handing off a controller. She looked back blankly.

"*We can't beat this.* Doesn't matter what kind of machine we have... We just can't."

"...We can't...*answer the question*... We can't...*settle our past...*"

For a moment, they looked down as they spoke. But only for a moment. Then they gazed into Til's eyes with smiles of heartfelt fun... Yes, they looked into those pale blue eyes, which were hotter than red-hot yet had been quivering with naked fragility. The fire that had smoldered, *I won't accept it*, and, *I won't give in*...rebelling *passively*. The eyes at last lit with a will that could no longer be shaken...*I want to win*—

"But, Til—I think, *now*, you can answer. Right?"

"...Til...*why did you run...?*"

"——!"

Yes...the *third person* at whom Veig's question was directed, the main heroine—his niece, Til. She could do it, they said. But Til peered back into Sora's eyes as if trying to determine the truth behind his words.

"Hey. Even if you build an airplane to fly, that doesn't make you a bird."

—Sora, *the dark sky*, spoke back.

"But birds don't build airplanes... Why do you think that is?"

—The sky of a color higher than blue, from beyond the greatest heights, smirked back.

"FYI, there are things you can only see when you're lower than anyone."

"...Let's blast off...so high...together, *higher than the birds.* ♪"

They invited her where she'd begged to go.

—Til looked down and grinned.

"Heh, heh-heh-heh. Heh, I say. Excellent, then, leave it to meee!!"

—If it was a place reachable only by the most inferior—

"There's no spirit-arm artisan worse than me in the worrrld, there's not!!"

—then no one but she could get there!! She shouted forth her zeal and her thirst, and the absolute truth—namely!

"For I——am as smooth as a dolphin, I aaam!!!"

"Hey, okay, I sort of get it, but just let me say this: You are talking about *beards*, right?!"

Sora cried out just to make sure, but he was no longer in the scope of Til's concern... Seeming as unstoppable as a fired arrow, Til violently kicked open a hatch of the cockpit and flew out.

With blinding speed, she started fixing her cracked hammer...

⏻ Chapter 5: For Answer
Pragmatism

And so,
the puppet fled to the sky the chick
so desired,
to that cramped, dark world.
Yes...
A sky for the puppet to be safe from hurt,
to smile from the heart.
A place where no one would trample
them, no one hurt them,
no force compel them, no need to change.
A new world where they could fly.

That day,
The chick knew well enough it likely
would never be.
The chick implored the puppet, who vowed
to fight:
No sky is worth seeing you hurt.
So the puppet, too, fled to that same cage.

Until we find a way to create that sky,
so thought the puppet in the
stifling world.
Thought and only thought...
Doubtful and wavering,
finding nothing sought,
the puppet still thought about that promise:

That day,
in a new land, gazing at the heavens above,
seeing the baby bird spread its wings
and smile,
the empty puppet —the sky —Sora —

…A stage filled with the echoing eruption of the Holy Forge…the waste disposal site.

A giant silver humanoid machine took heavy steps through the subterranean ruins buried in metal refuse. Tears welled in Veig's fiery eyes as he muttered desolately with his life's first worry.

"… Have I, of all people, really done something so very wrong…?"

He recalled the two souls he'd smashed after an unexpected struggle—the soul of that weirdly tough little weed with the excellent tits, and the soul of that incomprehensibly toxic viper who had cracked his sword for the first time. Gloomily swaying, wobbling ahead, he thought:

…What in the blazes have I done…?

Veig could remember being thanked, but never being blamed. Yet all he felt now was a mysterious sense of guilt etched into his soul too deeply to deny. Now here he stood, in front of the fallen metal mass, the machine lying on the ground with its limbs totaled.

* * *

"...Ho... I did say I'd be late, but to take a *nap*, you've got gumption, have ya?"

Veig looked keenly down at the broken frame. Through the comm system, he accused its pilots of *playing dead*.

In this game, attacks caused no direct damage to the opposing machine. Therefore, any damage must have *occurred* through rite failure or misfiring—or been *self-inflicted*. And truthfully, it was both. Veig's intuition told him. He lifted the broken body and howled.

"Hey, I'm talkin' to you!! Your opponent is me. Don't roll over and die. Have ya no sense?!"

Indeed...Sora and Shiro never did stand a chance against Veig in a battle of spirit arms. So *it was inevitable they would lose*. Still, though—

"Ya aren't plannin' to just clam up without sayin' a *word* about your soul, are ya?!"

Yes—they'd stood up to Veig with an unthinkable storm of bullets. But it carried *none of their soul*—the barrage was all too brittle. All it did was *reject* Veig's attack and say *No* to his soul...

It spoke nothing. It admitted nothing. Their soul had only rejected his and *remained steadfast*. Veig ground his teeth. *If they could do this much, then why——?*

He pulled up the wrecked frame as if by its collar and raged:

"When are ya gonna answer my *question*?!"

And he did at last get an answer.

«...*Right now, I will. I'll give you your answer, I will.*»

... A voice murmured across the line.

"————Whuh?!"

The wreck suddenly retaliated by blowing up, unleashing a mad torrent of soul. It answered him with powerful imagery that momentarily robbed him of his consciousness.

* * *

—......

It was at the bottom of a small hole, dark and cramped. Veig knew the girl who wept, looking up at the sky alone. He knew her well...the *flightless girl*, who more than anyone admired the birds that flew so high.

A paradoxical girl, she *knew she could not fly* and yet looked up to the sky... *Wept though she'd given up...* The world *interrogated her with unanswerable questions*—why she fled, why she didn't try—and then asked her why she cried...and despised her for it. Left her in this dump...unwanted...

The lone girl...*swinging her hammer through tears......* He—

—......

Veig tried to reach out...but *blam*—the explosion shook the cave and stirred him from his reverie. As soon as he took a look around, maybe sooner, he guessed what was going on. He grinned and howled with wild anticipation.

"What a joke... Ya never had anyone in there from the beginning? *It was remote-controlled...?!*"

Now that you mention it, there was no rule that said you had to pilot the machine...was there? If they controlled it from a cockpit *outside the frame*, they could chuck it around without compunction.

But even if it was remote-controlled, they had to be connected to their spirit arms. Which meant that blowing up their own frame so carelessly would have repercussions. And indeed, the ground shook with a chain reaction of explosions one after another throughout the waste disposal site.

Generated spirits drew lines of light as if flowing through circuits etched into the stage. The circuit of light would converge—to show it:

The *real unit*—!

Eager to see where the real cockpit lay, Veig followed the spirit light to its destination. It turned out to be at the center of the quaking stage, so far away that his zoom function was just barely sufficient to make it out. At the top of an especially tall plant, his eyes found their target—and they opened wide. It appeared to be a girl he knew well, standing on the seat of an opened cockpit.

«*You ask why I ran from* this *bloody world, do you...? ...It's a foolish question, it is.*»

But it was a girl he didn't know who murmured to him. Her eyes, blazing with unquenchable fire, looked far down—down at his machine. The girl with a hammer-shaped piece of junk in her hand spoke as if laying down a declaration of war. From her heart, she spoke her soul...not objective fact, but her feelings:

«It's because——I *despise* that world, I do.»

Til's voice, resolute, was yet like her limbs...jittery. She couldn't help but tremble, because of what she saw down there from the open cockpit—Veig standing there in the venue that still quaked from the blasts—and because of the sparkling hammer in her right hand. Regardless—

"Don't worry. We'll blast off with you. We promised, didn't we?"

"...Brother...always...keeps, his promises... Trust us, okay?"

—Sora's and Shiro's voices intoned from the seat in front of her, joyful but firm. And Til felt them holding her left hand tight. She broke into a smile to realize her trembling had somehow stopped... and she continued with her eyes fixed straight ahead on Veig's machine, all the way through to the man inside.

"...I hate this country. I hate Hardenfell, I do."

She reaffirmed her feelings—her belief. This arrogant world told her not to run. This oppressive world told her not to be ashamed. Til looked up at its tireless way of life and sneered at it.

"I love the sky, I do... In this country...*the sky is closed off*, it is."

The cave's ceiling reminded her; lost and confused, she'd ended up in this dump before she knew it, and the world asked her, *Why did you run?* Now, Til knew the feeling of a hand in hers. Now, she knew another world—that of those two. Now, she could say it:

Ah...there never was a place for me here.

—Screw this place—!!

So—!

"I also hate the chieftain of this country. I *hate* you, I do...!"

The hammer sparkled ever brighter as Til's words spilled out uncontrollably, with the *pain that burned her up*. What came back was a lonely, sorrowful chuckle. Til ground her teeth.

...She'd known—no, she'd had a hunch—that he'd say that. What he was saying. As if it was everything—

"I hate that...how everything's just as you expected... I hate iiit!!"

Her voice impulsively swelled with the *pain* that only grew:

"I hate how you act like you're so great, I do! I hate even more that you actually are, I do!!"

The dam had burst, and her feelings could no longer be contained.

"I hate how you advertise yourself as a genius, I do! I hate how I can't argue because you actually are a genius, I do!! I hate how you look down on me, I do! I hate so much that it's only natural because you're above me, I do!! I hate how you're so hairy!! You shaved too much, you say?! So what? Are you trying to rub it in? I wish you'd go to hell, I do!! I hate you, I hate you, I hate you—U-Uncle, you're a pervert!! **I hate you very, very, veeery much, I do!!**"

«*Whoa!! Come on, stop already or I'm really gonna cry! Goddamn!*»

The momentum had flushed out everything Til wanted to say. Inattentive to the tearful begging over the comm system, Til caught her breath. As the shaking of the stage and the sparkling of her hammer and her pain all grew in speed, she wiped her tears. With a sharp, firm voice, she mulled over her words carefully and gave her answer:

"I hate you. *That's why I run.* If that's not enough for you to understand—"

Then in the spirit of the game:

"—I'll sock it to you like this—and then I think you will understand, I do."

Yes—seeing behind her eyelids the place the feeling of those two had taken her as they held her left hand, that black sky with a white bird, Til laid down the gauntlet sonorously.

"I fled to *win*—to honor my promise, I did."

…A tactical withdrawal was made when one had a chance of victory… She had been just lost, but *now it would be redefined*—no. Each time another explosion went off, the spirits *converged into her hammer*, and it was that pain.

——And now it *had been redefined*—!!

That pain had turned her conviction into that of the past. Til savagely swung her hammer as she—

—bellowed forth her soul with the stirring of a power beyond all normal conception throughout the venue.

"I fled for the sake of this day, when I'd *surpass you*, I diiid!!"

It was a power that all feared instinctively. The memories sleeping deep in their blood awakened. An outrageous power of a whole different rank, a whole different status, a whole different order of magnitude—quite literally a different level. The future brought on in the next few moments by this power beyond reason didn't take someone like Veig to foresee. It was a strike from the heavens that sneered at every one of *heaven's gifts* crawling atop the earth, judging them likewise of null value. No one could mistake that power. It was——

——a Heavenly Smite……

"Hey, whoaaa! I thought the Flügel wasn't—hey, isn't that against the rules?!"

From his machine—his cockpit—Veig screeched, blanching. Someone who wasn't in the game—with magic that wasn't even a seal rite!! His one eye searched in a panic for the Flügel, but in the next moment—

—he realized that the center of the crawling power…was *Til's hammer*. And his one eye was opened by the roar over the comm system and the unheard-of shock that followed… Yes:

«Ultra-large-scale spirit-arm expansion—connect all!! Ariiiise!!!»
Til's face wrenched in agony as she brought down the hammer. There was a flash as it bore through the cockpit…and through the plant below. With that, there came a moment of silence to the blast-stricken venue. And then…

"——?!!"

…a vertical oscillation unlike anything that had gone before tossed them. A heavy shock came from behind Veig. He dodged instinctively on the spot, but from the mass of metal that had only grazed him flowed a tempestuous soul.

——……

A girl who wanted to imagine things that could not be imagined. A girl who wanted to fly though by no effort could she fly. Saying she could do nothing, she chased the bird in the sky for which there was nothing to do…

They said she was just running. They mocked that it was impossible. Her soul…

«I…knew it! …I knew it!! Better than anyone, I did…!!»
The transmission helped Veig crawl back to reality. But another—no, ten more—no, a hundred, a thousand, ten thousand—innumerable storms of metal whipped through the stage and assaulted his unit like squalls.

Just scraps, they hadn't much in the way of force or even speed. But every time the fierce soul contained in them scratched by his frame, it left residue. As Til's voice, wheezing in agony, continued to come through, it pounded at Veig's will, hard, so hard—

* * *

«*So…you wanted me to live like you…? Fa-kew!!*»

To live like them. Like a Dwarf. Without giving up. Without going astray or tiring. To try to overcome natural gifts. To live without shame or retreat. Indeed… Putting themselves on pedestals, *though they couldn't overcome Veig*!! Looking as if they understood, talking as if they knew!! They'd called her rubbish, and then!! They'd all said it. They'd basically said this…

—*Everyone else is doing it, so you should, too.*

—*You can dream you'll be rewarded. Just do it—*

——*just* shut up and do your work——!!

«*I don't like a world that tells me what to do… I hate it, I do!!*»

I'll never give in…

I'll overcome the chieftain and destroy *those dictates—!!*

I'll use measuring instruments and Elven theory. I'll use anything to find a different way!

I'll show him… So she thought…

«*But…no matter what I did…I just…couldn't find anything!!*»

Just piling up failures. Bathed in error, lost, confused, making one mistake after another. At last surrendering to a false resignation, as paradoxical as ever. Unable to say anything in return… At some point…she came to think she'd forgotten those feelings, and just wandered, pathetically.

«*…But—hee-hee… Now I know what to say—I do…*»

Weeping, sobbing, yet the *two souls* grinned. At last Veig realized the true nature of the maelstrom of metal pounding his unit. And for the first time in his life, he said, *It couldn't be*—he doubted his own intuition.

"……Hey… Ho. I must be hallucinating, ain't I?"

He saw the whirlwind of metal *converging*. Not the ground shaking, *but the stage moving*. Not the metal flying, *but just gathering*. The parts, the catalysts were joining and coupling and assembling. The majestic waste disposal site was rising as one. The stage itself was wakening—and standing up. That was his impression. It was confirmed by Til's announcement to everyone watching in Hardenfell, *I'll tell you*, and the thing that towered before his eyes—*a thing inconceivably gargantuan.*

«*You forge ahead without shame...as you will—but I, too...will do as I will, I will!!*»

She'd led a life of *shame*—failing, contradicting herself, getting lost without end. Today, this moment, was what it had all been for, and for that she was proud. She trumpeted to all the world that had rejected her, just as they were taught:

«**Shut up!! Your stupid world can eat shit, it can!! Pft!**»

Having asserted her *freedom to rebel*, the girl crumpled. The siblings embraced her and kept her from falling. Veig gaped at last.

It wasn't from finally observing the giant object towering over him. It was the girl held by the siblings in the now-empty cockpit at the top...the girl weeping tears of heartfelt joy that she was not alone—a girl beyond his knowledge, who looked down at a bird from heights beyond its knowledge...with a dazzling smile... beyond all knowledge.

«*...Uncle, did you...ever imagine...this...?*»

She asked him whether *this* was a sight that effort and sensibility could get to—and that moment, a torrent of violence descended upon Veig's unit...

Neither Veig nor any of the Dwarves watching through all of Hardenfell had ever imagined it, most likely. However, aside from Dwarves...the three who were watching at Til's hideout did not seem all that surprised. Their eyes still on the monitor, they spoke admiringly...

"...Wow... *A city can walk*, can it...? Oh, is that also a spirit arm?"

"To be more precise, it is a spirit-arm expansion connected to her hammer, on which she engraved my one-percent Heavenly Smite."

"Observation: Height 9,700 meters. Length 74,200 meters. Cannon count 982. Definition: High-maneuver fortress class. Evidence of brilliance of Master. Excessive. Zero maturity. This unit loves that part of him, too... Blush."

Steph knew those siblings... She'd imagined they'd do something unimaginable. No, she'd known it. So she watched the screen with a sense of resignation, as a shadow desperately ran from the storm falling from the mountain of steel...

■■■

At the venue, rain fell from the heap of scrap—torrential rain deep underground where there was no sky. Each drop sliced the wind, pierced the ground, and created a deeper depth below the bottom.

"What a *little* man you are, Veig!! You talk big, but you're the one who's smaaaall!!"

It was a hailstorm of scrap that accompanied the raucous laughter.

"You called this stage our *hunting grounds*?! What puny thoughts— what a tiny imagination!! As would be expected from someone so small-minded as to only appreciate big boobs—ah, it's a veritable microcosm of your life!!"

"...You said...*we could use any machines...and do anything with the venue*, didn't you? ♪"

Towering with a sneer on top was a giant mecha of junk—of the unwanted. Of unvalued failures and rejected scrap.

This was the gathering place for the things that might have not been mistakes. This was their home turf, they indicated with a sneer.

"Who's gonna take the time to hunt their prey after they've already lured them in?"

Sora uproariously exposed the truth that was now assaulting Veig.

"If you're gonna lure in your prey, obviously you're gonna go straight to a trap, aren't you, you scrub?!"

It was a cage, a trap. The junk itself, the venue itself, the soul of a girl who had patched failure to error itself—

"Ladies and gentlemen—*the venue itself is our machine*!! How do you like that?!"

"…We of Blank call it…the *Spirit of Mother Til…* ♪"

It literally looked down on Veig, nine hundred seventy times his size. Sora and Shiro cackled, back at the reins for their big counterattack.

—*Come, O ye who declare yourselves infallible, those of the righteous world. Now our patchwork heap shall speak with iron and lightning and fire to test our Mother's spirit. We shall now question the refuse that you have shorn away and discarded in your quest to forge. We ask: On what grounds did you reject us—?!*

"Personally, I'm not as into the NEXTs as the Arms Forts built by average schmucks to confront them."

In fiction, raw size is destined to be overthrown.

Which is how we know that *reality is different*!! Indeed—!!

"***Raw mass is the secret to defeating genius*, biiitch!! We haven't designed this bullet hell with any place to hide! You trap 'em and smash 'em with sheer numbers! There's no better tactic!! All you gotta do is *win*, baby, win!!**"

In reality—*overkill is all the better*!!

Seated in the cockpit, Sora and Shiro controlled the massive body and filled the screen with projectiles.

«*The fock?! How'd you get such a crazy machine?!*»

Veig screeched as he just barely managed to demi-shift from one empty location to another.

«*What kinda Dwarf has the power to run a barmy monster like that?!*»

Between that and the Heavenly Strike, Veig was sure now there were some spirits involved far outside the regulations. He raged at their perceived violation of the rules.

……Ha. His opponents laughed in unison. They knew it: Dwarves were the perfect negative examples. After all, they were just half-right. Just as he guessed that the stage itself was their machine, *but that wasn't even close to enough.* On Sora's lap sat Shiro—*and on her lap* sat a girl whose face was scrunched in pain, but who still sneered with fearless irony—

"Chieftain… You ask that now? I couldn't even *start up our first machine* without boosting, I couldn't."

It seemed he had still overlooked the trick in Shiro's arms. Yes, it was the murmuring of Til, the *real* trick, most impossible of all—

"To *begin* with…I can't even *use magic* without boosting, I can't."

———

«———*Huhhh?!*»

—that made Veig cry out in long-delayed recognition. Sora chuckled. Yes, a Dwarf so great as Veig probably couldn't have imagined such a trick. Til, by nature, couldn't even use magic, much less operate a supermassive spirit arm. For Til—

———was as *smooth as a dolphin*———!!!

Dwarves used catalysts because of the spiritual overload caused by their mithril—to *synchronize externally.* But Til didn't have that mithril!! She wasn't subject to such overload, or even load for that matter!! That was why she used *boosting*… Yes…the hidden truth that astonished Jibril when Til used her shift. Til couldn't use magic without boosting. Conversely, that meant she could if she used boosting…

…*It meant she could use boosting.* For example: She could chain boost to boost on the chain reaction of explosions of the huge number of demi-shift anchors they'd planted, funnel the spirits into her hammer on which she'd engraved a Rite of Heavenly Smiting, and synchronize it *into* her body! With the vast amount of spirits thus summoned under her control, she could operate this leviathan assemblage of parts, this scrap on the stage on which she'd engraved seal rites…!!

* * *

… Yes, if a normal Dwarf tried this, they'd blow right up. It would be impossible and meaningless. Just as Til said, it would be as perverse an idea as building an underwater breathing apparatus for a fish. But for such an abnormal dwarf, it was both possible and essential. For Til—

——was as *smooth as a dolphin*——!!!

«*Wha—? Wait, whoa—* Niecey, *don't tell me* yours still hasn't growwwn?!»

"Heh…heh-heh, Ch-Chieftain…I'd like to see you burn in hell! I would…"

Listening to their exchange, Sora, to be honest, was fairly sure by now this was not the case. But he still insisted: they *had* to be talking about beards!! So anyway—!

"Heh, this is the *difference in natural gifts…* Bow before the absolute wall you cannot overcome, Veig!!"

«*Fock!! How can a Dwarf's body endure that shite? You wanna kill my fockin' niece?!*»

The transmission to Sora roared full of naked rage. Understandable. One percent of *Jibril's* power—the power to run a supermassive machine like that—was as reckless as pouring rocket fuel into an automobile. Therefore…

"…Didn't you say *no mercy*? A man's word isn't worth much these days, huh?"

«————!!»

…Sora saw that Veig was thinking of taking a bullet and losing the game for Til's sake, and Sora stopped him, making a face. If Til died, it would probably spell death for Sora and Shiro, who were holding her, too. Til was barely conscious, but still she held firm to her hammer and smiled.

—*Veig meant to lose intentionally.*

This man didn't seem to understand what a humiliation that would be—!!

"To hell with your patronizing sympathy!! This is a trap—there's *no place for you to hide* and *no room for you to choose*!!"

Sora's howl what seemed like a signal to that which sat somewhere in the supermassive machine behind the giant cannon that opened its mouth with a roar: *another machine*. Sora and the operator *inside the additional cockpit* announced savagely:

"There's only one future: *Til's complete victory*!!"
«*Whyyy, it's time for the showwwdowwwn.* ♥»

That moment, the *light of the Holy Forge* flashed from the barrel, and suddenly a *metal glob* blocked the opening. Connected to the muzzle, the object sparkled—and this time, Veig froze, mech and all. It was another legacy of the past that he could not mistake.

"Can you dodge a *bomb*? If you know a way, as a gamer, I'd very much like to know!"

A bomb indeed, leaving no place to hide. A bomb called…yes, that's right:

…The *E-bomb*…

In the cockpit behind the blazing E-bomb was Fiel, smiling.

"Why, you'll note that we've followed the rules to a T. And in a most sustainable way, if I might add. ♥"

No magic other than seal rites. You lost if your core broke. And the players *here were everyone*…

"Anyone can very well recycle the unit we lost in, caaan't theyyy? ♥"

True, Til could connect and use Fiel's unit. Also:

"Incluuuding the seal of protection of that boorish fire, and incluuuding the seal rites on the unit. ♪"

Fiel had in mind the *seventh player*, and their fifth *trump card*.

They hadn't bothered with any seal rites for the specs, but they *had* bothered with seal rites.

They had implemented an eighty-four-fold rite using the seal of protection of an Old Deus. And they'd used the Holy Forge, *the power of Ocain*, to enable shifting.

Til had subsumed Fiel's unit and commandeered it under the protection of Ocain. And there was no rule that Til couldn't use *that* thing shifted from her hideout!! Chlammy asked suspiciously of the merry Fiel, who occupied the same cockpit:

"...Fi, I've been wondering: Whose idea was it to use the seal of Ocain's protection?"

She'd heard of the "rites of spirit-breaking" or whatever that they'd used in the War, such as Áka Si Anse—spells that used seal rites to call upon the protection of Kainas, creator of the Elves. But it was said they were no longer usable after the Ten Covenants. In that case, *this* thing Fiel produced must have been newly compiled, after the War.

...Who would have implemented a seal rite to call upon Ocain, of all gods? For that matter, even having grown up in Elven Gard, Chlammy had never heard of a spell that could un-quasi-shift such a large mass.

"Mmm, I don't know, myself. It's been the Nirvalens' ace in the hole for generations."

Fiel tilted her head. Yes, and they'd said this...

"They said trump cards are trump cards because you don't reveal them until the showdown."

Howeverrr... She gave Chlammy her greatest smile as she continued.

"Why, my ultimate trump card is you, Chlammy. ♪"

Fiel had gone to such lengths as to reveal her family's secret. She smiled at her best friend: *They had lost—and that therefore was the victory planned.* Chlammy beamed and reflexively looked away, embarrassed.

"If you say we can't win…why, then we can't win."

Yes…from the moment Chlammy had concluded that they couldn't win…

…Fiel had *resigned from this game*…

So, they had requested of Sora and Shiro a *friendly* token of appreciation for their *friendly* cooperation. It was a condition of the deal, in other words: No matter who won—

—Veig must be commanded to *bear shame for the rest of his life*…

"Whyyy, it doesn't matter what you do as long as you win!! Our objective is to convict that thing, the offender! In which caaase, it doesn't maaatter who uses whose power to win. As long as the crook gets his just deserts, we have wooon!!"

Fiel's bright demeanor made Chlammy chuckle.

"…Well, we do have to regret a little we didn't make good on our chance to win directly."

"But we must count ourselves blessed to have been able to pummel you a bit. ♪ After allll—"

"Yes. We are really *perfect outsiders to this matter*. We're not even friends, you know?"

As they snidely echoed Veig's remarks, Chlammy had a thought.

—They could win an unwinnable match through someone else's power. Then how might they answer an unanswerable question?

"*We'll make others answer for us…* In other words, as usual, we win through sophistry."

—Having had their past questioned: *Have you paid your tab?*

—They answered with their future: *I will when I can…*

……

"…And so the puppet continued building the sky… The sky only they still could not see…"

In the cramped cockpit, Chlammy smiled subtly as she gazed upon the sky before her. They'd opened it for her, for Fi, for Jibril, the Werebeasts, the Old Deus, and Ex Machina… And now…

"They're opening up *Til's sky*... Going on until they find their own..."

■ ■ ■

At last, brilliant, blinding light.

Til had gathered things from *outside*—welded them, forged them, patched them together in one wrong way after another. Now her fire melted them all together, and cast them as *ingenuity*, which she used to reach the sky.

"...Uncle...have I...kept...my promise...?"

The spirits raged, and her body ached as if it was about to break.

"Have I...reached a sky...that no one has seen before?!"

The heat threatened to burn out her spirit corridor junction nerves. But alas, Til smiled regardless...

"...Do you...want...to know...what it's...like...?!"

By now, only one thing entered her muddied consciousness: the distant sky Til was sure she'd never imagined, and that no one else ever had—the feeling of floating in a deep, black sky, Veig too far behind to see, uncertain of whether he could hear the voice she wrung out, or even whether it was coming out at all—

Still, she'd fulfill the promise of that distant day. She'd vowed that she would surpass him—and promised something to the bird of that day. She spelled out the wish she'd held in her heart, that her words, her smile would reach their destination.

"You piece of shit, you'll never understand, you won't!! *Serves you right,* **it does!! Pft!"**

«*Niecey!! You got to get back at me, huh?! Ain't ya imitatin' me?!*»

Veig's transmission came through at trace volume. Til did hear it, though, and she closed her eyes and grinned.

...Please. I'm about to fall under the delusion that I have become a bird, I do. But I know...that it's just an illusion, I do. By tomorrow, perhaps even by one second in the future, I'll be made to know——

——*Very well then…!! Making mistakes is my only specialty—!!*
—*Assuming I can… Assuming that nothing's impossible! I'll fail again, and build up my mountain of mistakes, I will!!*

She'd lose her way, she'd get confused, she'd blunder—and every time, she'd cry and wail and gnash her teeth in vexation! Til would take the long way around like a perfect fool, getting lost repeatedly, pathetically drenched in tears and shame. She might never even know if it had meaning. But there was a sight that could only be seen by taking that foolish path.

It could never be seen by those born with natural talent…by the birds that didn't build airplanes.
It could never be seen by the birds that had never felt that obsession: *I want to fly anyway.* There was such an entertaining sight to see, to be found in a place no one imagined.
…*I'm ready to make as many mistakes as it takes. I can say that now, I can…*

And so, while Til went limp in Shiro's arms—
"…Well, bet this is news to you smart folks. Here's the common knowledge of the weak. Listen with gratitude, yeah?!"
—Sora howled at the shell of the E-bomb, which glowed like a star to announce it was ready for blast-off.
"…Generally speaking, things in the world *don't go the way you imagine…*"
Just as they had sailed for India and mistakenly arrived in the New World; as they had tried to prove everything with mathematics and mistakenly refuted their mathematics; as they had built rockets to reach the moon and mistakenly dropped them on Earth…
…As far as humans were concerned, perfection was a waste of time. They'd mess it up anyway. To seek mere perfection wasn't going to do it. Therefore—!!
"Your thinking is too damn small!! If you want to fly, you're not

gonna have a chance unless you have the guts to go past the damn moon and crash into Mars by mistake!!"

Well…yes…?

"Even if you get *up and down backward*, you might be able to go through the planet to the sky at the other side, right? ♪"

You might end up with a *result better than perfect*, right?

«*…You fockin' with me? Shit*—»

A man born with natural talent… A bird that flew by sensibility alone…transmitted back with a sense of awe at the unknown he'd never had before—or not in a long time at least.

Indeed…they couldn't use the E-bomb. So he didn't know what it was they were on the verge of launching. He didn't know what it was to accomplish. He didn't even know a thing about the heights where his niece floated now.

But even so! There was one thing he was sure about. He howled with a longing he'd never felt.

«*So you're saying* you don't know what the hell will happen. *You're bloody* daft, *aren't ya?!*»

If it *might* be the case that Til couldn't take it—!! That instant, Veig's unit appeared to get blown away and then vanished from sight. One soul raced forth through the air, with maneuvers uncapturable by Sora's eyes, or by the venue's cameras. It left no trace; the unit broken down, it raced past its limits, riding the force of a fist.

—*I'll overcome even that*—

Detecting the single strike to end it, Sora smirked and answered inwardly.

—*Yeah. That's right! That's how we live, as fools incapable of anything but straying and failing and erring. Bet it's a breath of fresh air for smarty-pants jerks like you who live with all trial and no error, huh?*

What's gonna happen? How the hell would I know?!

"That's why you gotta *test* that shit! That's what we idiots call *science!*"

Sora sneered and activated the *contents* of the E-bomb in the muzzle, and a moment later Veig unleashed one soulful strike that pierced the shell.

■ ■ ■

It was a full-on collision of Veig's and Til's souls, entangling, stirring, radiating white. No one could tell whose soul it was anymore. Everything raced through the catalysts and through the minds of all present...

——......

...The man had been born with outstanding sensibilities. Everyone knew him to be a genius. He too knew this, not as a matter of presumption or conceit, but as a proud matter of fact. He swung his hammer without guile, yet with ferocity. To create a work that was better—no, the best. An unprecedented masterpiece. A divine revelation!! He would enter that realm only one before in the history of Dwarf, his ancestor, had laid eyes on. His eyes reflected the back of that genius who had laid his fingers on *creation*—the alteration of concepts. He would reach that extreme none had approached in six thousand years. The man who kept piling up successes was the second coming of that sublimity. Everyone was certain he would be the next chieftain. Amidst all this, the man was hurling invective at a *strange kid* who was following him around:

"Hey... Get lost already, would ya, fockin' brat?! You're gettin' in the way of my work!!"

"I'm not getting in the way, I'm not. I'm seducing my future husband, I am."

The one contradicting him as if it was nothing was, at the time, a little girl. The one who called herself his future wife.

"If you think I'm getting in your way, that just proves you have feelings for me, doesn't it, Uncle? Doesn't it?!"

"Niecey, you're gonna stand there winkin' and blowin' kisses at me like some bloody fool? I've feelings, *harsh* feelings!"

She was the precocious daughter of one of his older stepsisters, and she'd taken an inexplicable shine to him.

"I ain't got no interest in some kid who ain't even got any hair grown in yet————*can't bear to look at ya. Piss off*," he commanded.

The child shuddered at the man's sharp one-eyed glare.

That was that. Everyone kept their distance from him. His eye had the gift of ending the conversation. Even children always grasped the point that he lived in a different world...*until* then...

"H-how do you know that I'm smooth?! Have you seen it?!"

But this child shuddered because she suspected he had looked at her naked. Incidentally, this was the fifth time this exchange had occurred. In other words—

"You peeped on me?! You licked me all over with your eyes, how can I get married now, you should take responsibility, and then I'll be the wife of the chieftain, what a way to marry up, it is! Come, come, come, Mr. Sir? If you'll marry me, I can show you my body *aaany—*"

"I can see from your face you ain't got no *beard*, all right?! Don't blush. Why are ya strippin'?!"

"Ah!! No, I don't want to be the wife of some pervert who lusts after children, I don't!!"

"Listen to me, will ya?! Wait, didn't you just say you were seducing me? What do you want?!"

No matter how he tried to get rid of her, she kept coming. The man clutched his head.

—*The hell's with this fockin' brat?* His niece had a strange way with words. But more than anything, it was his own sense of discomfort

that confused him. Never having experienced failure or discourage-
ment, the feeling was altogether unfamiliar to him. It would be a
while before he realized it was his first experience of anger.

"...Listen, Niecey. I'm a fockin' genius. And that makes me a
bloody fine man. You followin' me?"

"Ah! S-so you mean, when I marry you, I'll be a fine woman?!"

"Argh, that ain't it at all. This is the problem. You ain't good for
me, is what I'm sayin'."

Back then, he had concluded thus:

"You'll never be a fine woman."

———

"...Uh-huhhh... What is a fine woman...?"

"First of all, she's an adult with hair. You're out of the question.
And she's a woman who fits me. Let's see... So first, she has big
boobs. And then, if her spirit-arm craft ain't at least on my level, I
ain't messin' with that, either. Otherwise, hmm, she's *damn* beautiful and *damn* chaste and *damn* sexy as far as I'm concerned. That's
what it means to be a fine woman."

"...Uncle, that's just a fantasy woman, it is."

"——Rngh?"

"I-I—I mean, there are no Dwarves with big boobs, there aren't!
And everything after the 'Otherwise, hmm' is exactly what my
aunts told me virgins fantasize about, it is! Uncle, are you a virgin?
By the way, what is a virgin?!"

"Shut up! What's wrong with an outta-this-world man wanting an
outta-this-world woman? Those fockin' sisters of mine!!"

And then:

"Heh, you're hopeless, you are. I'll just have to become a *fine
woman* for you, I will."

......Suddenly...

"In another thirteen, I'll be an adult, I will. I'll be downright
bushy, I will!! I'll be beautiful, and oh so chaste, whatever that means,
I will! Then you just have to get me sexy, and that's that, it is!!"

...the child whose pale blue eyes sparkled as she spoke started to feel extremely dissatisfied.

"I'll do my best to make spirit arms like you, I will. If you just give up on the big boobs, I'll be such a *fine woman*, right in front of you! And I'll help you stop being a virgin, I will!!"

She smiled as if to ask: *So what is a virgin?* He thrust back feelings he didn't understand himself—

"It ain't happening. Such a good-for-nothin' ain't ever gonna get how to make spirit arms."

...And that—

——was the man's first *misreading*...

"......A good-for-nothing...? ...What? You mean me...?"

...*What? What's with those teary eyes like you can't believe what you just heard?!* The man felt ever more uncomfortable.

"Wh-why nottt? I-I'll d-do my best, I will."

"Your best ain't gonna do it...!! Why can't you see?!"

Ah—the child truly didn't understand.

Dwarf was a race that created exactly what it imagined. But she didn't see that she didn't see what he saw. She'd never even imagined she might not have talent. The man stood bewildered as to why that was so uncomfortable for him.

"...I...I just don't—understand, I don't... A-after all..."

She rebutted between sobs.

"...Uncle, *you don't understand why I don't understand*, you don't!"

And at last the man had his answer.

"U-Uncle—*you can't overcome the limits of your own imagination*, you can't!!"

———.

"R-really...I've already surpassed your imagination, by being unimaginable to you, I have. I'll make a spirit arm that surpasses you *easily*... S-see, I've won the argument, I have!"

...Indeed...the man himself did not understand the child. He couldn't imagine what she was thinking, what she was feeling, what...she was crying about... The man she admired over all others had told her she was good for nothing. But she argued against that absolute pronouncement and declared that she'd yet overcome it, weeping and despairing while her eyes burned with blue fire. It was that paradox that baffled the man who never strayed or erred:

...He *feared* that unimaginable child...

...The man had been born with outstanding sensibilities. They grasped even that divine realm only his ancestor had seen. And thereby he became the first in history to reach the extreme that in over six thousand years no one had been able to approach.

——*And then? What next?*

The man could only imagine following in the footsteps of his ancestor, but still he had a *hunch*. Given all this, what was it that his ancestor had seen before he reached this realm?

He *couldn't have been a normal Dwarf*. He must have been different, something unreadable, incomprehensible, unimaginable... Rather like that well-endowed lady his ancestor was said to have loved...or—

"I—I *promise* I'll make a spirit arm that surpasses you, I do."

—like the paradoxical child declaring this *irresolute resolution*—

"...Arright then. Go make a spirit arm that surpasses mine and bring it back here."

—to overcome six thousand years of Dwarven stagnation...and the limits of sensibility—

"I'll be here waiting for the damn fine woman who can beat me. It's a promise."

—to become a *damn* fine woman.

The man and the child joined pinkies in a solemn oath. He didn't understand what was meant by her eyes, which looked up at him holding back tears. But he decided that, until he understood, until he was surpassed—he'd be the finest man imaginable...to be a good match for such a fine woman.

*　*　*

But the child fled...

She was still a paradox, while he still did not understand her at all, running even as he chased. The days and months passed idly—until one day...

...the man fell right into the trap of two strange Immanities. The otherworlders were winning while running from their past. The contradiction made the man sure: These two would know why the child ran.

...And his hunch was proven right. However—

"*...A damn ham-fisted resolution...* I was the one running, *huh?*"

—as their consciousnesses melded and the man touched the soul of the child from back then, he laughed at himself. He'd been called out on his limits—and he himself had run from overcoming them.

And from trying to imagine why the child had cried that day. Her eyes, heavy with unease, had sought—

—someone to be her place of belonging, to take her fumbling hand as she looked up to that sky where she knew she couldn't fly...in that darkness as deep as her will. That was all... The man shouldn't have waited to be surpassed. He should have sought with the child a way to surpass his limits.

"*... Really? Is that really how it is? You were running? Are you sure?*"

In their melding consciousnesses, the sarcastic laughter of a young man interrupted their thoughts.

"*You think falling into the junk heap with Til and becoming like Shiro and me is* not *running? You think that's being right? Yeah, maybe it is. But maybe it isn't.*"

Was the man running from his tab? From the paradoxical child who *hoped for what he couldn't imagine*? From his paradoxical self who *tried to understand a child he couldn't*? Chasing after the child who fled against his sensibilities that told him it was impossible, going so far as to *put us on the hook...*

So, what's the difference between running and running from running...?

■■■

And so...the impact that shook to the surface left the cave. The force that connected the parts of the massive body ceased, and pieces of metal fell like hail. Through the whirlwind of dust walked a man who carried an unconscious girl. A rusty man. His mithril had lost its luster due to spiritual overload, his hair and his beard now rusted over... But strangely it seemed to be the true form of a man with the surname Drauvnir. It seemed proof of the way of life of a fool, using and abusing himself to overcome himself, *not knowing what would happen*, unafraid of overload—the only one to overcome the limits of his race...

I won't let her die. The man had sacrificed his frame and overcome his limits to save his niece. But then suddenly—seeing her unconscious in his arms yet unwilling to release her hammer, looking genuinely happy, her chest rising and falling dramatically in sleep, smiling—

"......Ha...ha...! Haaa—ha-ha-haaa...!!"

—the man at last collapsed, like his *broken* soul sword, spread-eagled over the ground laughing.

"...Ahh... My fockin' niece beat me good... The future is hers... I've lost..."

Yes: Veig recognized his defeat. He looked up to the heavens—and at last, he and all the Dwarves watching the broadcast—

—saw...the *sky*...

An unknown sky, inconceivable underground...yet they saw it. That of which Til had spoken—just as that which had *closed off the sky* before had broken, for the first time in six thousand years, it was pried open—that which lay beyond the high blue sky...

"...You feel that, Veig Drauvnir? You see how small you are, how

shitty your taste?" asked one of the shadows peering down at him. The shadowy figure glanced at the group that Jibril had saved the moment Veig's core had broken.

"You gotta fight with people on your level. Sorry, man. You're just not up to playing me yet."

Ah, what a small man he had been. Veig looked up at Sora, seeing in him a very different kind of man.

"…Small boobs, big boobs, even humongous boobs; fake boobs and real boobs… They are all boobs…"

A big man… Such a big man. Sora eyed him calmly.

"If you claim to love boobs, how can you speak of right or wrong? Speak of love."

The big, big man's voice was so clear you could hear him all the way to nirvana.

"To reject boobs other than those of the uniform ponderous size you favor as fake, and to impose this view on others…"

No censure, no blame, no scorn or spite could be heard in his voice…only the sound of a man who had obtained enlightenment and imparted to the world the truth.

"To speak to such a soul is less than my soul is worth."

…Dost thou find it wonderful? Then may it be wonderful. No one can violate thy freedom to so find it. Then why, in speaking thy feelings, shalt thou denigrate others'? Indeed…

"Ideal tits? They're perfect if you work on them? Ahh, how small, how small!!"

It was he, Veig, who had lacked confidence. Whereas this immeasurable man, as vast as the sky, had stood from the beginning far beyond Veig, on a higher plane.

…He was one truly great virgin. Yes…

"If ya want ideal boobs, you're not gonna have a chance unless you have the guts to go for the *woman who goes way the hell past your ideals*, are ya?!"

Ah…it was just as his fockin' niece had said. The child that day had already surpassed him…and now she'd become a fine woman who surpassed his imagination. Sora smiled at this, too.

"…Yeah. It was my limit to pursue *mere* perfection."

Veig felt he'd seen for the first time what that child kept yearning for. She hadn't been looking at the birds. From the very start, she'd been looking at the sky in which they flew…

"…Ah, finally I can see what my fockin' niece saw."

That sky one wished for and longed for and pined for and yet could never imagine: that which he'd always pursued…the *ideal big tits that surpassed the perfect*… Ah, yes…

Bwoing…

Veig gazed innocently at Til as she slept, her rising and falling *chest*—her *humongous* boobs. Tits of such excess as to look a little unbalanced, allowing statuesque beauty to crumble. He smiled at this ideal he'd finally found, an ideal beyond limits. He was happy……

■■■

Indeed… Only two in history had seen that divine realm. A third who had opened the door without being able to see it was responsible for this by-product of a successful failure. In the E-bomb shell had been placed *two* false ethers to conceptually resonate.

"Hey—th-these are heavy; I can't even stand! 'Big' doesn't even describe these!"

"You see, Dora, this is the conceptual rewrite of 'big boob(?) essence'—"

"Analysis: Bust value of woman of unknown name. Provisionally categorized under handle 'megatits.' Very niche support.'"

"What are you talking about?! These are going to turn back, aren't they? I can't live like this!"

"Why, I'm fine if we don't turn back, insofar as I've happened to match Chlammy. ♥"

"You must be joking! Why do I have *even less now*?! I won't toler-ate having *no* boobs! Hey, Fi, saying your small boobs match me, are you indirectly dissing me?! Give me back my boobs!"

"Query: This unit's bust provisionally categorized under 'ample bosom'… Questioning conceptual rewrite of 'big boob essence.'"

"You see, it is not 'big boob essence' but 'big boob(?) essence'—"

And there the ladies cavorted, their boobs changing *randomly*. Exactly as in the experiment four days earlier, except that this time it worked without an explosion. The conceptual rewriter used Lóni Drauvnir's "big boob essence" *along with* one other false essence. Yes, just the same thing had happened as four days ago—instead of an explosion, it was *its by-product*. In other words:

"To summarize, it seems to be as in the experiment of four days ago, when, according to the sublime teachings of my masters, I engraved on unprocessed essence a seal identical to that for the big boob essence and activated this *unidentified essence*," Jibril rehashed for the two who hadn't been there. "I posit that a *two-way reaction* with the big boob essence has generated a composite conceptual rewrite."

Indeed…the principle was unknown. No one even understood how conceptual falsification worked. Thus, even Jibril was unable to explicate or elucidate this incomprehensibility. But she described it in words in such a rough manner as was possible. So:

"In short—*the conceptual rewrite is in the form of a question*: 'Are these big boobs?'"

"These clearly cannot be described as big boobs!"

"Yes, you see, it is 'big boob(?) essence,' such as to make everyone ask, 'These are big boobs?'"

——……

■■■

"For the record, this is the first and last time I'm gonna play Cupid for anyone, all right?!"

Sora paid no attention to the commotion. He took the hand of his sister, apparently the only one unaffected: *Big boobs? Where?*

"For God's sake, I'm still updating my years alive and without a girlfriend!! And now I'm supposed to help some d00d land a heroine?! And not just any heroine, but the one and only—the real thing—the brown legal Loli monster girl!"

"...I hope you find...happiness. ♪ That's one heroine...out of the running..."

The siblings walked away. Veig heard them loud and clear. He grinned softly at the sleeping face of his niece, who still smiled happily in his arms.

"...Ho... Bitches, I've heard your answer... I feel your soul..."

There was something the otherworldly siblings had never spoken of to the end. They hadn't put that answer into words, or even returned it in their souls. Indeed...

"I was wrong to question you. Thanks for showin' me...the sky..."

He got the sense that if they could beat this game world, they could say they'd *fled to win*... So:

"Lemme help ya build the sky of your future. Let's be *bosom buddies*."

They'd overthrow this game world, its rules, everything. They'd beat the world. Just you wait.

We're coming for you next, friggin' Earth...

And so the sun rose on the capital of Hardenfell. In a corner of that underground city, still buzzing in the wake of the epic battle that had broken the limits of the race, a group surrounded a table at a little tavern and raised their glasses high. It consisted of those who had dominated that battle. Specifically—

"Conference: First 'What Does Master Like Anyway?' Thorough analysis imminent. Yaaay."

"""""Yaaay."""""

"Hey, you're not really saying *yay*, are you?! Huh? Isn't this supposed to be a party, a *celebration*?!"

—it consisted of four women surrounding a screeching Sora.

...Fiel and Chlammy had left promptly, or perhaps simply evacuated to be more precise. In any case, those who remained were Jibril, Emir-Eins, Steph...and Shiro, too. Sora had been trapped in a tribunal under the guise of a celebration.

"And what do you mean, 'anyway'?! Didn't I say to love all boobs equally?!"

He quickly raised his objections, but their rejections came swiftly one after the other.

"Negative acknowledgment: Declaration pertains to freedom of thought, toleration of fetishes. *Awaiting answer pertaining to Master's fetishes.*"

"Also, Master, you mentioned that your soul was too proud to speak to his..."

"...So we conclude...you just, haven't...said what...you like... *obviously.*"

Then, as if lining up the exhibits to interrogate the defendant:

"Playback: '*You can grow big boobs, or get old and wrinkly, or even turn into a man!! Nothing could make your big brother not like you!*' '*Your brother loves you no matter how you look.*'"

"Who said you could record that?!"

"...Emir-Eins, I want, a copy...of that audio...!"

The brother and sister squealed for different reasons at Sora's statements from the prior game, played back at high volume. Still, Emir-Eins and Jibril calmly continued their questioning:

"Review: Master previously deduced to be a lolicon. Scope expanded to all ages and sexes. Requires reanalysis."

"That said, on one hand, the only ones my master has responded favorably to are those of tender age... But at the same time—"

"Revelation: Master enjoyed breasts of woman of unknown name. Action voluntary. Synthesizing above data—"

And so they laid out their deductive conclusion...thus!

"Conclusion: Fetish of Master is animal-eared, dark-skinned, big-boobed, cross-dressing male Loli hag...!"

"D00d, how effed up do you think I am?! What kind of trope monster is that?!"

Sora howled at the accusation, which made him wish they'd just say he'd take anything female. Regardless, Steph asked him bashfully, blushing fiercely:

"I-in that case, Sora... Why is it that you only touched...er...my chest?"

Silence fell. They looked at him. Putting words aside, he looked up to the heavens and thought thus:

Why...? "The guy all the girls go for" is fiction—an entity whose sole purpose in reality would be to get stabbed and retire from life.

So why am I being treated like such a man?

Ungifted with the protagonist privilege of falling on girls, yet breathing the air of a harem smackdown, Sora answered...silently:

Why had he touched Steph's boobs?

Because his sister—*because Shiro had let him.* End of story!!

Sora had never done anything "Eh-heh-heh-heh" of his own will, with his own hands, not even once! Therefore, there was no commonality between Sora, virgin, eighteen, and the guy all the girls go for. Those surrounding him now failed to understand that. But even so, his superhuman ability to read people, his natural gift as a lying puppet, made him certain:

If he told them that now, *somehow* he'd be *trapped*...!!

"...... ♪"

Ah... That look on Shiro's face—*Come on, just say it*—proved it more than anything. *After all, your brother knows that face. It's the face you make when you're waiting for him to screw up.* But why? Just how was it he'd be trapped? What would make it Shiro's victory—?!

Sora panted under the stress of all the various gazes pressing on him. And in the end, out of the blue:

"Heh, heh-heh-heh, yes, heh!! I-I'm free, I am... I have escaped, I haaaaaah?!"

"Tiiil!! Ohhh, I've been waiting for you! I was about to dieee! What took you so looong?!"

He leaped to the savior who had appeared in the bloodthirsty court of the tavern. *Tsk*, the females could be heard to click. Til had no way of knowing its meaning of remorse for their force-quit trial with the arrival of the guest of honor. She struggled to catch her breath and bowed deeply.

"I do apologize for my late arrival, I do. I was a bit held up by a *pursuit*...I was." Til saluted and restlessly justified her tardiness. "Wh-when I awoke...for some reason a horde of Dwarves was coming...I almost got *kidnapped*, I did; I was so scared, I was! But I happen to be a pro at fleeing, I do; they won't catch me, they won't!!" Now full of confidence, she declared it boldly—yes! "Th-they want to rub out this grubby mole who defeated the chieftain, they do!! Heh-heh, but I won't let them, I won't!! Y-you won't let them, will you? H-help me..."

...Save me...

Seeing Til look up with frightened eyes and plead to them, Sora and Shiro exchanged grins.

"Of course we won't let them rub you out. Because no one can anyway."

"...Everything...in this country...belongs to, you...you know? ♪"

——.

Til looked back blankly.

"...Uh... Um? I beg your pardon, I do?"

"Huh? D00d, the wager. Think back and remember the wording."

The one who would collect the *payment*...that is, everything Veig owned, i.e., the country...was the victor. In other words:

"See, all Veig's shit belongs to the winner—so it belongs to *you*, right?"

"...Yes. Everything... Including, of course, the position, of agent plenipotentiary... In other words—"

In any case, Sora and Shiro had to sell the medicine to Veig. All that was left was whether he would pay—and here, he'd paid. Indeed:

"—the spirit-arms artisan who surpassed Veig—*you*—are the new chieftain. ♪"

""Excuuuuuuuuuuuuuuuuuuuuuse me?!""

The above cry arose from both Til and Steph.

"What? In—in that case, you two *haven't gained anything at all*, have you?!"

Then why had they played this game? Steph shrieked to know. However—

"Hunh? They have, haven't they? *Everything they wanted.*"

—the answer came from the *other* guest of honor, his feet languidly tapping toward them.

A man in his wedding attire, a sword in his right hand and a bouquet in his left. A man of rusted mithril, who had known peerless talent, limits, and reaching for heights. A Dwarf combining arrogance and humility, pride and reverence—now, having put himself together, displaying himself as such a faultlessly *fine man* as to make Steph gasp unwittingly and Sora cluck reflexively.

He went on to clarify...

"I'd already lost by the time they trapped me. All that was left was *whether we could become friends...*"

That's right—from the start, Sora and Shiro's objective was not domination, but *unity*. They'd never had to accept this game. For that matter...

...they'd never had to win it... It was just—

"And now we are *bosom buddies*. I swear on my soul. I'll support ya."

—a matter of whether they could answer Veig's *question*... That was all. He'd figured that Sora and Shiro would step down if they couldn't answer. So if they did answer his provocation, he just wanted to hear the answer of the one of whom he truly wished to inquire, that being Veig's "promised girl." He wanted to fulfill the promise he made with her...

"Huh?! Uh. Me, the chieftain—the agent plenipotentiary of Dwarf? What? I can't possibly, I can't!"

"Yeah, ya probably can't alone. But you can do it with me, can't ya?"

True—having paid his wager, Veig had lost everything. Everyone except for the gaping girl to whom he now proffered a ring on bended knee. As he'd promised...he'd work with her as *husband and wife*—as *friends*...

"...All right, time for Cupid to leave for now. The *celebration*—"

"—comes after the *ending*... We're...gonna go home."

Sora and Shiro stood. Jibril and Emir-Eins followed their lead, whereupon even Steph got the picture: "Ah." She smiled congratulatorily, and she turned. Then, leaving behind a brief *flash* while the man's voice continued, Sora and Shiro walked away. Hand in hand, they pondered...

"...Let my place be inside you."

"......!"

Yes... Just as Sora needed Shiro and Shiro needed Sora, Til needed a *bird*...and Veig needed a sky... A bird danced in the unimaginable sky but could not create the sky. So—

"Show me what I can't see. Then each time ya do, I'll show ya *something greater.*"

As Til would surpass Veig, Veig would surpass Til in return... *That's how it should be.* Sora looked at his bird with whom he held hands, and they exchanged smiles.

He exchanged fierce grins with the bird. The bird that you'd devise all manner of tricks to finally lay your hands on only to slip from your fingers and disappear into the distance the next moment.

"So, uhhh... Yeah, how do ya say this? Now it's time to pour the booze...and say the real damn words."

Excellent. I'll catch you as many times as it takes, the sky said with a smile.

Yeah. And I'll slip from your fingers every time. The bird smiled as well.

——*Because each time, it reminds us...that there are* no limits...

"Won'cha let me deliciously enjoy ya? Let's blast off together."

——*Was it really necessary...to call that back...?* N-no. He must've meant it like "lift each other up." Definitely. I think. Sora and Shiro went on their way, doing their best not to think that they'd just heard the true intent of the virgin who'd waited and waited for Til.

"Sir. **Not on your life**, I won't. I hate you very much, I do."

......?

"And *these*. There are limits to harassment!! **Pft!!**"

......*What's this...?*

Sora and Shiro stopped in their tracks and turned in confusion. They saw that Til looked even more confused and was holding back big tears. *She'd been given humongous boobs.* His proposal struck down peremptorily, Veig knelt frozen into stone.

...Hmm. I see.

So that was what that *flash* they'd sensed behind them had been about. In one mere day, Veig had caught up with Til and constructed *megaboob* essence. *Bwoong*, heaved Til's boobs under Veig's conceptual rewrite, as she looked into Sora's eyes.

"What? So, after they all called me rubbish all that time, now they're calling me their chieftain? They're chasing me enthusiastically as if none of that ever happened, are they? **Huhhh?** Do they take me for a fool?!"

She looked back to Veig, who was still frozen in his cool pose. Tears streamed down her cheeks.

"And, I mean... Eegh—you look at what I've accomplished in the last sixty years...and then you do it overnight and then sexually harass me some more... Do you enjoy teasing me that much?! Turn me back, Chieftain. I hate you, I do!! Sir, Ma'am, help meee, waaaaah!!"

The binding force of the Covenants restored Til's flat, smooth form. And at last Til flew at Sora and Shiro to wail to them. All present were lost for words...

"H-he's talking about going *inside* me and telling me to *show him what he can't see*... H-he's going to rape me, he is!"

——*Hmm... I see.*

So she interpreted it not as a proposal, but as sexual harassment—or indeed an announcement of criminal intent. It didn't sound as if it should be taken at face value, that much could be said. But Veig, still in his matrimonial getup, held out the ring—

"Wha...? Hey, but, Til? Remember the promise? About how you'd surpass me and..."

After all that lead-up, she doesn't recognize this as a proposal...? Sora spoke for everyone who was there staring dumbly. Yet Til was nonplussed.

"*My promise to build a spirit arm that would surpass you...?* What...about it?"

Having murmured this, Til seemed to faintly recall. Her face grew gradually whiter and whiter, her eyes wider and wider, as she shrieked:

"Wha? I promised…just to *build a better spirit arm*, I did…you know? Marriage… If that's what you had in mind, I don't just hate you; I'm terrified of you, I am!! I—I mean—"

—*Hmm. Now that you mention it…* A little late, Sora suddenly realized two things that were odd…

Til *hadn't once* been overcome by Veig's soul… And also: Til had *never said* she *wanted* to marry Veig once she surpassed him… Sora and Shiro thought together as the shaky voice continued.

"Are you saying you've been putting your big boobs on me since I was *five* not just to torture me, but to *prepare* me for this?! You gave me nightmares. You made me *hate big boobs*, you did! You've been waiting with blue balls for seventy-nine years as you tried to break me so I'd be the kind of convenient 'fine woman' you fantasized about and then you'd bang me?!"

…*Hmm… I wonder why…*

The man had been steadfast in waiting, always thinking of his niece, who had declared that she would surpass him. But when she put it like that, it was hard to dispute that he sounded like a pervert…

Everyone was speechless. Til sat with a *thup* on the lap of Shiro, who was seated on Sora's lap.

"I have a place to go back to now, I do!"

Then, with her next words, it wasn't just Veig, but this time Sora and Shiro who turned to stone.

"It's here, it is. *I'm the big sister of these two*, I am!!"

——*Huh?*

"My victory is our victory, it is. And! I've absolutely no use for this country—not to speak of you, Uncle! I'm handing it over to them, and they can do whatever they bloody well want with it for all I care, they can!! **Pft!**"

Til snorted as she delivered Veig the coup de grâce. Sora fearfully interposed:

"Uh… Excuse me. Can I say something?"

"Sir! Please say as much as you like! Tell this country how it's—"

"No, first—since when are you our big sister?"

"Wha…? Queen Shiro said she was 'Nýi's little sister'…so that makes me her big sister, correct? And necessarily that would make me your big sister, it would…wouldn't it…? Huh?"

…Am I wrong? Are you going to abandon me? Til turned all teary-eyed like a puppy. Shiro still hadn't recovered from petrification.

"……Uh… Look, Til…"

Looking at this rescued puppy recalled a matter that the two of them had previously shelved: what to do about Til's position after the *Welcome back*, and…

"Can you tell us your name again, in full?"

Shiro seemed to recall it, too, after Sora mumbled this question. She gaped and blanched… Yes…

—*Tilvilg by clan, Nýi—* ……Oh.

Shiro had cut her off back then, so Sora was asking the rest of her name, *but there wasn't any rest of it.*

"Sir. Tilvilg by clan, Nýi by birth, it is…"

Nýi Tilvilg looked at him questioningly.

…More precisely, Shiro's "final warning" had been: "I am, the little sister here! Me!!" *Me… Nýi.*

In short, Til had nodded vigorously and agreed unconditionally to—

Oh, that was how it was… So Shiro's little sister role was considered to pertain to *Nýi.*

Wait… But that wasn't enforced by the Covenants, was it?

Before Sora could ask, Til demonstrated her will, which surpassed the Covenants. She sat next to Shiro, who sat on Sora's lap, and looked up in Sora's eyes— Or rather…

"I like it here, I do. From here—*I can see the sky,* I can."

…she looked up at Sora and Shiro: the black-haired young man and the white-skinned girl.

"I can see a dark, distant sky…carrying a bird to infinity."

It was as if she knew Sora and Shiro's promise... The promise they hadn't been able to fulfill.

As if that promise was about to be fulfilled. A promise even they didn't know. No...

"I want to go with them to confirm that sky continues forever, I do."

...as if *she would fulfill* that promise which Sora and Shiro still didn't see.

"Just as you showed me the sky... Just as you showed me that all my past happened so that I could meet you... I now will do what I can, as your big sister, to show you *that sky*, I will!"

And she narrowed her eyes with a smile that made even Sora, even Shiro woozy.

"That sky continues even into another world—I'll prove it, I will!!"

Til's voice was resolute, but Sora and Shiro knew they heard the subtext. Yes...it was true, Til needed her *bird*—that is, Veig—but *here*...there existed a bird that flew through the unimaginable heavens and a sky that constructed the uncreatable heavens.

...The chieftain? Who's he? I didn't call for him, I didn't...

"Veig. Is this like one of those scenarios where...you try to create drama and you end up getting NTRed?"

...That shit happens. You set the flags for the true ending, but they turn out to lead to a creepy, depressing ending... Looking sincerely troubled, Sora gazed at the ossified Veig, still with his cool expression, and asked in earnest what to do now. But, standing at the top of the race that never erred...and therefore never was right, either, Veig answered with a question. He begged for instruction in that which he could not understand for the life of him, could not even imagine:

"...Hey, bosom buddy... What the hell is with chicks?"

"Ah... Dear friend. That is the one of the few problems that has been fully solved in our old world."

"…Really? Damn, other worlds are some shit… Come on, can ya tell me the answer?"

Ah, humanity—those who flew into the stars, destined to one day reach the farthest extremes of space. Someday, they would overturn every impossibility… Except for that one…

"—That is the one mystery that will remain when every other riddle of the universe has been solved…so they say…"

Sora informed him as much, convinced that this alone would stand to eternity. And there seemed to be an agreement:

"…I'm so, stupid! Why, didn't I see… Too many flags…!"

"Analysis: Cannot detect big sister attribute in entity claiming big sister status. Identified as camouflage. But target of love detected from object is Master and sister of Master—indivisible. Query: Do you swing both ways?"

"Wha?! Emir-Eins, can you analyze love?!" Steph asked.

"Well now? Then can you not identify the target of my master's love, as well as his sexual preferences?" Jibril followed.

————Gasp!!

Sora recognized a gasp that accompanied the tension running through the sudden silence. He also recognized that countless gazes were upon him, peering into his innards. But he didn't know *why* those sharp, piercing gazes were upon him. What had he done? He didn't feel he would ever understand. So Sora did as he'd always done. Without knowing where or why or what for, without understanding anything, he found just Shiro's hand, turned tail on the unwinnable game, and got lost…

■■■

After each went on after him in her own way, the only one left was Veig, still in his wedding outfit, stacking up empty bottles on the table all by himself.

…Til had given him commands between spurning his heartfelt proposal and chasing after Sora and Shiro. First, Til had implanted him with a lifelong feeling of guilt, according to the deal with Chlammy and Fiel. Then, Til had given him back everything, including the status of agent plenipotentiary, telling him she didn't want him or his country, with a clever parting line:

Go to the planet of big boobs before you talk to me. Pft!

Indirectly, she'd commanded him never to talk to her again, with special spite and rancor.

"...Ya got turned down hard, eh, boy? Ain't every day one gets to drink to your sorrow."

Suddenly, a derisory voice came from someone sitting beside him. Since when? Since the beginning? Its owner gulped down spirit oil with gusto. Veig responded only with a groan.

"...Sorry, I'm busy... Wouldja leave me alone, Big Papa?"

An aging man who was everywhere, yet nowhere—was the *appearance* of this concept that cackled at Veig with eyes and ripples like the Holy Flame. Veig heaved one good sigh and glared back. He told him to be sure.

"Those there are my friends. I've made up my mind about that. If you're here to bitch at me about it, piss off."

He reported his solidarity in a tone that brooked no argument from anyone.

"When have I ever told you kids what to do...? As ya like."

But Veig's force found as much purchase as it might on fire.

"But who woulda thought those woodland rascals would call on my protection? Those're some interesting folks."

The Old Deus guffawed all the more loudly, as lively as raging fire. The Holy Forge erupted grandly as if to manifest his concept.

Ocain, god of the forge... His laugh was as uninhibited as the creator of the Dwarves' should be.

"Arright, then leave me alone already. I'm as busy as I'll ever be in my life."

"Huh. Sure keeps ya busy bawlin' like a heartbroken little girl, does it? Keep at it, ya workaholic."

But Veig's retort to this snark silenced even the god of the forge.

"I gotta *go to the planet of big boobs!!*"

——.

"Ngaaah! Ya hear me?! I ain't even been *rejected*!! Anyone can see that. And in the first place, she didn't realize I was proposing, ya see?! And second!!"

Veig made as if to shake off the droplets that had formed in his blazing eyes, as if discussing it was making him sad.

"She said, 'Go to the planet of big boobs before you talk to me.' So *I can talk to her after I do it*, right?! She told me to go. She didn't tell me not to come back, ya seee?! That's why I'm so fockin' busy."

Veig's breathless spiel suddenly changed pace, his gaze keen.

"—I gotta plot with my friends. That's nonnegotiable. I can't toss aside my work."

He'd vowed that. He was looking forward to it. He grinned audaciously and continued:

"But right now I got to defend myself to my fockin' fine niece!! I got to seduce her all over again! I'm drinkin' hard so I can imagine some ideas for a spirit arm that'll get me to the planet of big boobs and back double quick—you think I'm not busyyy?!"

"*...Ah. Sorry then. You got a big job ahead of ya, don'cha?*"

The god of the forge gave in to Veig's desperate yell. Indeed, after all...

"*To go to a planet that don't exist—to push through a paradox even a god like me couldn't, I gotta give you credit.*"

"Ha! Lemme tell you something my bosom buddies taught me, Big Papa."

Unless you had the guts to go past the damn moon and all that...

"If it don't exist, you just got to build it—that's all there is to it, ain't it?"

——.

"All I got to do is go to a planet no one ain't gone to before—and *that's the planet of big boobs!!* I'll plant my flag there and name it that! It's my planet—who can tell me what to name it?!"

———.

"Ah, Big Papa, I can see what you're thinkin'. 'There ain't no spirit corridors in space,' right? But! I'm gonna take a lesson from my friend: Once ya blast off, the rest is *inertia*!! Then when I come back, I'll use the concept of false essence—— *Ah!!*"

What was it he thought of?

"I got it, I got it! I can see it now. Damn, I'm such a genius!! Arright, see ya later, Big Papa!!"

The god's child who ran off in a rush…didn't seem after all to have realized:

Go to the planet of big boobs before you talk to me. That command to go to a planet that didn't exist… That impossible demand *was not enforced by the Covenants.* He didn't seem to realize how meaninglessly he meant to *embark on the Ixseeds' first spaceflight.* And as for his means—the god of the forge just laughed heartily.

"*Ho, children of another world. It seems there are some real fools among my sons, too. You got somethin' to look forward to.*"

What was essence? Veig still didn't know. It was only natural… Ocain, an Old Deus himself, didn't know.

Yes—Lóni Drauvnir, Veig Drauvnir. And Nýi Tilvilg. That falsely ethereal *thing* only they three had found was not a "divine realm."

It was actually an artificial creation of gods…

Even the god could neither create nor imagine such a realm, yet not one of them realized this. He thought back to that Great War—to that Suniaster he'd sought in order to rebuild the world—and he chuckled.

"*…I'm just the god of the forge, after all… A clown who doesn't know anything but effort, I guess.*"

Yes…at last he understood those who'd declared they'd destroy space, and he understood his children. Snickering, he thought:

"*…To build a Suniaster your own damn self… That ain't occurred to me, I gotta say.*"

To build an omniscient, omnipotent concept... Interesting folks, all right. Wouldn't be bad to give it a try, huh? The god of the forge grinned. It was, after all, the duty of children to surpass their parents. And he hadn't even realized they'd already done that six thousand years before. *Looks like I'm quite the fool myself, huh...?*

■■■

As they then went on their ways, suddenly—

"...By the way, Sora? Did you actually deliver Mr. Veig his... medicine?"

"Sure. Jibril shipped it. Hey, I wouldn't try to screw over my friend..."

—Steph realized she'd never seen Sora and Shiro give Veig the goods. She sarcastically suggested they might have taken the money and run, but Sora answered no less sarcastically.

He'd want to give his friend a little extra if anything. He'd never felt such a bond of friendship as he did today with his fellow virgin.

Steph went on:

"Then don't you think it's time you gave me my medicine...?"

"Why should we? The price is your whole damn country. You're just a figurehead. How can you afford it?"

But it wasn't Steph who answered Sora's puzzled question.

"Detection: Price of 'whole damn country'—all assets—includes debtor's person. Therefore, *excuse*."

"I see... So returning the country to my masters is an excuse for little Dora to sell herself?"

"...Steph's...getting clever...now. We gotta, watch out..."

"That is *not* what I meant! If you've forgotten, I'll have you recall!"

The two servants and one sister looked at Steph distrustfully, but Steph raised her voice in protest.

"Elkia is still on the brink of death, thanks to your poison!"

There they were, acting as if everything was all neat and tidy now, while the biggest problem remained unsolved, its details yet unrevealed: Steph demanded the medicine to resolve the crisis of Immanity's impending doom. However...

"Yeah, don't worry. Elkia doesn't *need* any medicine."

"............Beg pardon?"

"Report: Approaching appointed time. Remaining time until *sequence start*: ninety-eight seconds. Heeere weee gooo."

...the answer came from the grins of Sora and Shiro, the calm, emotionless report of Emir-Eins, and the ripping of a hole in space of Jibril.

On the other side of the hole was Elkia's parliament, various nobles in the assembly hall with the Commercial Confederation behind them.

"Hey, Steph? What are the other countries trying to find using these guys...?"

"They're trying to find the truth about you two—Blank—and your 'unbeatable trump card' that can take down gods, aren't they?"

Sora asked as the representative of those looking at the scene with icy smiles, and Steph answered.

"Sure. But, look. If we really had an unbeatable trump card..."

"...*We could have beat their impossible game*...beat the Commercial Confederation's coup...right? ♪"

"_____!!"

Sora and Shiro's grins only widened further. Their words shocked Steph.

"We, Blank, abandoned Immanity, declined the game, and left the throne empty..."

"...Then *where's*...the unbeatable trump card? *Whose*, is it...and who, got it?"

Yes—once Sora and Shiro disappeared, lost even to Fiel and Chlammy, a fierce espionage battle would begin in Elkia, now espionage heaven.

...A battle to figure out who was hiding " "...who held the unbeatable trump card.

"Then they'll start betting info they normally wouldn't dare. It'll be a real mess of an espionage battle."

The trump cards of each race, the rigged games, the races who didn't need them—if all this sensitive information got out, it wouldn't be long before someone found themselves backed into a corner, facing certain defeat. Therefore, to Chlammy and Fiel's question one week earlier, Sora had answered thus:

What was going on with Elkia? *He didn't have a clue.*

However…he did know how that mess would *play out.*

"Countdown: Eight. Seven. Six. Five—"

Sora smiled giddily as Emir-Eins began to count down.

"Hey, Steph. You know what the name of the poison we used is?"

Once she reached *Zero*, suddenly, at the back of the hole in space, the majority of the assembly together stood up and spoke, and Sora explained with a sneer.

"…*Truth serum.*"

"I have been secretly communicating with Demonia. I shall now reveal everything I know step-by-step."

"I have been secretly communicating with Elf. I shall now reveal everything I know step-by-step."

…Yes. Their faces showed confusion, panic, and terror as their mouths moved against their will. As if in chorus, they made the same confession simultaneously, word for word except for the parties with whom they'd been communicating: Fairy, Lunamana, Dhampir, Dragonia… Steph inwardly howled.

…Why—how did I not realize?! Sora and Shiro caused *the insurrection and* made *the Commercial Confederation issue convertible notes… I saw that much, but how didn't I notice the* method *by which they* provoked *them?! The* oppression *they applied just before closing the castle and announcing they were resting for a turn!!*

That's right…the commercial associations. The current Commercial Confederation—the traders and the nobles.

Sora and Shiro had challenged them to a game. *A nonnegotiable one… So…*

...they'd been forced to sign documents by the Covenants.
That was where they'd put the poison: in the documents!!

"...They don't do their research on potential spies... We're sur-rounded by n00bs, aren't we?"

Sora could see what the gasping Steph was thinking. He piled on the sarcasm with a smile.

"Well, I guess we can't *blame* them, though, since we erased their memories, destroyed the documents, and had them make new ones. ♪"

So those spies engaged in that fierce espionage battle were actually double agents...

"They didn't realize it. They didn't remember it. But they were very loyal in reporting the intel they gathered to us through the currency in a code they themselves didn't understand. True patriots, amirite? Even though they didn't realize it. ☆"

Indeed—they didn't remember it, or realize it, or *even recognize it.* It had been their decision and their desire to issue convertible cur-rency. The covenant had foreseen that. There was no way they would doubt their behavior, nor could they see through it with magic. Only Shiro held the encryption key, so even if they got wise, they still wouldn't be able to crack the code. Most of the information flying around made its way to Sora and Shiro, and:

"This allowed us to locate every one of the spies who infiltrated Elkia in the guise of the Commercial Confederation, and then?"

"...Almost all...of the races...involved—were in checkmate. ♥"

Sora and Shiro carried on while Steph could only gape. Jibril fol-lowed up:

"To stop the confessions, medicine is required—a word in *Japa-nese. ♪*"

Precisely—That was why the name of Dwarf did not surface in the confessions. Thus, Jibril revealed the true nature of the medicine she'd shipped, conveyed to all the spies.

"Result: Purchase of medicine before *step-by-step confession.* Devastating information leak. Inevitable. Brisk business."

"Yeah, we got some brisk business from those goons who realized they'd been played. ♪"

Leaving Steph speechless, Sora and Shiro thought:

—In other words, Veig had received the national missive they'd sent to all the races involved. And he'd just had a hunch about all this... He'd sensed there were just two choices: pay up with your whole damn country, or charge into an ugly battle of attrition among states and races and before long go under. He'd even had a hunch about where to find Sora and Shiro—and even got the irony.

Sora and Shiro shivered. That Veig was a monster. Still—

"But 'your whole damn country'... It's not a price anyone's gonna cough up so easily, huh?"

—even as such a monster... Veig Drauvnir's imagination had made clear to him that if he did charge into an ugly battle among states and races, *he would go under*. The two siblings, together, thought of the opponent that had made him so sure, and they savagely, confrontationally thought with twisted grins:

—Yes, it was the common knowledge of the weak: Generally speaking, *things in the world don't go the way you imagine*. For better or for worse.

Excited and drenched in a cold sweat, Sora declared:

"Come—let the games begin...suckas."

■■■

This day occurred exactly one month after the domestic insurgence. A few days later, the country that had *disappeared from the map*—as it changed its name from the Kingdom of Elkia to the Republican Dukedom of Elkia—this time disappeared from the *ground* as a voice answered the two's hopes. An echo against the spatial phase boundary, which everyone inhabiting that land heard, namely:

——a Sprite Tune......

⏻ AFTERWORD

Yuu Kamiya here. It's been quite a while—one year and one month since the last volume, *Practical War Game*. About a year and a half since Volume 9, not to mention all those delays. I'd like to take this opportunity to apologize deeply to my readers and all concerned...

But we know what my editor is going to say to that.

"...I have a feeling I saw something like this in the afterword of Volume 7. Is it just my imagination...?"

Yes, I knew it. I expected you'd tell me that. Of course, it is 100 percent my fault that the manuscript took *foreverrr* to get in and the release date was delayed as a result. Under the circumstances, I am aware I have such a dearth of room to argue as to make the amount of white space in that weird character 魚魚魚 (which I think is pronounced *sakana ga sakan na sama*) look vast. However, please allow me to say:

—What *do* you want me to write, then?! (Defensive rage)

Talk is cheap, right?! And I'm not even talking, but writing, right?! So! What if someone rattles off a bunch of fancy, polite, formal words of apology—but inside, they're thinking: *Damn, shut up already!* What should one do to make people believe?! Will the readers understand if I explain the circumstances? Will it fulfill them if I beg their pardon?! The best I can do for the readers who have kept waiting despite the repeated delays—

—is to make them think "it was worth the wait"...

To make it such a work as they'll think was worth it—and to pray that they think so. Don't you think?

......

"...That sounded so plausible I was almost convinced. Regardless, it doesn't justify you bypassing the question of why it was late, does it...?"

——Uh, well... Ummm... Remember the movie that came out last year? Now *No Game, No Life Zero* is coming out on Blu-ray and DVD, the same month as this volume.

"You get editor points for such a natural segue into the promo material. Oh, do go on?"

It's, uh, yeah... It's incredibly well-made, and...you know? Uhhh... It makes me think, like, I better step up, and, like——

"So basically you just got in your own way and fell into a slump again, didn't you?!"

I'm sorry, I'm sorry, check out the second volume of the manga, which is coming out this month, too! I'll get the next volume's manuscript in faster, so if you would, please... S-see you laterrrrr!!

SUDDENLY, ELKIA'S BEEN SWALLOWED UP BY A SPATIAL PHASE BOUNDARY, " " WITH IT!! WHO LAID THIS TRAP? THERE'S ONLY ONE WAY TO ESCAPE THE ENCLOSED SPACE— AND THAT'S TO USE A MAGIC LOLI-FYING BAG...?!

SORA HAD WISHED TO BE TURNED FEMALE, YET NOW HE FEELS HE WOULD LOSE SOMETHING AS A MAN. WHAT WILL HIS DECISION BE—?!

No Game No Life, Volume 11

—LET'S SIT BACK AND TALK GAMES WHILE SURROUNDED BY LOLIS—

NOW IMPLORING MY EDITOR TO LET ME WRITE THIS SO I CAN CHURN OUT THE MANUSCRIPT FASTER!

THE AUTHOR IS SICK OF COMING UP WITH COMPLEX PLOTS!! AND THE ILLUSTRATOR IS TIRED OF DRAWING BIG BOOBS!! A STORM OF PENT-UP RESENTMENT IS UNLEASHED ON SORA FOR NO GOOD REASON—